English Knight

Book 1 in the Anarchy Series

By

Griff Hosker

English Knight

*Published by Sword Books Ltd 2015
Copyright © Griff Hosker*

*The author has asserted their moral right under the Copyright, Designs and Patents Act, 1988, to be identified as the author of this work.
All Rights reserved. No part of this publication may be reproduced, copied, stored in a retrieval system, or transmitted, in any form or by any means, without the prior written consent of the copyright holder, nor be otherwise circulated in any form of binding or cover other than that in which it is published and without a similar condition being imposed on the subsequent purchaser.
A CIP catalogue record for this title is available from the British Library.
Cover by Design for Writers*

Contents

English Knight	i
Prologue	3
Chapter 1	6
Chapter 2	11
Chapter 3	19
Chapter 4	27
Chapter 5	33
Chapter 6	43
Chapter 7	50
Chapter 8	58
Chapter 9	67
Chapter 10	74
Chapter 11	81
Chapter 12	90
Chapter 13	95
Chapter 14	101
Chapter 15	111
Chapter 16	118
Chapter 17	126
Chapter 18	134
Chapter 19	141
Chapter 20	149
Chapter 21	157
Chapter 22	166
Chapter 23	173
Chapter 24	180
Chapter 25	187
Chapter 26	196
Epilogue	206
Glossary	208
Historical note	209
Other books by Griff Hosker	213

Dedication
To the team at Sword Books who help me to do what I love; write.

Prologue

Constantinople 1120

I am Alfraed, son of Ridley, the leader of the English Varangian Guard in the Emperor's court in Constantinople. I was named after the last descendant of King Harold Godwinson who was killed at Battle Hill in 1066. Aelfraed had come with my father and fought for Emperor Alexios. Aelfraed was dead these many years and the Emperor had recently died. My father had decided that, as he was getting older, we should return home back to the land which was now called England.

We stood aboard the Genoese ship which would take us to Frankia and I watched the land of my birth fade into the east. Constantinople, or Miklagård as my father's men named it, was the only place I knew. I did not want to go. I did not want to leave my pampered life. I had been happy in that exotic city. All my friends lived there. I had many friends and a wonderful life. I was familiar with all of its ways and now I was being dragged reluctantly to a new home in the west. It was unfair! I glanced at my father who was now white, shrunken and frail. He had once been the most powerful English Varangian serving the Emperor but now time and age had caught up with him. He had fought in his last battle. He had led his last warriors. I had to return with him to the home he had left so many years earlier. I owed my pampered and exquisite life of joy to him but he was taking me away from all of that.

He had been a sad, quiet and lonely man for these past twenty years. His wife, my mother, had died giving birth to me and he had withdrawn into himself. I think that he found it hard to talk with me. He was used to warriors. The only people he had ever loved were Aelfraed, my mother and me. The only time he spoke to me was to tell me the tales of the two of them as Housecarls fighting first the Welsh and then the Normans. I knew of all the battles in which they had fought and heard of every enemy they had slain. I knew of their journey down the Rus rivers where they had fought Pechengs until they had entered the service of the Emperor where they had fought the Normans. Once Aelfraed had fallen in battle it seemed that my father did not record the battles. They seemed not to matter. Only those where Aelfraed had led seemed worthy of remembrance. He was a modest man. I only knew of them through his oathsworn who followed him as he led the English Varangians to fight the Emperor's enemies. Six of them followed us now. Two were too old to fight, Ralph and Garth. Like my father their fighting days were done. They acted as companions and servants to my father. The other four would not have much longer to fight but they, like the others, were keen to return home to England to die. All of them were now Christian; the Emperor had insisted. Inside, however, I knew that the seven of them still held on to pagan ideas. They were forever touching amulets. The seven of them were a throwback to a bygone era. I did not feel like I had much in common with any of them.

We were travelling in style for my father had acquired a vast fortune while serving the Emperor in Constantinople. He had maintained a friendship with two merchants whose lives he had saved and they had invested his money well. We were rich even by the standards of Constantinople.

What concerned me was the home we were returning to. My father had been driven from England as an outlaw. He had neither land nor title. William the Bastard had taken Coxold, which my father had held, because of his opposition to him. He was now dead and my father deemed that Henry, who now ruled, might have forgiven his rebellion. We would travel through Frankia to Normandy where the King of England spent most of his time.

And what of me? I was nothing like my father. I had my dark looks from my mother. I had my education from Byzantium. I could speak English, Norman, Norse, Greek and a little Italian. I could read Latin as well as Greek. Unlike my father I could ride a horse well; he just sat on one. I rode mine. I could use a lance and a sword. I had been considered one of the finest swordsmen in the city. All of that was behind me now. All of my friends were in Constantinople and I felt like I was just watching over seven old men to make sure that they did not fall overboard before we landed in Frankia.

I trudged to the cabin I would share with the others. My life could not get any worse. What future did I have in a land I did not know amongst strangers and with all of my friends on the other side of the world? A world filled with barbarians and only one step away from a pagan hell of indescribable proportions. For the next weeks, my world would be bordered by the sea and the small Genoese ship which was taking me inexorably away from the place I wanted to live. Every day I woke to the torment of knowing that the life I had known was over.

Chapter 1

"What's the matter, Alfraed? It is an adventure we go on. You are a young man; you should be excited."

Wulfstan was the youngest of my father's oathsworn. He was not yet forty summers old. He had been with my father for ten years having lost his lord who had hired out as a mercenary for the Normans. Of all of my father's men, he was the one I could talk to, a little at least. "We are leaving the greatest city in the world, Wulfstan, to go to the back of beyond. We go to a place where people still live in mud huts and they have yet to hear of baths!"

Wulfstan chuckled, "Those that are lucky have a mud hut. Most of them lie beneath a bed of straw at night."

I believed him, briefly, "Truly?" The grin told me that he was teasing me. "Your humour is wasted on me! Besides if it is such a wonderful place to live then why did you and father leave?"

"I left because my lord left and I was his man. Your father followed your namesake. A great hero."

"You did not know him!"

"No, but I served in the Guard and heard his name spoken with reverence. Your father is the last warrior left alive from the battle of Stamford Bridge and they helped to win that battle for King Harold."

"It did him little good. He lost the battle for England did he not?"

Wulfstan looked west and nodded, "Aye and that is why my lord left England. The land of the Saxon became Norman overnight."

"Then why are we returning?"

"Things are changing, the Bastard is dead and they say that his son is not as bad as his father." He tailed off lamely. Then he turned to look at me. "Your father, as well as Garth and Ralph, wish to die in their own country. I understand that. It is the clay from which we are all made. All men wish to do so. You will do well there."

I shook my head. What did this fool know? He could barely read and write. I doubted that he had visited the baths once and would be happy eating cabbage soup each day. "Why on earth should I do well? Do they have libraries? Are there baths where I can be bathed, oiled and massaged? Do they eat exotic delicacies from the four corners of the earth?"

He shook his head, "No and I must say that I do not see the need for such things. They are not what makes you who you are. You are a fine warrior. Everyone knows that you were the best swordsman in the city. You would have been a strategos in a few years."

"Exactly!"

"In England, there is the opportunity for war; not with the barbaric Musselmen but with knights such as you. You can lead your own warriors and carve out your own empire."

"I thought that there was peace there now."

"There is never peace. There are wars against Anjou and the Franks. There are raids against the Scots, the Welsh and the Irish. When there are not those wars then lord fights lord for little morsels of land. Fear not, Alfraed, if you choose the right men to follow you then you can become a mighty and powerful leader."

"I will believe that when I see it. Besides we have the whole of the land of the Franks to cross first. Apart from you and I, the rest are old men! We will not make it twenty miles from the coast. We will be attacked and robbed."

"Do not dishonour those warriors. They may be old but they are skilled. If anyone is foolish enough to attack us then they will learn to their cost that white hair does not make an easy victim."

That evening as we ate our meal my father actually took the time to talk to me. He normally talked at me and told me what I was doing wrong. I was glad he spoke because it meant I could ignore the slops that they had served up as food. "I know that you are not happy about this voyage, Alfraed." I flashed an angry look at Wulfstan who merely shrugged and continued eating the foul-smelling fish stew before us. "Do not blame Wulfstan. He is my oathsworn and his loyalty is to me." He sipped his stew seemingly oblivious to the smell which was almost making me sick. "We had to leave the new Emperor. I am old and I am not the leader I was." He chuckled, "Some would say that I was never a leader."

Ralph shook his head, "Do not say that, strategos. You were a good leader."

"But I was no Aelfraed was I?" They all shook their heads. "But that matters not. I saw weaknesses in the defence of the Empire."

"Weaknesses? The walls are high and powerful. No enemy can ever breach the walls of Constantinople."

"Strength lies in men and not in walls. The warriors who come to fight now do so for the coin they can take. They are not loyal. We go where gold will not buy men's hearts. I would have warriors around me like the ones here, around this table." He nodded at each one of his men. They all gave a slight bow back. "But the real reason is that I am dying and I would be buried in my land close to where I was born. Life is a circle and I am coming back to the beginning here at the end."

"But what of me? I was not born in that land." I pointed to the east. "I was born there! England is not my land; it will never be my land."

I had raised my voice to my father and I saw the anger flit across the faces of Garth and Ralph. My father smiled and shook his head, "You have England in your heart. We just need to find it."

I slammed my spoon down and drank the beaker of wine. Ralph laughed, "And you will not find wine like that in England. You will have real ale! Then you will know you are home."

If he thought he was cheering me up then he was wrong. My father wiped his mouth and said, "When I am home and when I am dead and buried then you can, of course, take my money and return to Constantinople. That is your choice. I do not think you will make that decision but by then you will know your heart."

I was bored by the journey. Once my stomach had become used to the tossing and turning, I managed to keep a little of the food down. It still tasted disgusting but it did not come immediately back up. The wine helped and, as we passed Sicily, now controlled by the Normans, I was pleasantly inebriated. That ended when we neared Naples. Wulfstan found me lounging on the deck and threw me my sword.

"On your feet, Alfraed. Your father thinks it is time you practised with your sword."

I saw, behind him, my father and the other oathsworn watching me. I took the sword from its scabbard and waved it before me. "I do not need to practise. I am the finest swordsman on this ship. You said so yourself."

He nodded and balanced himself on the balls of his feet. "Then you will be able to defeat me in two passes and you can get back to your drinking."

I stood. The rolling motion of the ship made it hard to balance and I wondered how Wulfstan was managing to keep so still. I noticed that the crew were also watching us. We were the amusement for the day. I decided to show them all just how good I was.

"Very well then, Wulfstan, but don't come crying to me when I defeat you with a couple of swashes!"

He gave a slight bow and said, "I am ready for my lesson, my lord."

I made a swing at his head. If it had not been for the motion of the ship it would have been a perfect strike; as it was I slightly overbalanced and felt the flat of Wulfstan's sword strike me on the buttocks as I landed on the wooden deck. I heard the laughter and I began to colour. I tried my backward spin manoeuvre. I reversed my direction to hit him on his unprotected back. Unfortunately, I fell over and landed flat on my face. There were hoots of laughter and derision. I looked up and saw that my father was not laughing. He was watching me sadly.

"Why don't you stand still?"

Wulfstan gave an annoyingly patronising bow and said, "If it will make it easier for you then by all means."

I watched as he braced himself. This would be easy. I put my arm behind me for balance and lunged at Wulfstan. His feet never moved but his body swayed out of the way of my sword and I found myself falling forward. As I lay on the deck my father's foot came down on my hand. I looked up at him. "Unless you work at becoming the warrior you were and foreswear drink for the rest of this voyage you will never beat even an old man like me."

He turned and walked away. Wulfstan put his arm down to pull me to my feet. "I am sorry Alfraed but your father wanted you to learn a lesson." I was about to say something pithy when he held his hand up. "He told me that the warrior he followed, Aelfraed, had brothers who became like you. They were spoiled and arrogant. He did not wish his son to be so humiliated. Here it was only his oathsworn who saw you fall. You can begin to become a warrior again."

"It was the pitch of the ship!"

"No, it was the drink and, in your heart, you know it." He took the sword from my hand and sheathed it. "When you have sobered up then we can practise. The captain says we have many days before we make landfall."

When I did sober up, and that was made easier and faster by the sniggers from the crew who had been watching, I decided that they were right and I swore to become fit once more. I had no baths to help me purge my body but I took to exercising every morning alone before sparring with Wulfstan. We used the heavy wooden swords I had used when I had been younger. A blow from one of those was enough to wake you up. The first two days saw me suffering at the hands of Wulfstan but I soon became quicker and remembered all the moves that had made me so famous. On the seventh day, as Wulfstan poured a bucket of seawater over me to refresh me I realised that it had been many months since I had truly exercised. I had been full of self-pity at my father's decision to exile us. I began to feel much better about myself and by the eighth day, as we neared our destination, I had Wulfstan running hither and thither. I had found my skills once more. I would be ready for this journey into hell!

Chapter 2

We had chosen the ship in which we travelled because my father assured me that the Genoese were allies of the Emperor. Further west there were enemies who might decide to take revenge on these Varangians. The surly faces which greeted us did not seem to be that friendly. We had many chests to be unloaded and Ralph and Garth went to negotiate the purchase of horses. I asked about servants when the two white-haired warriors wandered off into the bustling port to negotiate.

"Servants? My son, there will be no servants until we reach England."

"What about cooking and grooming the horses?"

"We will do that." I think my mouth must have dropped open. I was certainly speechless. Groom my own horse? It was unthinkable. "We have many leagues to travel. If we hired servants here, they would, in all probability, steal from us and return here. When Aelfraed and I travelled down the mighty rivers of Rus to get to Miklagård we not only cooked for ourselves we hunted, rowed and even pulled our ship. This will be luxury for we will have horses to ride and, occasionally, inns in which to stay."

Whenever my father said Miklagård I knew he was talking of a different time and place. That had been the old name the Varangians gave to Constantinople. There had been a time when I had been amused by such things. Now it left a sour taste in my mouth.

The two retainers came back with a string of horses. Old Ralph shook his head. "They are robbing bastards here, my lord. We have paid far more for these horses than they are worth."

My father shrugged, "They are worth what we pay for them. We would have to walk and carry our armour else."

As we packed the leather travelling cases onto the horses I asked, "Will it be wise to travel without armour? We are travelling through a strange land. What if we are attacked?"

Garth had laughed, "If we are attacked it will not be by men in armour it will be by bandits. We will leave the armour in the chests. If we cannot handle a few bandits then we deserve to end our lives in a foreign forest. Just keep your sword by your side and your bow handy Master Alfraed and we will get through this journey." I saw him exchange a look with my father. "Aye, and we may all come through it better men."

Inevitably Ralph and Garth led the string of horses loaded with our goods. They were the senior retainers and my father's closest warriors. Wulfstan and Egbert were the youngest but they rode some way ahead of us while Athelstan and Osric rode behind. As we headed towards the distant mountains, I asked my father about this.

"It is simply a matter of choosing the best warrior for the task in hand. Ralph and Garth are like me; they are past their days of fighting. Once they were the fiercest warriors who ever fought in a shield wall. But now? Our senses are dulled and our hearing is fading. Wulfstan and Egbert have the best eyes, ears and noses. They will sniff out any danger."

"How long will it take us to reach our destination?"

He laughed and suddenly looked much younger. "Ah, the impatience of youth. In all honesty, I do not know. I have never travelled here before. The captain told us that it would take three long days to reach Turin where there will be lodgings for us. The first days will harden us for the long journey ahead."

"This may be too much for you, father." I was genuinely concerned for my father was no longer a young man.

"I am not fated to die on this road. I dreamed a dream and saw myself dying in England. It is meant to be. I had a sword in my hand. This journey will help to prepare me."

We rode in silence and I wondered about death. My father seemed resigned to it. I wanted to live and enjoy life. He appeared happy to embrace it. I did not even see the country and the mountains through which we rode; I was contemplating a life in the west, far away from the joyous life I had known.

We rode until dark. Wulfstan found us a small dell by a mountain stream and we made camp. I dismounted and dropped the reins of my horse. Ralph's voice stopped me, "Master Alfraed your horse will neither unsaddle itself nor will it water and feed without assistance. Unless you look after your own beast then you will be walking before any of us. We have no spare horses!"

I looked at my father for help but he merely nodded his approval at Ralph's words. This was getting worse. In our home in Constantinople, we had had slaves and servants to do everything for us. I had to watch the others as they unsaddled their beasts of burden. When I had laid down my saddle, I followed Egbert to the river where he led his own horse. I noticed that he spoke to it.

"Why talk to the beast, Egbert? We will get decent ones when we get to England."

He laughed, "Until we get to England, Master Alfraed, these are the decent ones. Get to know your horse and treat him well. He may well save your life."

"But you were not a horseman, Egbert. What do you know about them?"

"I spoke with the troopers in the Tagmata and they instructed me." He nodded at the others. "When we knew we were returning home we prepared."

I detected a hint of criticism in his words. In the months before we had left, I had spent my time drinking and giving all the pretty girls as much attention as I could. I did not doubt that some of my seed had taken. Now I wondered if my time could have been better spent. I looked at the horse as it drank from the stream. It was a chestnut colour with a golden mane and on his forehead, there was a white cross. I realised that I had been given a fine-looking animal. I glanced over at the others and saw that mine was in the best condition. Why had they given me the best horse? I idly stroked between his ears and his head came up to nuzzle my chest.

"Good boy." He whinnied and, for the first time since leaving Constantinople, I did not feel alone. The men with whom we rode were my father's men. This horse was mine and the nearest thing I had to a friend. "That's a good boy and what shall we call you? It needs to be a noble name for you carry a noble knight. Should I call you Bucephalus? Do you carry another Alexander?" Annoyingly the horse went back to drinking from the stream.

"He will tell you his name when he is ready. For now, he will answer to good boy."

I looked around and saw Wulfstan watching me. "And are you another one who learned about horses by asking others?"

"No, Master Alfraed, I rode when I served with my former liege lord. We rode to battle and fought on foot."

I was learning much about myself and my companions. I was not asked to help with the cooking and I watched the men as they organised the camp. I envied them their easy manner and their banter. They were a little too familiar with my father for my liking but he seemed to relish it. The food was bland but marginally better than on the ship. Perhaps my hunger helped. I was about to roll into my blanket on the hard ground when my father said, "You and Osric can have the first watch, Alfraed. See you in the morning."

I looked in horror as the others all rolled into their blankets. Osric chuckled. He was a big man with a wild mop of golden-red hair. He looked like the lions that they had in the amphitheatres. "You'll get used to it, Master Alfraed. The secret is to keep busy. Feed the fire; check the horses; pee regularly. The time will soon go." He gestured for me to follow him away from the fire where we would not disturb the others. He took his cloak and fastened it about his neck. It seemed prudent to copy him as there was a chill in the air.

"How do we know when our shift is over?"

"You don't but I will. You get the time in your head. We don't cheat each other. We all take it in turns. Your father has been kind this night. He has given us the best shift. The worst is the middle one when you are woken from a comfortable sleep to freeze in the night and then have to try to get back to sleep when you wake the last sentries."

He began to pick up dead branches from the forest floor. I copied him. "You are used to this?"

"Aye, on campaign we guarded a whole camp not just a handful of warriors. There you never know if enemies are coming to slit your throat." I looked around fearfully as though an assassin might be creeping up on me. He laughed, "Do not worry, our horses are good sentries. They will alert us to anyone who is close."

Osric was right, the duty did pass quicker doing small jobs. I learned how to keep the fire just right, neither too fierce nor in danger of dying. I also learned much about my father. Osric was in awe of him as a leader and I learned more in that one shift than I had discovered in my life so far. I was so tired when our shift ended that I barely noticed the rock-hard floor.

The next day we passed through beautiful mountains. I saw snow on the peaks in the distance. It was spectacular scenery. I spoke with my unnamed horse far more and I listened to the banter of my companions. Wulfstan was the one with the sharpest and wittiest tongue. He had the ability to make them all laugh. It became obvious to me that when they had faced death, fighting for the Emperor, it had bonded them. These were brothers under the skin. We had little danger on the road but I noticed that when we approached other travellers, they all became alert. Ralph and Garth moved closer to my father and their hands were never away from their swords. I began to see that while their faces smiled at the strangers we met, their eyes did not. Once we had passed them then Athelstan and Osric hung back and watched for treachery. I was riding with warriors. They might be old but they had not forgotten their trade.

By the time we reached Turin with its high walls and promise of comfort, I was in a happier frame of mind. Once this journey was over and I had returned to Constantinople I would have some interesting stories with which to regale my friends.

We stayed in an inn and our horses were stabled. It was still *'good boy'*; he had not yet told me his name but I had come to know my horse and I almost missed not having to care for him when we stayed in the inn.

Osric took me out to buy clothes for the mountains. I had thought that we had already crossed them but Osric pointed to the west where the snow-covered mountains rose to the skies. "It will be so cold up there, laddie, that you could lose your fingers or your toes."

For the first time since our journey had started, I was actually needed for I could speak a little Italian and I was able to negotiate a price for the goods we bought. I could see why my father had chosen Osric to go with me. He was the largest of his warriors and with his golden mane, he seemed to tower over the locals. We were not cheated and, in fact, they seemed pleased to have us out of their markets as quickly as possible!

Wulfstan had been busy when we returned and discovered the route we would be taking. We had to buy a mule to carry the extra clothes and provisions. It would take us four days to cross the mountains and reach Lyons. As we left the next day, I was just grateful to the Romans who had built such fine roads. They made the journey much easier. Wulfstan allowed me to ride ahead with him for part of the way. I wondered why.

"The man in the inn I spoke with told me that hundreds of years ago the Romans had inns called a mansio and they were spread out along the roads for visitors to use."

That intrigued me. The night in the inn had made me realise the pleasure of a roof and a soft bed. "Are there are any remaining?"

"There are some but we cannot count on them." He suddenly turned in his saddle to look up at the mountainside.

"What is the matter Wulfstan?"

"I do not know and that is what worries me. I feel as though we are being followed or tracked and yet I can see nothing." He rubbed the back of his neck. "I just have a feeling."

I stared around and it all seemed normal to me. "I can see nothing."

He laughed, "And you have yet to fight. You do not know danger."

He was wrong. "I have fought! I have used my sword and my dagger in combat!"

He shook his head, "No, Master Alfraed you have not. When you fought there was no danger of your dying. When you are close to death you find senses, you did not even know you possessed."

We rode in silence as I listened for these hidden dangers. "This is why my father wanted me here. You are teaching me."

"Your father is a wise man. He has been travelling through dangerous lands since he was younger than you were."

I looked at him in surprise. "How do you know?"

"Others told me. He and your namesake were legends. He was not made an outlaw in England just for poaching a deer. He and Aelfraed led a rebellion against William the Bastard. He has fought the Norman horsemen and beaten them. Do not let his white hair fool you, Master Alfraed. You are being trained so that you may become a shadow of the warrior that your father is."

We did not find a mansio; at least not one which stood whole. We found a building that had four walls remaining but neither roof nor people. It did, at least, give us some shelter from the biting wind and the fire had a hearth in which to burn wood. That night Osric and I had the middle shift. It was the first one I had had to take. Osric had been right; being woken from a warm blanket to stand in the cold was not a pleasant experience.

Egbert took us to one side. "We saw nothing on our shift but I shall sleep with my sword next to me."

"Wulfstan was right then?"

"I think so, Osric. I saw nothing but the horses are nervous. I would keep your swords to hand."

The words were not addressed to me but they were intended for my ears. Osric nodded to me as Egbert rolled into his blanket. "We move away from the fire. Let us find a tree to stand next to. Wrap your cloak tightly about you."

As we stood some thirty paces from the glow of the fire and I shivered I wondered what this danger was. I went to speak but Osric shook his head and held his finger to his lips. I was learning to heed these warriors. I was in their world now.

It was my horse that alerted us. He whinnied. Osric touched my arm and then drew his sword. He pointed at my eyes and then the forest. He wanted me to watch. I nodded to show that I understood. He walked back to the campfire; I assumed to wake the others. Where was this danger? I peered into the forest. I could see nothing! Then I caught the slightest of movements. Had I not been warned of danger I might have thought it an animal of the night but Osric's touch had set my senses alight.

I saw a shadow moving towards the fire. I was hidden by the tree and I stared as the shadow became a man and I saw that he had a long, curved blade in his hand. Other shadows began to move towards the camp. I began to step forward when I felt Osric's touch on my arm. He shook his head and led me away from the fire and into the forest. For a big man, he was silent. I could now see the ten or so men who walked towards the fire. It looked as though my father and the others had not been woken or they had, at least, not risen.

I raised my sword but Osric shook his head again. What was he waiting for? I stared in horror as the men walked into the camp and stood over the blankets. When would Osric do something? As if he had read my thoughts, he nodded to me and, lifting his sword he ran at the nearest warrior. I pulled my arm back and stabbed at the man nearest to me. He had only been two paces from me and my sword sank into his flesh. I felt it grind against bone and it made me shudder. I pulled it out. The man turned and raised his sword to me. He was not dead! Osric's sword slashed around and sank across his back. The man dropped at my feet dead.

I looked up and saw that my father and his oathsworn had risen like wraiths and their attackers lay dead at their feet. I saw the last two assassins as they ran into the forest. I was going to follow when Osric's ham-like fist grabbed my arm. "Let them go. They can do no more. Fetch the bodies into the light and let us examine them."

The eight bandits were searched and money and weapons taken from them. My father looked at me for signs of injury. He nodded when he saw that I had none. "You have had your first brush with death. What have you learned from it?"

I looked at the dead men. "That I can see better in the dark than I thought."

Osric shook his head, "That is not the lesson you should take from this. If you have an enemy and the chance to kill him then do so or he will kill you. Had I not been there then you would be lying dead in the forest and not him." He put his arm around my shoulder. "You did not like the feeling as the blade ground against the bone."

"How did you know?"

"It was the same for all of us when we first killed. If you stab upwards then you will avoid many bones. Still, you did better than I could have hoped. You did not make a noise in the forest and that is a good thing." He pointed to my horse. "And he is a fine animal. He warned us. He would make a good scout."

And that was how my horse got his name. He became Scout. He seemed to like it and responded every time I used it. Of course, Wulfstan gave me the trick of giving him a treat of an apple or patting him on the head as well but that night saw a bond between my horse and me, I could not have believed back in Constantinople.

Chapter 3

We had been riding for a day when I finally asked Wulfstan about the attack. "Why did Osric let those two bandits escape?"

"They will spread the word that we are not easy victims. We will now reach Lyons safely."

"And was it right to strip their bodies of their valuables and weapons?"

"Spoils of war, Master Alfraed. You take what you can when you can. Who knows what awaits us?"

My education began as we descended to Lyons. Lyons would be the end of the Holy Roman Empire and then we would begin our journey across Frankia. We would draw close to the lands of England and Normandy; our final destination.

Lyons was a border fortress. It was the most familiar town I had seen so far. I recognised the hands of the Roman builders everywhere. Here were the knights of the Holy Roman Emperor. They looked a little different to the knights from home but I recognised them for what they were. They wore mail here but the helmets were full-face helmets. My father and his retainers still used the old fashioned open-faced helmet with the nasal. They had the kite shields my father had faced in the wars in the east. My father and his men still clung to their round shields. When I saw the knights I felt happier.

It seems that my father's name was known in Lyons and we got to stay in the great hall of the castellan, Hugo de Montfort. He was of an age with my father. Count Hugo called me over. "Well, boy, will you be a warrior like your father?"

"I hope to be a knight, sir." I was not very happy about being called a boy. I had a beard and a moustache; I had bedded women!

Count Hugo looked in surprise. "You do not wish to stand in a shield wall as these fine fellows once did?" he did not wait for my reply. "I fought for the Emperor when I was a young lance for hire. How well I remember your father standing like a rock with his warriors beside him. The Normans shattered their lances and had their hearts broken. They could not penetrate the wall of wood and steel."

My father laughed and suddenly seemed young again, "And then you and your horsemen drove them from the field and returned rich men."

Count Hugo gave a loud guffaw and spread his arm wide, "And then I came here to become the most powerful castellan on this side of the border!" He quaffed his wine. It was good wine. It was deep and red. It was so rich you almost needed a spoon to drink it. His voice became lower and more serious. "You have a most difficult part of your journey to come. King Henry spends much of his time in Normandy. Rouen is his main castle. But you will have to cross France first. Louis the Fat is not the king his father was. This one rules with a strong hand. He knows the Norman ways and fought alongside the Dukes of Normandy."

"Are you saying we may not be welcome?"

"I am saying, old friend, that you need to be careful and diplomatic. I will give you an escort across the border. The king does not keep a standing army as the Emperor does and he relies on his vassal lords to watch his land. Archambaud of Montlucon has a powerful castle on the Cher River. I know him. My men will take you as far as him and then you will be on your own."

I was confused. "Count Hugo, why does the Emperor not impose his will upon the land?"

Count Hugo shook his head with a sad smile upon his face. "This is not an Empire such as the one you have left. Here the power lies in the castles and the warriors who serve the Emperor, or the king. A strong king can control his lords but there are lords who will try to take power from their masters. Here the treachery is not done behind closed doors but behind a wall of steel, a wall of armoured knights. If you have skills as a knight, young Alfraed, then you will do well." He went on to tell us of the young knights who would ride in a conroi under their liege lord. They did not fight in wars against barbarians as they did in the east but they fought men mounted and armed much as they were. This was a noble kind of war.

I looked around the hall and saw knights younger than I. They were sat around tables sharing the camaraderie of the young. I was with old men. I would never enjoy the life of a knight in a conroi. I found myself being envious of them.

"I will send one of my household knights, Geoffrey of Coutes, with you. He is a good warrior. I would advise you to wear your armour for your journey across Frankia."

I looked at Wulfstan. "I had been told that we would only encounter bandits who would not wear armour."

Wulfstan did not seem put out by my implied criticism. Count Hugo nodded, "Up until now that was true but now you travel across a land with castles and petty lords. They may decide to challenge your crossing. You will be under my protection until Montlucon. After that...." He shrugged.

We bought two more horses from Count Hugo. Two of the ones we had bought in Genoa would struggle to carry an armoured knight. I caused something of a stir when I emerged in my armour. It was the overlapping lamellar armour favoured in Constantinople. It was lighter than mail and more effective. The young knights I had seen the night before all came to examine it and ask me questions. They were envious of me. My shield was a smaller version of their kite shield. It did not cover as much of my legs but they were protected by more lamellar armour and mail. Finally, my greaves gave my lower legs protection. I carried my helmet which had a face mask and aventail also of lamellar construction. It felt good to be in armour once more. I could face the dangers more confidently.

As we headed northwest I noticed that all of the knights had unique designs upon their shields. Mine was plain. I asked Wulfstan about the designs. "They identify the knight and his lord in battle. See how that all look different but each one has a boar's head on it somewhere. They show that they are Count Hugo's men."

That made sense. In Constantinople, we had not needed such things. All of the warriors bore the shield of the Emperor. Here men fought in smaller groups. I thought I would ask my father to have the same designs put on our shields. We were a conroi of sorts.

The land through which we travelled was good farmland. It was clearly very fertile. I saw terraces on the hills with vineyards there. I could see that this land was worth fighting for. The mountains through which we had passed were only fit for barbarians and bandits. Now we had reached what passed for civilisation. The only wooden buildings belonged to the peasants; the Count had called them villeins. The hills were dotted with fortified castles made of stone. Each one had a raised mound and a ditch surrounding it. This was all so different from my home.

Montluçon had the largest castle we had seen since we had left Lyon and Count Hugo. Geoffrey of Coutes spoke with the castellan and explained who we were. Sir Geoffrey left, eager to return to Lyon before dark.

The castellan was a small powerful man. "I am Eugene. The master, Lord Archambaud, is out with the household knights. They are teaching one of our neighbours a lesson. Pray, stay the night. He should be back in a day or so."

"We are anxious to reach Normandy."

Eugene shook his head, "I cannot give you permission to cross the land of Lord Archambaud. You will need to stay here until he returns." He saw the looks exchanged between Ralph and Garth. "I have no doubt that he will grant you permission but Lord Archambaud is sensitive about such things. He likes matters to be conducted properly."

It was a pleasant castle to visit. We stayed in the hall normally used by the household knights. It was empty for Eugene just had the ten men at arms to guard the castle. They wore leather armour but all had a helmet, a spear and a shield. When we ate, that night, I asked Eugene if this was a typical castle.

He smiled, "You have not seen Frankish castles before?"

I shook my head. "Constantinople and its mighty walls are my only experience of such buildings. These seem so small by comparison."

My father snapped, "Alfraed, do not be rude to our host."

Eugene laughed and waved away the apology, "I am not offended. I have heard of the mighty walls of that great city. No, my young friend, we do not compete with a large castle but we have walls we can defend with a small number of knights and we can control large swathes of land from here with our knights."

"How many knights does his lordship lead?"

"He has three conroi. Each one has ten knights. The ten knights have their own men at arms and they are mounted too."

I took in the information. "Father, is it the same in England? You and the others fought on foot."

Before he could answer Eugene said, "We often fight on foot too. The horses are the quickest way to get to a battle but a man fighting in armour will soon tire a horse." He laughed, "Your son is most curious, Lord Ridley."

"I apologise for him."

"No, it is interesting for me to meet someone who looks like us and speaks our language and yet is a foreigner."

I liked Eugene. He told wonderful stories of fighting with his master Lord Archambaud and carving out this little domain of theirs. It seemed that Louis the Fat was increasing his control over the lands and eventually there would be conflict with Lord Archambaud. Eugene did not appear to be concerned about the prospect of war with a king. "There have been strong kings of France and weak ones. We shall see. I have lived a long time, Alfraed son of Ridley, and I have learned to take life as it comes. I would advise you to do the same."

Lord Archambaud returned at noon of our third day in his land. He was a most imposing knight. He shunned the new style of helmet and still wore the same kind as my father did. I noticed that the knights of his conroi all had the mail which still had a detachable face piece; it was called a ventail. I knew then that Lord Archambaud liked things done the old ways. He and my father got on famously for they had both fought the Normans. I think we could have stayed there for some time but my father was aware of the passage of time.

Lord Archambaud seemed to understand. "I will have my conroi escort you to the edge of my land." He laughed, "I doubt you will have any trouble for I have imposed my will on my neighbours. They each lost household knights." I had noticed the wagons and horses which he had brought back into his castle. Frankia did not seem a dull place to live.

He left us at a small village. There was no accommodation but there was a wooden wall around it and the presence of the knights of Montluçon ensured that we were welcomed. As we ate our frugal meal my father told us what he had learned from the Lord of Montluçon.

"It seems there is a battle to control the parts of Anjou, Normandy, Poitou and Touraine." The names meant nothing to me. My father, who was always patient with me, said, "They are the duchies through which we need to pass. Henry is close by his borders with Maine. He is supposed to be hunting but from what I have discovered he is looking for an opportunity to enlarge his kingdom."

"Are the lands through which we are to travel not safe then?"

Ralph laughed, "Of course not! We are just as likely to be taken for brigands and bandits as travellers. The next days will be dangerous, Master Alfraed. You will be using your sword before too long. Of that I am certain."

As I went to sleep that night I could not help but wonder about the draw of England. My father was risking death to reach his home as were his retainers. I suppose in my arrogance I thought that I would be immune from swords and arrows for I was young. I was wrong.

For five days we saw few people as we travelled along the old Roman Road. There were occasional merchants and, once they discovered that we were peaceful, were happy for us to travel with them. They moved too slowly for us, however, and we left them after we had enjoyed some of their food. The merchants ate well. We were not far from Tours when we hit trouble.

We had found a ferry to ford the river. We should have known that trouble was waiting for us. The ferryman seemed very nervous about dropping us off. He kept glancing to the west. Wulfstan nodded to my father. "I will take young Master Alfraed and we will scout ahead. Come."

I followed Wulfstan and noticed that he donned his helmet. It seemed prudent to copy him. The road wound along the river but Wulfstan led us up a gentle slope towards the north-west. I could see that we followed an ancient trackway.

"Why are we leaving the road?"

"The ferryman seemed nervous about the west and besides our route is to the north and west." He pointed to the track we were following. "This is earlier than the Roman Road. Often they are the best way of travel." Above us, the slope became steeper and was rounded. I saw treetops above the slope. I glanced behind and saw that my father and the rest were just half a mile away. They had the pack animals to lead and could not travel as swiftly. As we reached the summit of the slope I saw, about two miles away, a small castle. We had seen many such castles on our way north. Wulfstan stopped and pushed his helmet back. He peered at the castle which stood next to the Roman Road we would have travelled.

"See, Wulfstan. Had we stayed on the road we might have been able to stay at the castle."

"We have passed many such castles. Since we stayed at Montluçon how many have opened their gates to us?"

I had not thought about that but now I realised that none had opened their gates. "None but that does not mean that this one will not."

He laughed. "This is not a peaceful land. You saw the Lord of Montluçon; he was busily enlarging his lands and taxing all who passed by. We will wait here for your father and let him make the decision."

I heard the horses as they jingled and jangled their way up the slope. Suddenly I spied the gates of the castle open and horsemen and foot soldiers emerged. Wulfstan jammed his helmet down. "Lord Ridley we should make for the trees."

"Very well."

I was going to argue but the rest all rode to the trees. When Wulfstan spoke they tended to listen. Once we reached the top of the rise they all jumped down and took their shields and weapons from their horses before hobbling them in the tree line. I was surprised at the speed with which the old men did so. Osric chuckled, "Come along, young sir. Prepare yourself."

I did as they did but I knew not why. "This is nonsense. They might well be coming in peace."

"In which case, my son, we have lost nothing by preparing for war."

I saw that they all had their shields slung easily across their backs. Only Ralph and Garth had their weapons out for they wielded axes and needed two hands. As I turned I saw that the horsemen were much closer. There were four of them and they had a Gonfanon with a golden star on a red background. They also had the same design on their shields. The eight men at arms who followed them all displayed the same symbol. The four horsemen reined in as their men at arms hurried to catch them.

Their leader raised his helmet and lowered his ventail so that he could speak with us. "Who are you that dare to cross my lands?" I saw that he was a little older than I was.

My father took off his helmet. "I am Ridley of the Varangian Guard and we are travelling to England."

"Then you are spies of Henry brother of Curthose, the sons of the Bastard! Lay down your weapons. You are my prisoners!"

My companions did not seem at all discomfited by the young man's words. "We cannot do that for we are not spies. What is your name?"

"I am Guillaume Fitzbois and I hold this demesne for my father Guy du Bois. Surrender or die."

In answer, my father swung around his shield and drew his sword. "You may try to kill us but as right and God are on our side I do not think that will happen."

The angry young man wheeled his horse and rode away. Was it over? Had my father's words discouraged them? Osric said, "They are going to get enough space to charge us, Master Alfraed: be ready."

I noticed that Ralph and Garth stood on either side of my father whilst the other four flanked me. Wulfstan murmured quietly, "Follow through with the blow if you have to strike. These men will try to kill us. Be in no doubt about that. A wounded man is twice as dangerous!" He nodded to me. "Listen for Osric's commands. When he speaks obey him instantly and we shall all live."

The four riders halted and then lowered their spears. Behind them, the four archers pulled back on their bows. As soon as the arrows were released the four horsemen, followed by the four men at arms with spears, charged towards us. I felt the ground shake as they thundered up the hill. The arrows fell ineffectually short. I saw how clever Wulfstan had been in choosing this defensive position. The slope was rounded like the bottom of a pot. The horses slowed as it became steeper. They would reach us at barely a walk. The young Guillaume Fitzbois was outstripping his peers and I heard Osric chuckle. "What a fool he is!" We held our shields up and the second flight of arrows thudded into them.

The riders headed directly for my father. I feared for him. The spear was lowered and pulled back ready to punch into my father's mail. I could not believe that he stood there so calmly. As the spearhead was pulled back a number of things happened all at once. First Osric shouted, "Charge!" It seemed bizarre for we were outnumbered and on foot. They were on horses. I obeyed and we ran towards the advancing soldiers. The next thing was that Ralph and my father locked their shields and met the spear and thirdly Garth swung his war axe. It smashed into the side of the head of Fitzbois' horse. There was a loud crack as the horse's head was crushed by the head of the axe and Guillaume Fitzbois flew over the head of his horse.

Ralph swung his axe and it smashed into the shield of the second rider who fell at the feet of Egbert. Egbert's sword was pricked into his ventail in an instant, "Surrender or die!"

The knight had no option. He put up his hands and said, "I surrender."

Osric's war axe smashed through the spear which was jabbed at him and Athelstan stabbed the surprised spearman in the stomach. A second spear came at Wulfstan who flicked it contemptuously to one side and then brought his sword down across the neck of the spearman.

Behind me, I heard Guillaume Fitzbois yell, "We surrender! Quarter! We yield! You have won."

I turned to see my father with his sword at the throat of the felled knight. We had killed two men, a horse and defeated four knights and none of us had a scratch. How had seven old men and an untried boy managed to achieve that feat?

Chapter 4

We left after the young knight had sworn to do penance in Tours Cathedral for his unwarranted attack. I saw hatred in his eyes and he would remember us, however, he had lost face in the eyes of his men and we were safe; for the time being. Of course, we quickly hurried out of his land for there was little point in tempting providence. My father left Egbert to watch our backs. The young knight had been humiliated and who knew what he might do.

I rode at the head of the small column with Wulfstan. "How did Garth stand there with the horse charging? And how did he manage to strike the beast?"

"Most horses will try to avoid you. Of course, if it is a solid line of knights then you rely on the locked shields before you and behind you. In a skirmish, the horse will swerve because it can. The difference is if a knight charges on a warhorse, a destrier. They are trained to trample and bite. The young knight rode his second-best horse, his palfrey. Because Garth was on the extreme right and we were to the left the horse would have veered towards the gap. It meant its head would be travelling towards the swinging axe. Timing is a matter of practice. Garth has a good eye for such things and he practises swinging. A horseman who falls from his horse is helpless." I took that information in. Perhaps these old men had something to tell me which might actually be of use. Wulfstan looked at me. "You did well today but I still sensed that you hesitated. You must be confident that your blow will end the combat. It may not but if you deliver with the full force of your arm then you have an excellent chance of ending the combat. Remember we have the finest armour of any warrior that we will meet."

"But you and the others wear the old fashioned helmet."

He laughed. "We like the open face. It means we see well. Of course, you are right, an open helmet invites a spear thrust or a blow from a mace. We have fought like this since our fathers fought. It is too late for us to change."

It was a pleasant land we travelled through and we rode in silence. I had learned to keep my eyes open and to watch my horse. Scout had already proved his skill at sniffing out danger and I was growing fond of him.

"Why did you and the others not help Garth and Ralph to defend my father? You are his oathsworn."

Wulfstan closely examined my face as he answered, "We are your oathsworn too. When your father no longer commands then we follow you. Until then we guard you," he smiled, "Your father is still a mighty warrior while you have much to learn." I was not certain I liked that but I had to believe Wulfstan for, so far, his advice had been sound. It seemed I needed the others to watch over me.

We spent the next three days avoiding all settlements and, especially, castles. We camped in the woods and ate frugal meals. I learned how to cook. It was summer and Athelstan was a good hunter. I found the food we ate blander than my palate was used to and lacked the variety I appreciated but it took the edge from my hunger. We met a few travellers and when we discovered that we were close to Le Mans my father ordered a detour to avoid that huge castle. Wulfstan sent me to the rear, to my father, when we began the detour. I had long ago realised that I was still little more than a child in their eyes and I obeyed.

It was obvious my father wished to speak with me. "How do you feel about this journey now? Do you still hate your father for bringing you so far from the comforts of your fabulous home?"

"I do not hate you." I smiled, "Although I will admit that I was not happy about travelling to the end of the world."

"Your destiny is there." He looked wistfully to the west. "I had not even seen ten summers when I followed Aelfraed and his uncle. I left my home to follow the sword. It was not a happy home and I never looked back. I hoped that you would not regret leaving your home." He put his hand on my arm. He had a gentle touch for a hardened warrior. "I learned to be a warrior. I lived amongst warriors such as these." He gave a deep, heartfelt sigh. "I yearn for those carefree days before the Normans came." He tightened his hand over my arm. "I learned about myself in those years. When we fought the Welsh and faced charging horses I learned to be a man and a warrior. I was proud of you the other day when you did not flee. That was the first time you had faced a charging horseman and I know the temptation is to run. Already you are changing."

He was proud of me. He did not say that normally. I looked at him and saw that he had become older already on this journey.

"When we meet this king I will have to abase myself before him. I do not wish to do so but it will be necessary. Aelfraed and I were thorns in his father's side. He will not forget that but I hope he will forgive. If not then you and the others may be on your own."

"No! I stay with you."

"The important thing is for you to get to England. My home was in the north and from what I have learned from travellers it is an empty land now that William the Bastard has scoured it. I hope that we can carve out our own demesne there. The land has many hills and a warrior can build a better castle than the ones we have seen so far. We have money and can hire cunning builders who will make our new home impregnable. Then we will hire warriors."

"Mercenaries?"

"No, my son, warriors who will fight for us. The payment will be their due. It worked in Constantinople and I see no reason why it should not work in England."

I gestured with my arm towards the warriors and spoke quietly. "These men fight for you because they are oathsworn."

He laughed, "And I pay them too. They would fight for me whether I paid or not but they deserve payment do they not?"

We rode in silence as I took in his words. I had taken so much for granted. Of course, they would be paid. They were not slaves to work for nothing and they deserved their coin.

"What happens when the money runs out? How do we pay them then?"

"Unless you waste it then that will not happen for some time. We have enough for many years. By then you should have farmers who will produce crops and rear animals. You share in the profit of the men who work your land."

I had not thought about money before. When I lived in Constantinople I always had coins to use and bills were always paid. Life was going to get more complicated. What did I know about farming? Or running an estate? I was destined to be a warrior. I had felt a rush of blood when I had fought the men from Anjou. I had had time to prepare and to anticipate. Wulfstan was right, I had been hesitant but I would not make the same mistake twice.

We knew that we were in Maine and that was now a vassal state of Normandy but it was not a settled place. Bands of discontented knights still disputed with the King of England who had taken both Normandy and Maine from his brother. Anjou to the south and Blois to the east were also unhappy about the expansion of the belligerent Henry. We would have to proceed carefully. We kept a keen watch about us and I listened to Scout. He had proved invaluable in identifying danger.

It happened that we were leading our horses. We did not always ride them for we had far to go. The ground was climbing, albeit gently and we were keen to conserve the animals. They were faring better than they would have in the east. Here there was plenty of good grass on which they could graze and I had found an increasing number of apple trees which Scout appreciated.

Wulfstan always had an answer to my questions. When I asked him about the walking he pointed to mighty Osric who was striding ahead of us. "Osric and the rest of us fight on foot. We have powerful legs and strong arms. You saw how Ralph despatched the horse with one blow. If we ride too much then our legs and arms become weaker. We rode until now because we needed to make time. Now we are nearing our destination. We will need to be warriors."

"We will have to fight the king?"

"I hope not for he will have the best warriors in the land and many of them. No, when we get to England there will be many who will not wish to see a Saxon with land."

"How will we get land?"

"Your father has a claim to the manor of Coxold in the north of the land. He will ask the king for the land given to him by King Ethelred."

"But he is Norman, why should he help a Saxon?"

"Your father is an honest man and he may be able to persuade the king. If not then we will find a lord who may take us as vassals." He sighed. "This is really about you, Master Alfraed. Your father can count his years left to him on one hand. He has already outlived all of his fellows. You must learn from him so that you can prosper and carry his name and yours on."

That was an awesome responsibility. I had thought about my father dying but it was something which was in the future. It was like marrying, becoming a father. It was there but it was a long way in the future and not worth worrying about. If my father had a mere five years left then I should get to know him more. Suddenly Scout's ears pricked and he slowed. "Wulfstan!"

"I saw." He gave a low whistle and the others stopped. I was slower than the rest but they all hobbled their horses and grabbed their weapons. I had learned now that we fought on foot. I donned my helmet and my world shrank. I could see the advantage of a more open helmet. Luckily my mask merely covered my eyes and not my ears. I watched as Osric waved us forward and we moved through the woods. I could hear the clash of arms. Someone was fighting ahead.

As the noises grew I drew my sword and pulled my shield around a little tighter. There was a dell and a stream ahead and in the middle were five hunters. They were being attacked by eight knights and ten men at arms. There were the bodies of four dead hunters and two men at arms and the remaining hunters were getting the worst of it.

I would not have known who to side with but my father did. He roared a challenge, "Varangian!" and hurled himself down the slope towards the men at arms. They were taken by surprise as was I. I ran as fast as I could to catch my father. Three men at arms turned to face him. He had outrun Ralph and Garth. I watched as he deftly deflected one sword whilst stabbing at a second man. The third brought his sword around to strike at his unguarded back. I did not hesitate this time. I brought my sword over my head and sliced through the soldier's shoulder and arm. He fell screaming to the ground. Ignoring his dying throes I punched the other warrior with my shield and when he fell at my feet skewered him to the ground. I stood before my father looking for another enemy.

I heard Ralph chuckle, "You can leave your father to us now Alexander! There are enemies aplenty for you."

I glanced and saw that they protected him with their shields. I saw a knight rushing at me with his mace ready to strike me. I notice that he had a longer shield than I did. He was more used to fighting on a horse. I know that I should have been less reckless but my blood was up and I had just killed two men. I ran straight at him. He swung his wicked-looking mace at my head and I barely managed to get my shield up in time. The blow numbed my arm but I was inside his guard and I stabbed blindly at him. My hands are fast. I felt my sword grate along his mail. He stepped back. I saw anger in his eyes but I could not see his mouth for it was covered by a ventail. I was tiring a little but the practice with Wulfstan on the ship had prepared me well.

I stepped forward and brought my sword over my head. He swung his mace at the same time. He was trying to break my arm and he struck my shield a second time. My shield had been made by the finest armourer in Constantinople. It had cost a gold talent. Strips of metal were cunningly concealed below the leather covering. My shield held. His fared less well and I saw the wood beneath the leather. The blue shield with the yellow stars and single fleur de lys was looking a little worse for wear. I used my shield offensively and I smacked it hard at his hand which held the mace. He recoiled and the anger was replaced by fear. I feinted with my sword and he pulled his shield up for protection. I spun around and brought my sword into his unprotected back. This time the sword bit through the mail and the padded tunic. When I pulled it away I saw blood on it. I punched him in the back with my shield and he fell at my feet. I was about to ask him to surrender when he swung his mace at my leg. Had I not been wearing greaves he might have broken it. As it was I jumped and he only caught my leg with a glancing blow. I was so angry that I swung my sword and decapitated him.

I was out of breath with my exertions and I looked for my next enemy. There were none. The other knights and men at arms were on their knees.

I turned to see my comrades. Their helmets were pushed back and they were all grinning at me. My father came over and clapped me on the back. "Well fought, my son. For a moment I thought I was watching my old friend Aelfraed. He too had fast hands and a sword which was like lightning."

There were four hunters remaining. One looked to be of an age with Osric and he was the only one who appeared to be without a wound. He had a grey flecked beard and looked to be the leader. He held his hand out to me. He spoke in Norman. "Thank you, sir. That was a well-fought battle." I nodded my thanks for I was still out of breath. I took off my helmet and felt the cool air on my sweating face. The man looked surprised. "And yet you are little more than a boy!"

I was about to snap a retort when my father stepped forward. "This is my son, Alfraed and I am Ridley of Coxold and Constantinople."

The man frowned. "A strange combination. Coxold is in England is it not?"

"Aye, sir. Do you know it?"

"I have heard of it. I am Henry King of England and Duke of Normandy!"

Chapter 5

My father dropped to his knees as did the others. I was a little slower. My father said, "Then it is you, sire, that we seek."

The king said, "Rise, Ridley of Coxold, although you claim false title. I will deal with these rebels first." There were just four men at arms left and three mailed and well-armed knights. I noticed that they all wore the same livery as the knight I had killed. "You, Guy Fitzwaller, shall go back to your father's castle and fetch me a ransom of fifty gold talents. When it is paid then you can have your father's body. He has paid for his treachery with his life. You will pay with gold. You will bring it to Caen where you and your brothers will swear fealty to me on the tomb of my father." The young man nodded and, leaving his sword there, he mounted his horse. His ventail was lowered and I saw the look of anger on his face as he glared at me. He might swear fealty to the king but I was his enemy. That was two enemies in Anjou already!

"Come, we will ride to my hunting lodge. Have you horses?"

My father nodded, "Aye, we do." Wulfstan led the others to retrieve our horses. When they returned the bodies of the dead hunters were draped over their horses and the mail and the arms from the dead men were strapped to the knight's horses along with the body of the leader. They walked.

My father rode with the king. I said to Wulfstan. "Will they leave the bodies there?"

The king laughed, "Until they have paid the ransom they will have no choice. I think Guy Fitzwaller will be at Caen before we are." He turned to me, "Come boy and ride next to me and your father."

I did not like the term boy and Wulfstan hissed, quietly, "He is the king! Hold your tongue."

I nodded. "So Ridley of Coxold, how do you claim your title? That estate belongs to Odo and has done since before I was born."

I almost held my breath. The king owed us something but my father's story could result in us joining the men of Fitzwaller in the donjon at Caen castle.

"I was given the estate by King Ethelred but I fought against your father."

"You were at Battle Hill?"

"No. I was at Stamford Bridge where we fought Tostig and Hadrada." He looked defiantly at the king, "But we fought against your father's men when they came north."

The king frowned. "You fought with Aelfraed Fitz Godwinson?"

"I fought with Aelfraed, aye."

"I heard he died fighting the men of Sicily in Byzantium."

"Aye, he did. He has been dead these thirty years."

"And you named your son after him?" My father nodded. "If you had known who I was would you have done things differently back there?"

"No, for you were being attacked and it is my duty to defend the weak."

He laughed, "I do not think the King of England can be considered weak but I thank you for your intervention. It might have gone ill otherwise. What is it you wish of me, Ridley of Constantinople?"

"I wish to go to England where I can spend my days in peace."

"You cannot return to Coxold. Odo would not like it." My father kept his own counsel and said nothing. The king looked at me. "And you, Alfraed son of Ridley, what would you have?"

"My sword fights for my father against all of his enemies!"

I saw my father roll his eyes but the king laughed. "You are a belligerent cockerel! I like that. You could become one of my household knights. I like the way you fight."

"I serve my father."

Just then we saw a castle hove into view. "We will see. Tonight you will stay with me. That is for both your safety and mine. I had thought that this part of my land was safe to hunt. It seems it is not." I flashed a look at him. "Oh do not worry, Alfraed; you and your father will be rewarded for your actions. You saved the life of a king." He laughed, "Hunting is ever dangerous for my family!"

I remembered as we entered his small castle with him that his elder brother had been killed in England whilst hunting. Once inside the walls, he pointed to a small hall. "You can use my warrior hall. You will be safe in here and we will talk this evening while we eat."

Once in the hall, my father wagged a finger at me. "Do you see me becoming angry with the king? Have you no sense? He can have me killed out of hand as an outlaw."

"He would have to go through me first."

Wulfstan and the others all laughed. "There would be a story to tell around the campfires how the King of England was slain by a youth who had barely started shaving!"

"Do not encourage him! This was *wyrd*. It was meant to be. We were guided to that forest and to find the ambush. All will be well."

"I hope so father. I am not as optimistic as you. We cannot have Coxold; what else is there?"

"I can give you the estate of Fitzwaller for your own. I would like doughty warriors like you defending my borders here."

My father shook his head. "A very fine offer, my liege, but it is England I desire. I could have stayed in the comfort of Constantinople else."

"It does not do to haggle with a king! Especially when you are a rebel and an outlaw."

"I was a rebel but I have repented my sins in the Hagia Sophia. The Church has forgiven me."

"Hmph, the Church can be bought for the price of a pyx! But I do owe you something. I might have been captured and had to pay a ransom. If it was not for your son then Robert de Waller might have won." He finished chewing on the leg of the game bird and threw it over his shoulder to the dogs that lay behind him, waiting patiently for such scraps. "Coxold is in the north is it not?"

"Aye, my liege. North of Jorvik."

The king laughed, "We name it York now." He held his goblet out for some wine. "My father cleared all who lived north of the Tees. They were like you, Ridley of Constantinople, they were rebels and outlaws. There are many estates there and I need my borders protected. My cousin, David, casts avaricious looks at my northern marches. The best ones, the ones that can grow wheat, are all gone but I have some which are north of the Tees. They can only support barley and oats. They are not much in demand. How say you to an estate there? I have some empty lands which are north of the Tees. My father swept the rebels from it many years ago."

"England is all that I desire, my liege."

"Then when we reach Caen I shall have my clerks write the documents and you can swear fealty to me in Caen Cathedral."

"Thank you, my liege."

"Now you can tell me about Constantinople. I had thought to visit it on the way to a Crusade but I have matters here to arrange first."

He was, despite his words to me, a genial host. He seemed comfortable in the company of warriors. He enjoyed the stories my father and his retainers told him.

When we reached Caen I was impressed. It had good solid walls and looked to be as powerful as Lyon had been. It would not be taken easily. The River Orne ran along one side; the gatehouse and the tower looked formidable.

His household knights viewed us with suspicion until they were told of our actions. From then on we were treated as heroes. They were especially keen to hear of the cities and warriors in the east. Guy Fitzwaller brought the ransom. His younger brothers had been stripped of their arms and their armour. They looked most unhappy. The four of them abased themselves before the king. When Guy handed over the ransom I saw the annoyance as the king had every golden piece counted out. It was a further insult. They were taken to the tomb of William where they swore fealty to Henry. I knew that they would now be tied to fighting for him whenever he asked. They might not fight very hard but if they broke their bond then they would burn in the fires of hell. As they left their hatred was directed at us and not the king. We had been the cause of their father's death and they would not forget it. At least we would be in England and away from their enmity.

We swore our oath on the holy book which the bishop held. It was a sacred oath but I could not see a problem in swearing it. We all needed a lord to follow and this Henry seemed as good a leader as any. It was also a guarantee of land in England and that was my father's quest.

Surprisingly the swearing of the oath made the atmosphere lighter. His clerks went through their records and found an empty estate remarkably quickly. It was the manor of Norton and had been owned by the de Ville family. It was close to the castle which the Bishop of Durham had used when he had first landed. Now he had a fine castle. "I give you this manor for it guards a crossing of the Tees and protects the Bishop's lands. He is your liege lord and you will be subject to his command. You may have the title of baron." He handed my father a ring which a cleric handed to him. "Here is the seal of Norton."

"Do I have permission to build a castle?"

"Hmm, that is an interesting question. Needs must you may have to defend the river crossing for me but you were an outlaw."

"I have sworn an oath my liege and I am never foresworn."

The king looked at my father. There was something about Ridley of Constantinople that made men believe him. Honesty was etched in every line on his face. "Very well. You have my permission to build a castle." He waved a hand at the cleric. "Brother John will give you the titles and deeds which you will need." He looked carefully at my father. "There is an opportunity for a man with the strength to build a position of power in those wild borderlands."

My father shook his head, "I have had power, my liege. I have commanded vast armies and wrested land from both Italian and Muslim warlords. I seek a peaceful land, a land for my son to come to love."

For the first time, the king seemed to notice me, "Ah the fine knight who has such a deadly and lightning quick blade. Then do you seek power and land, Alfraed of Norton?"

I was not used to such attention. I had to think quickly, "I do not know your majesty. All of this is new to me. This time last year my biggest worry was the style of my beard and the cut of my clothes."

All of them, my father included, laughed at that. "And so it is with all young men." The king looked at me sadly, "My son, before he was taken from me, had much the same attitude. You two might have been friends."

I bowed. There seemed no response I could make to that. Instinct gave my tongue words. "I will try to serve you on your borders as your son might, your majesty."

For some reason, that seemed to please the king enormously. He embraced me, "You have spirit and you have honour. Our meeting was a good one. You will be my men in the north and help the Bishop to turn back the Scottish tide."

Brother John was a small fussy man but he was always smiling. At least in the time, we saw him he always had a happy and cheerful countenance. He took us to his cell where he had maps. "If you are Saxon, my lord, then you know the area. There were Saxons both at Norton and Billingham but, as you may know, those people were all removed when King William chastised the rebellious earls." I saw my father frown. His men had told me of the upset he had felt when he had heard of the slaughter. Many of his servants and friends had died. Brother John continued. "Your land goes from the river north to the borders of the Bishop's lands and farms here." He jabbed a finger at the map. "They go as far north as the land of the De Brus around Hartness and to the east as far as the marshes."

My father peered at the writing on the map. "Wulfestun, here, is that a separate manor?"

"It was but no longer. King William incorporated it into Norton."

I ventured a question. "Will there be any dispute over ownership?"

My father and Brother John looked at me curiously, "A strange question, my son."

I shrugged, "If King William cleared the land of the former owners and installed his own baron then will they not dispute our ownership?"

Brother John nodded, "A fair question. They were raided by the Scots and the men slaughtered. The women were taken as slaves. There are no heirs to dispute the land."

"But the women."

"Have no claim." Brother John shook his head, "Here Salic law rules. Women may not inherit. It is not like the East. Even if the slaves were freed they could not have any claim to the land."

The cleric spent some time refining the exact boundaries and giving us the number of farms on the land. He could not give us the names as they would be in the church on the manor. Seemingly satisfied the cleric told us that the documents would be ready the next day. "Are there any further questions?"

His friendly attitude had emboldened me. "If the king's son is dead then who will be the next king?" It was as though I had sworn in church. My father and his men glared at me and Brother John's face fell. "We should know this father for we do not want to lose this land. The king might be dead already but for our intervention."

Now that he understood my question Brother John's smile returned, "Another fair question. The king is young enough to marry again but he has made plans. His daughter, the Empress Matilda has been named heir. The matter is still raw because the young prince has only been taken from us recently. Even as you were leaving Constantinople his son was drowning in the English Channel."

Wulfstan said, "*Wyrd*!"

Brother John made the sign of the cross and said, "The will of God."

"But she is a woman. This Salic law you mention means she cannot inherit."

"You have a sharp mind. As her father has named her as his heir she can but in all likelihood, it will be her sons who reign."

"How many has she?"

"None but she is but eighteen summers old. You will like her, young sir. She is clever and she has a witty tongue. Some say too witty for an Emperor. They have no children yet but she is young." He waved an impatient hand having gossiped more than he had intended. "I must get on with the documents you need. It is good that you can read for many of those you will meet cannot!"

We left the brother and wandered the mighty town of Caen. "We will buy two slaves here, Alfraed, we have done the difficult part of the journey. We do not need to travel as quickly."

We bought many items which my father thought we might need. Already, just since arriving in Caen, I had noticed the chill winds which whipped off the sea. I was not used to such a climate. The cloaks we bought were thicker and warmer than the fine ones we wore to show off in the east.

"When we reach England we will have some boots made. Your days of wearing sandals are over, sadly."

"Thank you Wulfstan, you are a constant source of good news."

He shrugged, "I never liked sandals anyway."

We also bought the pots they made here. They were of a better quality, or so Osric said, than the ones we would find in England. More importantly, they would be cheaper.

There was not a great deal of choice at the slave market. I was more used to the huge bustling markets of Constantinople than the one in Caen. There seemed little variety of skills. I left it to my father and Ralph to make the decisions. They knew what they wanted. They just watched without making a bid. Others went to examine teeth, hair and arms but the two of them just stood. We bought some of the local wine and sat at a table to watch.

Eventually, Ralph went over to a woman. She looked to be younger than Wulfstan but older than me. She appeared to have all her teeth; that was always a good sign. It was hard to judge her age accurately but she looked to be thin. It looked as though she had not had a good life. They brought her over to us. "This is Faren. She is English and she can cook."

"How do you know?"

My father looked at me, "She told me." I was about to ask how that was proof but I saw Wulfstan give a shake of his head and I held my tongue.

They went back to the slave market. There were far fewer of them left now. They eventually approached a youth of no more than fourteen summers. He was thin and wasted. I wondered if he would even last the journey across to England but my father seemed satisfied, after speaking with him, and he paid the money and brought him over. "This is Aiden. He will look after the horses. He was born in Ireland but raised here." He turned to the two of them. "You are now my property. I am Ridley of Norton and this is my son, Alfraed. We will be travelling to England in the northern marches. If you serve me well then I will be generous and may even grant you your freedom for I am not a cruel man. If you try to run then you will be blinded."

My father's voice and face were so honest that even strangers trusted him. I saw the two slaves nod eagerly. Perhaps they were used to being threatened with blinding. They looked to me to be the runts of the litter but the others seemed happy enough. When I became the holder of the purse strings I would buy better slaves than these two.

My father anticipated that the deeds and titles of Norton would be ready on the morrow and we arranged passage on a cob which was travelling to London. The ***Maid of Rouen'*** looked nothing like the ships we had in the east. She was almost round in shape and had no oars. However, my father assured me that her capacious and empty hull would accommodate the horses and Ralph had negotiated a good price as she was bound for London anyway and this would save the captain taking on more ballast. The high tide would not be until noon the next day and I hoped that my father's judgement of Brother John was a correct one.

The documents were ready by first light and my father insisted that I be there when they were presented to him. "You will be the lord of the manor once I die. You must be there when they are presented in front of witnesses. I want no dispute over the claim to the land. I lost the manor of Coxold. I will not lose this one too."

There were a host of clerics and officials when we returned. The king, it seemed, had gone to visit his newly acquired estate. The estate of Fitzwaller might lie in Anjou but it was owned by King Henry. I had learned that he had acquired Normandy by first defeating and then imprisoning his elder brother Robert. Anjou was ruled by Fulk of Anjou. He was however in Jerusalem carving out a kingdom for himself there. His son, Geoffrey Plantagenet was only eight years old and the duchy was ripe for plunder. Henry had his beady eye upon this juicy morsel already.

The Bishop of Caen performed the ceremony conferring the title of Baron of Norton and the deeds to the manor of Norton on to my father and his heirs. My father and I had to swear fealty to the King and to promise to supply knights and men at arms should the king require it. As we left my father said, "How many knights and men at arms would be required by the king?"

Brother John smiled, "The king understands that you do not know the land. It is just three knights and twenty men at arms at the moment." He lowered his voice, "However if I were you, Baron Ridley, I would have more available. The northern march is a dangerous place."

As we boarded the ship to wait for the tide I asked. "We only have two knights, father; you and me, where will we get the third?"

He pointed to Wulfstan. "Wulfstan is a fine warrior. He will be the third."

"Can you do that? Can you make an ordinary warrior into a knight?"

"I am the Baron of Norton. Subject to the king and the Bishop of Durham I can do whatever I wish. Remember that Alfraed. This is your road to power. We have been lucky or perhaps it was just *wyrd* but our meeting in the forest with the king has given us a path to a home in England. When we left Constantinople I knew not how it would come about but it has and we should take advantage of it."

As soon as the ship left the estuary I began to vomit. The huge waves we saw terrified me. They seemed to tower over the ship and threatened to send us to the bottom. Each wave drenched me to the skin. How could men sail in such a storm? By the time I was retching drily Wulfstan had fetched me some water. "This storm is an omen!"

He laughed. "This is not a storm. The waves you see are the normal ones for this stretch of water."

My eyes widened and I forgot the sickness, briefly. "Truly?"

"Truly. You will get used to this. It will take the better part of a day and a night to reach the safety of the mighty Tamese."

I could not endure this ship for half a day let alone a day and a night. I suddenly remembered something Brother John had told me. "Is it true that William Adelin, the king's son, perished when his White Ship foundered in these very waters?"

"I believe so."

"It is an omen."

I sank to my knees and rested my head over the side. That way I could be ill without too much movement. The less movement I made the better. I heard Faren's voice and it sounded gentle. "My lord if you drink this it will make you feel less ill."

She proffered a pot beaker. I shook my head. "Thank you for your kindness but I could not keep anything down. The water I just swallowed to cleanse my mouth has rejoined the sea."

I saw her smile and realised she was not as old as I had first thought. "Trust me, my lord, it will work. I promise."

She was a slave and if she displeased me I could have her whipped. She might be telling the truth. "Very well." I dared not look at the liquid in case it brought on the retching again. I lifted it to my lips.

"Drink it down in one and then look out to the horizon. That helps too."

This sounded like witchcraft to me but I had little choice and I complied. There was a brief moment when I felt my stomach churning once more but, as I stared at the horizon I began to feel better. My stomach stopped hurting. I smiled, "Thank you Faren. It works. I shall go below decks and see my father."

Both she and Wulfstan shook their heads. "Better to stay on deck and stare at the horizon. We will keep you company."

I was in their hands and I did as I was bid. That, in itself, was something of a miracle. I rarely listened to anyone for advice. I was, however, ignored for the two of them chattered away. I suspected that the slave was taking advantage of my good nature for she was not working while she and Wulfstan spoke. However, I allowed it for their presence made me feel much better.

Chapter 6

By the time we reached London I had got what Wulfstan laughingly called my '*sea legs*'. I had even managed to keep down a little stale bread. As the horses also looked well when we landed them I concluded that my father's choice of slave had been good. Aiden had cared for them well.

We landed in the early hours of the morning before dawn. The walls of the city were still closed and so we headed north directly. We had no reason to enter the city. There was a Roman road which ran from London all the way north to our new home. The others were all in good spirits for they were home. Ralph and Garth actually kissed the ground when they landed. I was just disappointed. Apart from the white tower, I could see next to the river the buildings looked mean and small. If this was the capital of this land what was the rest of this godforsaken land like?

We were well north of London when we met our first travellers. They were heading south for London. It was what we would have called, in Constantinople, a caravan of merchants. There were armed guards surrounding the pack horses. In truth, I could have taken them with the old men of my father but they viewed us with suspicion and the guards nervously gripped their weapons. I almost laughed as they tightened their grip on their shields and poorly made spears. Perhaps my father was correct and this was a land of opportunity.

What I had noticed was that it was a land of cold. It was only late summer but I was colder than during the worst winter in Byzantium! Even when the sun came out it did not warm the bones. You were always chilled. The wind whipped through your clothes. I almost contemplated putting on my armour to protect my body from the elements. As I looked at my father I could not believe the change in him. From the moment we had seen the coast of England he had been a different man. During the journey through Frankia, he had stooped less but now he looked stronger. He seemed to be taller. How could that be? He looked more like the warrior who strode around the Varangian barracks with a confident gait. What was there in this land to inspire him so?

He spoke to me, when we stopped at an old Roman mansio on the northern road for food, about England. "This is the road that we marched up with Harold Godwinson in five days to fight the battle against the Vikings and traitors just outside York. We will not do it in five days but I fear that particular march cost Harold his country. Many Housecarls lay dead at Stamford Bridge and Aelfraed and I were wounded. Had we been at Hastings then William's bones might lay upon the field and not Harold."

Osric had been listening. "And yet, my lord had you not gone to Constantinople and fought with Aelfraed of Topcliffe then you would not have met young Alfraed's mother and he would not be here. You would not be returning now a rich man. Perhaps this is *wyrd*."

My father looked at me and smiled, "Perhaps you are right. We had to march north to face Tostig and Hadrada. Who knows, if we had not been wounded and marched south, then we would have died there at Hastings." He laughed and slapped Osric about the shoulders. "You are right and we may not make York in five days but we shall not dawdle."

The road was neither friendly nor hostile; it was just empty. There were inns that had grown out of the deserted mansio left by the Romans. They had some of the original stone but repairs had been made in wood. Still, they provided food and shelter and they speeded our journey north. They were not, however, welcoming and the further north we went the more warnings we received of the dangers therein. The forest around Nottingham and Sheffield, called Sherwood by the locals, appeared to be particularly dangerous and then, we were warned, there were dangers from Vikings and Scots. The castle on the Don appeared to be the last safe place we would find before we would have to risk the forest and the men of the woods as the outlaws were known...

My father, of course, laughed such things off. "This is my land and we will be safe there."

I felt intimidated as soon as we saw the huge green swathe stretching out on either side of the road as far as the eye could see. Even the others like Wulfstan were a little apprehensive. "Let us, at least, put on our armour. It does look like a place of ambush."

My father had looked mystified, "Who would ambush us? We are in England."

"In the last mansio, someone spoke of the hooded men who rob travellers upon this road."

Strangely that seemed to make my father chuckle. "Very well but it will not be necessary."

I certainly felt better once I was in my armour but, of course, it meant we walked more than we rode. Once we entered the forest I saw that it was less dense than I had expected. These trees were ancient oak, beech and elm. It was lighter than some of the thick forests of Frankia. Perhaps my father had been right. I almost began to breathe easier. The arrow which thudded into the shield of Ralph led me to believe otherwise. I had my shield around to protect me in an instant. I noticed that Athelstan protected Aiden while Wulfstan put his shield before Faren. We were under attack; it had to be the outlaws.

My father handed his reins to Garth and stepped forward. "Who is it that stops the progress of Ridley who was of Coxold and fought with Harold Godwinson?"

Silence filled the forest until a voice from the forest shouted, angrily, "You lie, Ridley and Aelfraed fell in foreign fields fighting the fierce Norsemen."

"Then I must be a ghost and you cannot kill me. Come and face me like a man. I like to see the face of the man who promises to kill me. I swear that we will not do you harm if you approach in peace."

The hidden voice laughed, "Three youths, a woman and five old men do not worry me!"

"These old men are Varangian Guards and you should fear them but I give my word you shall not be harmed."

We were all standing in a defensive circle. There was no movement in the woods neither was there a flurry of arrows. Eventually, half a dozen men with bows, dressed in leather approached from the woods to the west. They all wore hoods and I took them to be the hooded men we had been warned about.

My father took off his helmet as they approached. I wondered if this was a foolish gesture but, amazingly one of the archers lowered both his hood and his bow. "It is you, my lord!"

"Branton! You are still alive." They ran towards each other and embraced. The other hooded men did not know how to react but they lowered their bows. We lowered our weapons although Wulfstan still protected Faren. I felt obliged to follow my father but I still felt threatened by the men hidden in the woods. I had no doubt that we had seen but a portion of their force.

"Where is Osbert?"

The grey-haired bowman who stood next to my father shook his head. "He has been dead these twenty years. William the Bastard's men hanged him." He pointed behind him. "There is his son, Harold Osbertson." A man my age stepped forward and nodded.

"I can see his father in him. And do you have sons, Branton the archer?"

"I did but they were taken in the plague along with my wife."

"My wife and daughters were taken too. This is my son, Alfraed." I stepped forward and clasped the man's arm. "This is Branton who led Aelfraed's archers." He embraced his old friend again and laughed. "This is *wyrd*."

"It is my lord. And do you return to Coxold?"

"No, the king has given me the manor of Norton on the Tees."

The young man who had led the hooded men from the woods picked up his bow again. "As I thought; Normans!"

Osric stepped forward, "Hooded Man, you may have more men in the woods but if you say that again then you will find your head separated from your body. We fought the Normans when you were still sucking on your mother's titty! The man you insult fought at Stamford Bridge and was named an outlaw. Think before you speak."

The one called Branton snapped, "Enough Robert of the Woods! These are friends. You do not rule this band yet."

My father turned to the young man. "The Normans are here now, my friend. All the ranting and the raving cannot shift them but there are still English men and we will reclaim this land but not by force of arms. My son may dress as a Norman but he is an English knight. And soon there will be more of them." He spread his arms towards the hooded men. "Any who wish to follow me may come to my new manor on the Tees. I know not what we will find but I can guarantee land and Scots to fight. What say you?"

Branton stood behind my father. "I was ever your oathsworn."

He nodded and Harold Osbertson joined him. "And I grew up with tales of Aelfraed and Ridley, the housecarls. I will join you for I have had enough of hiding in the woods. I would be a free man again."

Four others joined us and Branton shouted, "Would any others join us?"

Six men came from the forest and stood behind us. Robert of the Woods looked distinctly unhappy but he gave a wry smile. "Then it seems I now rule the hooded men. I will be sorry to see you leave me, Branton and Harold but I will stay here and fight the Normans!"

Once our twelve new comrades had collected their belongings, which were meagre, they followed us north. We had to leave them outside of Nottingham when we went into the castle to buy supplies and more horses for they were known as outlaws. We also bought some short swords for them. My father was determined that they would be men at arms and not bandits.

The next few days were interesting for me as I saw a different father. He and Branton spent the whole journey talking to each other. He seemed to become younger. How was this possible? Occasionally they turned around to look at me. I guessed they were talking about me. Osric and the others kept their distance from the new men. Only Wulfstan spoke with them. I asked him about that, "Osric and the others are still bridling at being called Normans. They would fight the sons of the Bastard still if they could."

"But the man who insulted them is many miles south in the forest."

"Oh they will come around but it will take a few blows and harsh words first. When the air is cleared they will fight shoulder to shoulder."

"And yet you are friendly towards them."

"I lived longer under the Normans. Your father's oathsworn have spent most of their lives in the east and they have a distorted view of England." He nodded towards Harold Osbertson who rode behind Branton. "Speak with him. He is desperate for companionship and you are of an age." I wondered if I should. Wulfstan added, "He would make a good squire. If he lived off his wits in the woods then he will be handy and he is young enough to train."

He was right, of course. Annoyingly Wulfstan was always right. I nudged Scout to ride next to the young archer. While most of the new men walked we had had two spare horses for Branton and Harold. The young man glanced at me as came next to him and then fixed his eyes on the back of Branton's head.

"Will you miss the woods and the forest?"

He looked at me, "Would you?"

I shrugged. "I have never lived in the woods. This trip is the first time I have camped under the trees. It is summer and it is dry. If you did not enjoy the life then why suffer it? Surely there should have been somewhere you could have gone to make a living."

He shook his head, "I am sorry, my lord, but you know nothing. I was brought up to hunt and to fight. Both are forbidden by the Normans." He sighed, "I know not why Robert of the Wood spurned your offer. I would have followed your father anyway but as a retainer of a Baron I shall never be hungry again and I will get to hunt and to fight. This is one of the greatest days of my life."

"You do not show the same pleasure I would."

"That is because I have had nothing in my life so far and until I have lived for two moons in this Norton I shall not believe that my luck has changed."

"You believe in luck then?"

"Aye. My father, Branton and I have had nought but bad luck."

"My father says that a man makes his own luck. When he and Aelfraed left to travel through the land of the Rus and reached their Miklagård there were many times they could have turned back or given in but they were determined."

"Aye, I know. My father and Uncle Branton often said that they wished they had followed the Housecarls to the east. Their lives would have been better."

I realised then that I was looking at myself had my father not made those decisions all those years ago. Each day I was gaining more and more respect for the man I had taken for granted. He was quiet and unassuming but he had a rod of steel that ran through him.

We rode in silence. It was comfortable. Strangely I no longer felt like the baby of the group. Aiden did not count for he was a slave. Eventually, Harold turned and asked, "What is this manor of Norton like?"

"I have no idea. I suspect it will be a dangerous place. The last lord of the manor was killed and his family enslaved by the Scots."

He nodded, "If I cannot kill Normans then Scotsmen will do."

I laughed, "I like you, Harold. You speak your mind and that is good." He smiled at me and I risked rejection as I asked him, "Would you be my squire?"

He looked at me and frowned, "Squire?"

"I would have you help me to prepare for war and in return, I will train you to be a knight."

"You would do that? You would help me become a knight?"

"It is not an easy route, believe me. It is an easier life being a man at arms."

"I would rather be a knight. When the Normans came on their mighty horses and drove us into the forests I was angry for I wanted to fight back but I could not. Even with the knight killer arrows, we could not defeat them. I would like to be able to face knights equally."

"But we have sworn allegiance to Henry. We cannot fight Normans."

He smiled, "Who knows what the future might bring, besides it will take some time to train a bumpkin like me to be a knight but I will be your squire, Lord Alfraed of Norton, and gladly serve you."

I help out my hand and he clasped it. "Then you are my squire." I suddenly noticed that Branton and my father were watching us and they were smiling.

Chapter 7

We skirted York for the same reason that we had avoided Nottingham. We had also tired of comments about the armour and weapons wielded by my father's men. They marked them as Saxons and Wulfstan and Osric had had to use their strength to ensure our safety. We left a few bloodied noses and broken coxcombs in our wake. Besides which we had less than sixty miles to travel. My father and Branton remembered a narrow stretch of water we could ferry to cross the Tees and avoid further attention. The new men at arms were a resourceful group of men who could chop down trees quickly. They tied them together to make a raft ferry in less than half a day. That way we could reach the manor without encountering other Normans who might object to our presence. My father was being careful. He wanted a wall around us before he met his neighbours. Strong walls made for healthy neighbours. He knew that the Bishop of Durham was still in London and he could not upset him by failing to present his titles. Any clerics who might be unhappy could be ignored. The walls were what was important.

We made our wooden ferry to cross the Tees at a narrow bend in the river some twelve miles from Norton. We saw a walled farm on the escarpment and Osric was convinced that we were being watched. None of them knew the name of the settlement. This was not a friendly place. We rode north without speaking to our new neighbours. As Wulfstan pointed out, "They have been raided and attacked from the south and from the north. It will take some time to build trust. Fear not, Alfraed, your father is skilled when talking to people. They will trust him and come around to his viewpoint."

I was learning much about my father. In fact, the slow journey north had given me the chance to see him in a different light. In Constantinople, he had been the Emperor's man. Here he was his own man. King Henry was on the other side of the Channel. My father had more authority even though he commanded fewer men than he had before.

Since Harold had agreed to be my squire I had spent every moment of each day instructing him in the skills of a knight. We could do much from the back of a horse. I taught him the names of all the equipment he would have to service and clean. He had much to learn. He could use a sword but had no experience with a shield, armour, or a helmet. None of them were easy to use. They looked to be easy but in the hands of a novice, a shield could be a hindrance. Each night I devoted an hour to giving him the basics of a sword and a shield. I also had to show him how to ride properly. He knew how to stay on a horse and that was about it.

Wulfstan and the others spent the same hour improving the skills of the new men at arms. As archers they were peerless but they had much to learn about other weapons. We had time and we would use it. By the time we reached the stone church at Norton, we were ready to put down roots.

The church was unfinished. There were stone walls and a wooden tower. The half-finished roof was just covered in turf. We reached the site too late to begin work and so we explored the land. We would camp and when dawn broke set about building our castle. My father took me to the church while the others scouted the land.

"This will be where I will be buried Alfraed. We have to finish this quickly."

I gave him a sudden, worried look. "You are not ill, are you? I know that this cold climate is not good…"

"Fear not my son I have no intention of leaving you yet." He took out his sword and tapped the floor. It was dirt. "This should be a stone floor. The walls are stone but I wonder why it is unfinished?"

Perhaps my ears were younger or I was more alert but I heard the noise from behind the tattered hemp curtain which hung listlessly at the back of the altar. I whipped out my sword. "Come from behind there before I pierce your hide."

I heard a voice, full of fear, say, "I am sorry, masters, do not hurt me."

The figure which emerged from behind the curtain was almost a skeleton dressed in rags. I later learned that Peter was but two years younger than I was but it was difficult to tell that from his first appearance.

"Son, put your sword away." I sheathed it and my father waved the youth forward. "Come so that we can see you. Tell us your name and your story."

"I am Peter of Yarum. I served with the priest of this church Father Egbert."

"And where is he now?"

The young man pointed outside the doorway. "He died three months ago. He received a blow to the head when the Scots took the lord of the manor, Baron De Ville. He did not recover. I buried him and gave him the last rites."

"You are a priest then?"

He shook his head. "I was learning to be a priest."

"And why have you stayed?"

"The church was all that Father Egbert wanted. He saw it as a sign that civilisation had arrived."

"What happened here? We have heard that the manor was raided by the Scots. How did you survive?"

He began to well up. "I would have stayed when the soldiers came, but Father Egbert made me run and hide." He pointed to a large oak tree. "I climbed up there and saw them."

"Come we will go outside for you need food and I would sit while you tell me the tale."

Aiden had seen to the horses and Wulfstan had lit a fire. Faren was already preparing food. She looked up when we approached. "Faren, this is Peter and he needs food."

"That he does, master. Here, eat this to be going on with." She handed him some stale bread and a bowl of the thin soup she was making. She was a fine cook and the broth would be nourishing. When she had finished cooking it would be a hearty meal. He gratefully took the bowl and dipped the bread in to soften it. He closed his eyes and sucked, almost deliriously on the softening loaf. Father nodded to a couple of nearby decaying logs and I pulled them over so that we could sit down.

We waited until he had cleaned the bowl. Faren said, "You will have to wait now until the food is ready for all but you will need many more meals before we see some flesh on your bones."

My father laughed, "She has a sharp tongue, Peter, but she is kind. Now that you have eaten tell me all. I will ask questions when you have finished."

"They came from the north across the tidal marshes. His lordship had not thought an enemy would come across them for they are dangerous." He shrugged, "Perhaps they had a guide for they knew the secret pathways. I was woken by the noise of battle. They broke down the gate for it was not finished. That was when I was told to hide. By the time I reached the tree all of the knights had been killed and Father Egbert struck on the head. They took Lady Adela and her mother Judith of Norton. The slaves they took too but the men they slaughtered."

"Tell me, Peter, for you have lived here with the deceased Baron of Norton, how do you suppose that Scottish raiders managed to get here through the land of the Bishop of Durham and Hartness?"

The young novice looked at the ground and shook his head. "I am but a novice priest. I know not about such things."

My father nodded and smiled, "Would you still be a priest?"

His eyes opened in surprise, "Yes, my lord, but how? I am but a novice."

"You can read?" He nodded. "Then you can learn." He pointed to the church. "I will finish this church and you shall be my priest. I will get you ordained."

"You can do this, my lord?"

"Probably but you will be God's man first and then mine. Understand? You will be loyal to me!" Peter nodded and dropped to his knees. "Come, rise. You are no slave. Now as my man you must be truthful. Answer me about these Scots. How do you know that they were Scots?"

"I did not recognise their coat of arms and they spoke with an accent."

"Then they could have come from anywhere north of here. Possibly just over the other side of the tidal reaches."

"But that is Hartness and the land of Baron De Brus."

My father said nothing in answer to that. "Faren, see to some better clothes for the priest. Father Peter is now my man too. Alfraed, come with me and we will find Wulfstan."

We headed north towards the edge of the land that belonged to my father. "We will need good stone and a mason. I will also need to visit with this De Brus and see the Bishop's reeve at Durham. I need to sniff out the land. There is something wrong here."

"How will we get the stone here?"

"There are quarries close to Persebrig. We can sail them down and use carts to bring them the last four miles or so. That is for the future. We need more horses and we need our walls up."

Ralph and the others trudged up the bank. I saw that their boots were covered in mud. "It is treacherous down there my lord. There are muddy holes that will suck you down. We need not worry too much about an attack from this direction."

"And that is where you are wrong, old friend. Someone used paths in that morass to launch an attack on the castle. We need to make this side of our fort impregnable." As we walked back he told Branton and his other oathsworn what we had discovered.

"Then, my lord, when we have built the wooden walls we will scout the paths ourselves. I will become as familiar with them as any attacker," Wulfstan grinned, "and I am sure master Alfraed and his new squire can discover the joys of swamps too. It is all good training to be a knight."

My mouth dropped open, "How can that be good training to be a knight? We ride horses."

"Aye and when an axeman takes the legs from your horse and you are afoot then you will need to be nimble on your feet and know where the solid ground lies." He always had an answer.

After we had eaten, my father gathered us around. "We have two tasks this week. First, we make our ditch and our walls." He pointed to the church. "We surround the church with the walls and we make a roof. We will have to send to Persebrig for our stone. I would have a stone floor for the church. When the walls are completed and the church roofed then I will go with Ralph, Garth, my son and Harold and we will travel to Durham. The rest of you can build my hall."

Osric shook his head. "That is too few men to protect you, my lord. Take more of us."

My father rarely raised his voice but he had this ability to sound his words slowly so that each one was like the blow of an axe on a shield. "I am taking three good knights and a squire for protection. I need a hall building ready for the winter. We have much to do." He shrugged, "If there are any guards to be hired or bought in Dunelm then I will buy them. That is all that I can promise."

And so we worked hard. All of us, father included, cut the wood for the palisades and buried them in the ground. Then we dug a ditch all the way around and piled the spoil next to the ramparts. Wulfstan explained that when we acquired the stone we would reinforce the base with it and use it to build a gate and a tower. I could see that adding a curtain for the church would add to our work but father was determined. It took us a good ten days, working every moment of daylight to complete it but when it was finished we were safe; for the first time.

I was curious about the lack of interest in us. None of those who owed fealty to my father and worked the land came to see us. He seemed philosophical about the whole thing. "Their crops are still to be harvested as are their animals. When we are secure then we will tax them."

The completion of the roof of the church proved to be easier than we had expected. On one of his scouting expeditions, Wulfstan had found the remains of a Roman house. It had not been a fine villa; there were neither mosaics nor a bathhouse but there were still some stones and, best of all, roof tiles. We made a cart and carried them back so that, before we left for the Bishop's castle, we had a waterproof roof on the church and Osric had some stone for the foundations of the hall.

When we left we took Aiden with us to look after the pack horses and my father asked Faren what supplies she needed. Surprisingly there was little she asked for. "We are close enough to the sea to make our own salt, my lord and you have more spices than I have seen before. Perhaps some flour to tide us over until the crops are in."

We were up before dawn and ready to ride whilst it was still dark. There was a well-worn track that headed north and west to meet up with the old Roman Road. As it went to Durham and thence no further we took to calling it the Durham Road. We smelled the fires from the farms of our tenants as we headed northwest. We had yet to meet them but the smell of wood smoke alerted us to their position. We knew that the manor given to my father abutted the lands of the Bishop. Redemarshall and Bishop's ton were the two settlements Brother John had identified on a map.

The first dim light of the new dawn peered over the eastern horizon as we passed by the first of the villages which we owned. Thorpe had been settled by Danes. I wondered who lived there now. They had a wooden walled village and it looked to be a good defensive site. Once we were north then we were in the land owned directly by the Bishop. I saw little evidence of a military presence as we headed along the road which was still cobbled in places.

Harold and I led the small column while Aiden brought up the rear with the horses. We only spoke once it was light. Until then, we warily watched and listened for danger. I took the opportunity of examining my squire and his appearance. He was a better warrior now than when we had first met but he did not look like a squire. His leather armour was functional as were his leather helmet and sword. Until we had a smith working in the fort we would be hampered and have to rely on the weapons and armour we had brought from the east. He needed a shield. The other expense I needed to persuade my father to make was some better horses. Scout was a good horse but he was no warhorse. He would struggle to carry me in armour to battle. I needed a young horse which was much bigger than he was. I was not hopeful about being able to buy one. They were uncommon here in the north. I would need to win one on the field of battle. Somehow I doubted that Scottish raiders would provide what I needed.

I listened to my father speaking with Ralph and Garth behind me. If you did not know them it would be hard to identify the lord for they spoke easily with each other. My father had told me how often they had stood in a shield wall. There was little rank in a wall of death. It explained much.

"We will need a mason, Lord Ridley. Our skills in building are basic."

"Aye, but will we find one? I have not noticed many fine buildings. There will be masons in Durham but I suspect that they will be occupied working for the Bishop."

"And Osric is right too, lord, we have too few men. We could not defend our walls if we were attacked. We have barely enough men to hold the tower we have yet to build."

My father lowered his voice but I could still hear his words. "We must give my son a start. He is young but he is improving."

Garth chuckled, "Aye he is but have we enough days left to make him into his father?"

"He will not be his father. His father was a housecarl. My son is a knight. He will achieve more than I could ever have dreamed. He will take Ridley and his name into the future and bards will boast of his deeds."

"Your deeds are mighty, my lord and men sing of them."

"That is kind of you, Ralph, but we both know that we are forgotten already in Byzantium." He raised his voice. "Alfraed, take Harold and scout ahead. There is a forest coming up and it is the sort of place a bandit might use for an ambush." He laughed a little, "I am sure Harold will identify the perfect place for such an ambush!"

To be honest I was glad to ride ahead. The sedate pace of the three older warriors did not suit me. I kicked Scout on. He seemed pleased to be trotting rather than walking. "Where would you ambush us if you were waiting in the woods?"

"You see yonder, sir, where the road rises and then turns. That would be a good place for an ambush. A pair of good archers could cover the approach and they would wait around the bend. The others would wait in the ditches and the brush on this side of the woods."

"Not in the woods?"

"No, my lord. Most horsemen worry only about woods and they would not be alert until they entered the eaves. A good bandit can disguise himself and lie in a ditch and remain unseen."

"And were you a good bandit?"

He grinned, "Aye, my lord, the best. I think that is why Robert of the Wood was so angry about my leaving. I could hide in a ditch all day and not be seen."

"Have you killed up close, with a dagger?"

His face became serious, "Aye my lord; more times than I care to think of."

"Is it hard?"

"It never gets easy but in most cases, it was the man I killed or me. I survived. My father did not."

We had reached the bend in the road. Harold slipped from his horse and jabbed his spear into the murky waters of the ditch which ran along the road. I knew from those in the east that they were designed to be kept clean. Since the Romans had left no one had bothered. "And you could hide in that water?"

He nodded, "You have a reed through which you breathe. Normally you hide there just before the ambush. It is not long to wait and it guarantees success."

There were no hidden men and we waved on the others. The woods went almost all the way to the walls of Durham. When we emerged on the ridge to the south of the castle we halted. The road went steeply down to the bridge across the river. There was a gatehouse there and we saw the road climbed up to the castle and the cathedral which dominated the skyline. We could see the masons working on the magnificent structure. The river ran around three sides of the castle and the town. I could now see why the Scots had not bothered trying to take it. They would have lost many men. It seemed to me that the only way would be to build rafts and cross the river. Of course, an attacker would then have to climb the steep bank and face arrows and missiles from the walls. It explained why they had chosen the softer target of Norton.

Ralph, however, had a sharp, military mind. "The Scots would have needed to pass close by this castle to reach Norton. Why did the Constable not sally forth and bring them to battle?"

My father pointed to the west. "Perhaps there is a ford further west."

Ralph was not convinced, "Perhaps."

Chapter 8

The men at arms who presented their spears to us were not dressed in mail. They wore leather but they looked like men who knew their business. They looked insolently at my father, who smiled, patiently. When they did not speak he did so. "I am Baron Ridley of Norton, recently appointed by King Henry. I am here to present my titles and deeds to the Seneschal."

His tone and titles had an immediate effect. "If you would dismount then you can lead your horses up to the hall. The Seneschal is holding his weekly court. You will have to wait until he has finished."

We dismounted. I did not like the man's tone but my father and his oathsworn seemed happy enough. The hooves of our horses clattered across the stone bridge. It was a steep climb up to the tower and the hall. I noticed that the wall ran along both sides of the gate and it turned. It was not finished yet but an enemy would have to endure an attack from both sides if he was to take the tower. This was a castle that would be the equal of Caen when it was finished.

The cathedral lay to one side of the bailey. It had men scurrying up the half-finished tower. They had, seemingly, many masons here. There was a trough filled with water. "Aiden, water the horses. Harold, help him."

The four of us walked towards the Great Hall. The two guards saw our weapons and our armour but they parted to allow us entry. Inside there was a small man seated on a chair that looked far too big for him. This was the first time I saw the Seneschal of Durham, Geoffrey Fitzrobert. I came to learn what a clever and devious man he was. He would have fitted in well at the court of the Emperor. He knew how to play the game of politics. He was as shifty as quicksand. We stood at the back and listened to his deliberations. It would tell us much about the man. I was learning. The man who was brought forward to be examined was not a knight. His rough clothes showed him to be a workingman but a freeman. The Seneschal had a high pitched voice and I noted that he spoke in Norman. I wondered if the man could understand what was being said.

"William of Lincoln you have been found guilty of attempting to defraud the Bishop of four gold pieces. How plead you?"

Surprisingly the man spoke in Norman. It was halting but I could understand it. "My lord, I protest. I was paid that coin for work on the West Chancel of the cathedral. It was honestly earned."

The Seneschal smiled and it was an evil smile filled with cruelty. "Robert of Durham disputes that and maintains that he completed the work. He says that you did not do the work you were contracted for. He says that you spent much time with your wife. Are you calling the master mason a liar?"

I did not have much experience in courts but I knew that this was not something to say lightly. The accused's shoulders slumped, "I did the work."

"And Robert of Durham says you lie. We have no reason to doubt the word of the master mason. You are fined four gold pieces and banished from Durham. Pay my clerk." The mason reached into his purse and walked towards the clerk. "If there are no further cases to be heard then this session herewith ends." The strident voice echoed around the hall.

As the people started to leave my father whispered something in Ralph's ear; he nodded and left. The three of us approached the Seneschal who had stood and was watching the court empty. We waited patiently. Fitzrobert waved his hand at my father, seeing that he clutched documents. My father inclined his head and handed over the titles and deeds given to him by Brother John in Normandy.

"My lord, I am Baron Ridley of Norton and King Henry has endowed me with the manor of Norton. Here are my titles and deeds."

The Seneschal allowed a brief look of irritation to flash across his face before he adopted the smile of a serpent and began to read the documents. "It is good that good King Henry has appointed a lord of the manor for Norton. We were saddened when the previous owner, Baron Guy de Ville was so treacherously slain by the Scots." My father said nothing. "Would you and your companions care to spend the night in the castle? I am sure it will be more comfortable than a night on the road."

"Thank you for your kind offer, my lord, but my son and I need to get back to the manor. We have yet to build a wall around my hall."

"Of course. This is your son?"

I stepped forward, "Alfraed of Norton, my lord."

"Another Saxon name; how interesting. I suspect there is some story here. You must promise me that you will visit at Christmas time. We hold a winter feast and I would get to know you. If there is aught that I can do for you then please let me know. The Bishop is still in London and I rule in his stead."

My father nodded, "Thank you for your generous offer and hospitality. We will take advantage of your market for we have come north with few possessions."

"You have coin?"

My father smiled back at the question. "We have coin."

After we had left Garth said, "There is someone I would not trust out of my sight."

"You are right, Garth. Let us complete our business and get back to Norton."

I was surprised to see Ralph outside and he was talking to the mason. My father approached him. "William of Lincoln has my oathsworn here explained what I want of you?"

The mason nodded. "I did not lie to the court, Baron Ridley. I did the work but I had just finished my work and they wanted to rob me of my payment."

"The Seneschal and this Robert of Durham are working together?"

The mason shifted from foot to foot. "I would not wish to risk further censure. I have lost enough and I will keep my counsel." He raised his head to look at my father. "You wish me to build a church?"

"No, the church is built but it is crude and I would like it improved and I would have a tower built."

"I do not know you, sir and I do not wish to offend you but what is to stop you from withholding my payment too?"

Ralph began to bridle but my father restrained him. "No Ralph, he is right. And he appears to be an honest man." He looked at the mason. "I am Ridley of Norton and when I give my word I keep it. I shall house you and your family and pay you five gold pieces for your work. I give you my word but if that is not good enough then we will part."

As I have said my father had this way of speaking that made people trust him. I do not think I will ever have that skill. It worked yet again. William smiled, "I take your word and the work my lord. I shall get my family."

My father clasped his arm. "Garth, go with him and see that he is not molested."

"Thank you, my lord."

When they had gone my father shook his head. "There is much deception here. Come, we will see what the market has to offer."

We found little of value in the market. There were neither weapons nor armour and when we asked about a smith we were told that he only worked for the Seneschal. It was the same story with the horses. The one or two they had for sale were of a very poor quality. We bought some rye and wheat flour for Faren. In all, we spent but two hours in the castle. It was a disappointing expedition. However, the short time in the castle meant we could reach home before dark. When Garth arrived back we were ready to leave.

William had two sons, a daughter and a tired-looking wife. Judith. My father smiled, "Judith, wife of William, you should ride with your daughter."

"Oh no my lord, I could not."

"I insist. Aiden, help the lady onto the horse. William put your tools in the packs on the horses. I would be gone from hence." She looked relieved once she wearily mounted. Faren would have someone else to fatten up. It was not just the priest who was thin and emaciated. That was another difference with the east. In the east even the less well off were well fed whilst the rich were positively obese! This land of the north appeared to be constantly on the edge of famine. I had noticed the lack of animals in the fields as we had travelled north. The fields just grew rye, barley and various green vegetables. It would be a poor diet.

Although I was young and did not know England I too felt that we were in danger as long as we remained in the castle. Our weapons and armour were of a much higher quality than those we saw within the castle walls. There were many envious glances from the handful of knights that we saw. All of them still had the long kite shield and the old fashioned mail with the ventail. My lamellar armour attracted much attention.

As we left my father put Aiden, the mason and the pack horses in the middle. He rode at the fore with Garth and Ralph. "Alfraed you and Harold watch our rear. I do not trust these people."

We noticed that the guards at the gate over the bridge took a great deal of interest in the direction we were taking. There was only one road south but they may have been making sure that we did leave the castle.

We had plenty of time to return home before dark. Had we not left before dawn we might have struggled. I suspected that the younger child of the mason would slow us down for he looked to be barely six years old. I think Garth thought so too for he reached down to pull the boy before him on his saddle. Garth was a sentimental man. I saw him making the boy smile. He was just like a doting grandfather. He had been denied the opportunity to father children and he was too old to do so now. The young boy made him smile. The laughter of the child enlivened the journey home.

We rode at a little distance from Aiden and the horses. I wanted to be able to react to danger. Harold kept looking over his shoulder to ensure that we were not followed. I idly drew my sword and checked the sharpness of the blade. Harold looked at me, "You think we might need our weapons, my lord?"

"Let us just say, Harold, that I can feel the hairs on the back of my neck prickling. Wulfstan has taught me to trust such things." I ruffled Scout's ears. "Beside Scout here is a little restless and is looking around. He senses something and I have come to trust his judgement."

He nodded, "Wulfstan is a mighty warrior. Why does he not lead his own band?"

"He is oathsworn to my father."

"Oathsworn?"

"Aye it appears a little archaic I know but my father and the others remember when a man took an oath to fight for a man and he kept that oath unto death. My father swore one to your namesake, Harold Godwinson. It was only a wound that prevented him from keeping his oath. He was still at Stamford Bridge when Harold and his housecarls died."

"I think it is good to swear an oath and follow someone. Robert of the Wood always wanted my father to swear an oath to him but he said he had already sworn one oath and that was to Lord Aelfraed and so long as Aelfraed lived he would honour that oath."

Perhaps our conversation distracted us or it could have been that we were too far from the front of the column to smell danger but whatever the reason the first we knew of the ambush was when the arrows flew. Garth, at the front, was quick and his shield came around to protect the child. He was struck in the shoulder by a second arrow. Still, the warrior held his seat and protected the child.

My sword was already drawn and I yelled to Harold, "Follow me!"

I knew from what Harold had told me that the ambushers would be deep enough in the woods to hide and yet close enough to release arrows accurately. I guessed the distance to the hidden target and I leaned forward over Scout to make myself an even smaller target. I knew that I needed to attract arrows: I was armoured and Harold was not. Even so, it was a gut-wrenching ride through the undergrowth as I headed towards an unknown number of men. I was relieved when no arrows came my way.

To my surprise, these were not bandits but soldiers who wore both mail and leather. I discovered that when Scout flushed two of them from their hiding place as he galloped towards them. They came so quickly that I barely had time to react. I sliced at the nearer one to my right and was rewarded by my blade sinking into his neck. I jerked Scout's head around and the second warrior was taken by surprise as I sank my sword into his chest. Had I not had such a good seat I might have tumbled from my horse but I lowered my sword and allowed his body to slide from my blade.

My move had allowed Harold to join me and he shouted, "To the right my lord, they are heading for their horses!"

He held his spear like a lance and we plunged through the thinning trees towards the seven men who were running away from us. I knew not why they ran; we were just two warriors on horses but run they did. I watched as Harold pulled back his arm and punched the head of his spear between the shoulder blades of the man at arms who was tardier than the rest.

I saw the horses, there were ten of them. One warrior was mounted holding the reins of the others. I slashed down and laid open the back of the man who ran, too slowly, before me. I glanced at his body as I passed. His back looked like a freshly cut fig, oozing red. The others had reached their horses. As Harold thrust his spear again at one of the riders another tried to strike at his unguarded head. I kicked Scout and jammed my shield between the sword and Harold. I have quick hands and my sword stabbed into the mailed warrior's side. He tumbled from his horse. The blow to Harold had surprised him and he lay on the ground unhorsed. I watched in frustration as the remaining six galloped west.

"Secure the horses!" It was foolish I know but I charged after the fleeing riders. I felt all-powerful. Scout was a good horse and had nimble feet. His hooves danced around the roots of the trees. The last rider was not so lucky and his horse stumbled. It allowed me to close with him. He glanced over his shoulder and tried to pull his sword from its scabbard. He was one of the guards from the castle! I brought my sword down hard and was rewarded by seeing his sword bend. "Surrender or die!"

His answer was to strike with his bent sword at Scout's head. It infuriated me and I jerked Scout's head away from danger whilst swinging my sword horizontally. His head flew from his shoulders and bounced away through the woods. I looked up and saw that the other five men were too far away for me to catch. I grabbed the reins of the soldier's horse and led him back to the others.

My father and Ralph were attending to Garth's wound while Harold, William and Aiden stood with drawn weapons watching the mason's wife and the children.

"They have fled."

Ralph looked up and shook his head. "That was brave, master Alfraed, but exceptionally foolish. Had they turned on you then you would now be dead and we might be in danger."

He was right but I needed no instruction from an old man. I ignored his comment. "They were from the castle."

My father looked up, "How do you know?"

"The last man I killed was one of the surly guards from the gate."

I saw him frown. "Aiden, tie the horses to the trees and then you and Harold go and collect the armour, helmets and weapons from the dead." As they went off he smiled at me. "Despite Ralph's harsh words, my son, I am proud of you. Aelfraed would have done the same."

"How is Garth?"

Garth looked up and grinned, "Garth is feeling foolish. It will not happen again, young master." He nodded at me, "By God but you have quick hands. They are like quicksilver."

I smiled. All young men liked praise and I knew that this was genuine praise. Garth knew swordplay; he had practised it every day in Constantinople.

When Aiden and Harold returned my father looked at the haul. "Well, we have made a fair trade. One wound for five horses, two sets of mail, four swords and five bows." He looked at the collection. "Where are the helmets?"

Harold flushed, "I am sorry my lord we forgot them."

"Go and get them while we mount." As Harold turned my father said, "My son, the one you said you recognised, where is he?"

"His head is yonder."

"Fetch his head, too, Harold. We may have to return to the castle and have words with the Seneschal."

While they went off to complete the grisly deed I examined the mail and the weapons. They were neither of the finest quality but they were better than nothing and Harold had shown that he needed protection. "Father, there were no shields; I wonder why not?"

Ralph snorted, "They would have identified them as the men from the castle. Someone does not wish your father to rule Norton."

When Harold returned with the three helmets he had found he also brought the head of the dead man. The journey from the body to the ground had caused the head to smash into rocks and roots. It could have been the eyeless skull of any man. The identity of the man could not be identified for certain now.

"You are sure that he was the guard?"

"Aye father."

"Well we cannot prove it and so we shall have to bide our time but we will be on our guard and keep a careful watch."

The attack had delayed us and the sun was just setting as we neared our castle. After Durham, it looked small and vulnerable but it was home and we would defend it.

Faren, although a slave, was like a mother hen and she fussed over both the children and Judith when she saw their pitiful condition.

My father addressed his new mason. "For tonight, William, we will house your family in the hall but tomorrow I will have my men build a hut for you inside the walls."

"Thank you, my lord. I am your man." He paused, "I see no stone here."

"No, we need to go to Persebrig to buy some."

"I will accompany the buyers for some of these stone merchants will take the coins from a dead man's eyes."

That evening after we had eaten and the family had gone to claim a corner of the hall for themselves I sat with my father, his oathsworn and Branton. It was a council of war.

We had told the others what had happened. Wulfstan rubbed his beard. "I wonder why they did not send knights."

Ralph laughed, "I think they saw three old men and two boys. They probably thought that ten men at arms could do the job. They did not know the ferocity of young Alfraed here." He shook his head at the memory of my reckless charge. "Wulfstan he was fearless."

Wulfstan jokingly wagged his finger at me. "Make sure you are not so reckless when you face the Norman knights."

I laughed, "We saw off those in Normandy easily enough."

"We were lucky that time for they were careless and thought that we could not defend ourselves. When those men at arms return to the

Seneschal they will know your mettle and they may try to use your recklessness to their advantage."

"How do you mean?"

"They will feign retreat and when you follow they will turn and destroy you."

"It is how William the Bastard won when he defeated Harold. His knights ran and the fyrd followed. Only the Housecarls stood firm and they were surrounded and slaughtered. You need to use your head, Alfraed, as well as your sword."

Of all of my father's men, Ralph was the wisest. He understood war and his advice would be heeded.

My father nodded his agreement and said, "Alfraed, I would have you and Harold go to Persebrig and buy the stone for the castle."

I was both pleased and surprised, "That is a great responsibility, father. Can I be trusted?"

He laughed, "It takes a long time to finish a decent castle and it will be you who reaps the benefits, not I. Besides, it will teach you how to negotiate. I am sure William will be a good adviser." His face became serious. We now know that we need to be careful here. This is a land filled with our enemies. Until we have built up our strength we will need to tread carefully."

I was excited to be given such a task.

Chapter 9

We now had surplus horses and we took one for William as well as a spare. I began to head to the west but William said, "My lord we can save time if we head to the river. We will need a boat anyway. Carts are expensive and you have to hire drivers."

It was my first decision. I could not fault the argument my mason had used but it was hard to take advice from someone who was not a warrior. "Very well."

We took the track towards the Tees. It was south of us. I knew that Persebrig was to the west and I hoped we were not making an unnecessary journey. The track went over undulating ground and had not been built by the Romans. In winter it would become a muddy morass.

"Tell me, William, how do you make a living? I know that you are a mason and build churches and cathedrals but do you not have a home of your own?"

"All my children but William, my eldest, were born in Durham. We lived there for the best part of four years. I hoped for another three or four years of work. By then William would have been able to assist me and we could have taken on bigger jobs. I like not working for others such as Robert of Durham. I have my own ideas of how buildings should be created."

"And how long will it take to finish the church and the tower?"

"The church will not take long; it just needs a stone floor but the tower will take longer. It depends on how large you wish it to be."

"So you will be living with us for some time?"

"I hope so, sir. Your father seems like a fair master."

"He is the fairest man I have ever met and I know that he will treat you and your family well. He came from humble origins."

Harold looked up. "My father told me that the master had an estate at Coxold."

"He did but that was a reward for services to the king. He began his life as a humble soldier and then became a Housecarl. He has never forgotten his roots and the way he was brought up."

Suddenly the river was ahead of us. I had never seen it this far east and it was wide. There were a few huts there; all of them made from wattle and daub. What struck me was the small mound that was adjacent to the river. I realised it would make the perfect site for a castle. I reined in and the other two looked at me in surprise.

"My lord?"

"I am just looking, Harold, at the hill. William, would this make a good place to site a castle?"

The mason dismounted and picked up a handful of earth. He handed his reins to Harold and walked to the river's edge and then paced back to us. "It would, my lord. The ground is firmer than in Norton. We would be able to build in stone here."

"Good, then when we return we will broach the subject with my father. And now let us introduce ourselves to our people."

I suddenly realised I had no markings on my shield. It was plainly covered with a blue dye on the leather covering. We had been remiss and I needed a sign sooner rather than later. I needed people to know who we were. It seemed to me that there were many dishonourable men in these parts. I needed them to know that I was not one of them.

There were too few of us to worry the small village and the people came out to see us. I noticed that there was a smith here. That was good news. I saw, too, the sheaf of barley that marked the home of an alewife. Wulfstan had told me that he dreamed of finding some decent beer when we reached England. He would have his wish here. In the river, there were three small boats. Two of them looked like large fishing ships but the third looked to be capable of carrying cargo.

I did not dismount but I spoke in English. I was lucky that my father had spoken to me in that language since the day I was born. It sounded like a foreign language to me but I could speak it fluently.

"What is the name of this place?"

"It is Stockton."

I nodded, trying to affect the same pose as I thought my father might. "I am Alfraed of Norton and my father, Ridley of Norton has been granted that manor by King Henry."

I was disappointed that they did not seem enthusiastic. They began to drift back into their places of work. I began to redden. I had not dismissed them. "My father will be coming here in a week or so and we will decide upon the taxes that you will have to pay."

The blacksmith, obvious by his apron and huge arms, laughed. "The last lord of the manor took our taxes and the Scots took them when they killed him. Perhaps we should pay them directly to the Scots, sir and save time."

"Insolent wretch! We are here to stay and you will give us respect as well as taxes."

He did not seem at all put out by my tone. "We will see, young Alfraed of Norton. If you are still here this time next year then I might change my opinion. And now, good sir, we must get back to our labours so that we can pay the taxes you desire."

"What is your name?"

"I am Alf the smith and yonder is my place of work should you wish more conference with me."

I frowned. This had not been a good start. As we headed towards the river bank and the ships which stood there I began to imagine a castle here. Then Alf the Smith would have to take heed of my words or he would be punished. The thought brought a smile back to my face. I knew that the captains of the ships would need coin to take us upstream. I had plenty in my purse but I was keen to show how I could negotiate.

As we dismounted William said, "My lord would you mind if I spoke with the captain first?"

I frowned; was he trying to cheat me in some way. "Why?"

"If he is heading to sea or he has cargo already then he may not be suitable. It is better to discover such things first. Equally, we may be able to journey further upstream with the smaller fishing boats and save our horses. It would be best to discover what we can do first."

That seemed reasonable. "Very well go and ask."

As he wandered off I turned to Harold. I knew I could trust my squire. "What did you make of the blacksmith?"

He smiled, "He upset you, my lord?"

"He was insolent!"

"I think I can understand him. Many men live as outlaws because they do not wish to pay taxes and work for someone else. Those like the Smith who work to produce metal are content to pay taxes so long as they are protected. The former Baron did not protect them."

"But he died along with his knights."

"And that is the lot of the knight. He fights and he dies. Even I know that but the smiths and sailors go on with their daily lives. Once your father has shown them that he is here to stay and, more importantly, strong enough to stop raiders and predators then you will gain respect."

I knew that he was telling me the truth but it was hard to hear such truths. I did not expect to have to earn respect. We were the lords of the manor; it was our due.

William wandered over. "The captain is willing to take us to Persebrig and the quarries but he tells me there are no workers there. They were taken as slaves by the Scots."

"Then what is the point of going there if there is no stone?"

"There is stone, we just need to collect it. The captain and his crew are willing to act as workers, for a payment."

I felt cheated, William had negotiated for me. "Very well but I will settle the price." I paused and lowered my voice. "How much would you recommend?"

"A silver piece for the captain and two copper coins for each of the men should suffice."

Surprisingly they seemed happy to agree. "Harold, stay here and look after the horses. If we are not back by dark, then return to Norton."

"Aye my lord."

The river was wide but it twisted and turned through thick woods. Willows draped down to the water. It looked to be teeming with game. I saw many birds and animals which could be hunted; I would have to get a hawk.

The captain's name was Olaf. It seemed he came from a long line of seafarers. I saw Viking blood in him and he had a hard face but he was a pleasant man. He lived with his wife in Stockton. She turned out to be Alf's sister. Most of his trade was in carrying iron ore from the hills on the southern side of the river. He was almost like a ferry. I asked him why he did not bring goods that the villagers could use.

"They have little money. Norton is a poor manor, meaning no disrespect. The land is marshy and the farms are small. The nearest wheat farm is south of the river. It might not be so bad a living but the Scots raid and pillage every couple of years and the people have little hope of prosperity."

"Why does the Bishop not stop them?"

"Because he lives in London and the other lords, well let us just say it serves them to keep this river and its people frightened and wary. The Normans have long memories and it was the Eorls from around here who rebelled against William the Bastard. All of them were slaughtered but they are still suspicious of those who live hard by the river. My wife and her family hid close by the river to escape the slaughter. She was but a child then." He shook his head. "I know that you are not Normans but it will take some time to win them around. Be patient, my lord, they are good people."

I had much to think about as we sailed west. It was slow going for the wind was not in our favour but the captain seemed quite happy to tack back and forth. I could see why he had such a small boat. Anything larger would have struggled to negotiate some of the bends.

"She is a knarr. They do not make them now but my ancestors sailed them to Miklagård and back. They are a sturdy type of vessel. They can handle the ocean but they ply the river well." He pointed to the north. "There, that is where the quarries are. Persebrig is a couple of miles to the west but we can quarry and load from here."

He pulled his small ship close to the shore. There was no tide and he had his small crew tie us fore and aft to a couple of trees. William had brought his tools with him but he was confident that we could just pick up the stones that we would need.

We had a short climb up the bank and along a track. It was less than a hundred paces, all told, but the last part was quite a steep climb. We emerged through a hedgerow and I saw the quarry before me. It was not what I was expecting. The ones I had seen in the east were deep holes. This was more like the side of a cliff that had crumbled in a storm.

"There my lord; this is perfectly good stone for the church and the tower."

I only knew marble and granite and this was neither. It was a yellow sandstone. I was not so certain. "Why is no one here? Who owns this quarry? The Bishop of Durham could use this stone for his cathedral."

"No, my lord. This is good stone but it does not carve well. Your father wants stone to walk upon and to keep him safe. This is perfect for that." He grinned at Olaf, "Well captain, time for your men to earn their money. The sooner it is loaded the sooner we can get you back to your wife!"

I sat on one of the larger rocks and watched as they picked the stones selected by William and began to transport them down the slope to the ship. I was surprised at the speed with which they did so. Most of the stones were slightly bigger than my helmet and could be carried by one man but William had them carry some which were thinner and the size of my shield. "These will make our task in the church much easier. I will have less work to do on them." I saw the wisdom of using a man with such skills. I would have randomly collected all the stones. William chose what he needed.

And then we were loaded. I was alarmed at how much the knarr had sunk lower into the river. There appeared to be perilously little freeboard left. Olaf laughed at my concern. "Do not worry my lord. It will help us to sail better and this time both the river and the wind will be with us. We will fly back."

And he was correct. There was still light in the sky by the time we reached Harold and the horses at Stockton. He tied up to the bank and I saw that the tide was going out. "We will unload in the morning, my lord when the tide is higher and it will save my men wasting their energies." He held out his hand.

I was loath to pay him but I had little choice. I counted out the coins and he knuckled his head and said, "Next time my men and I will fetch the stone for you if you like. It will just cost one more silver coin than the payment this time. Now that we know what kind of stone your mason wants we will be able to work quicker."

I looked at William. "It is a good idea, my lord. We can always use the stone."

"Very well. I will return with my father and some carts to transport it."

As we rode back through the dusk Harold told me what he had learned. He had been to the alewife and she knew all. Raiders tended to come at harvest time. The local farmers had nowhere to hide and protect themselves. Most of them just fled into the empty part of the land to avoid the voracious predators. It explained why there were so few farms. It must have been soul-destroying to raise crops and animals and have them taken away before they could be used. He also told us about the different crafts who worked in Stockton. There the people used Olaf's boat to flee across the river when the raiders appeared. It seemed that the Scots had stopped attacking the settlement. It was not worth the effort. I saw that the manor of Norton was not what it seemed. It was an island surrounded by a sea of enemies.

"You have done well, Alfraed. From what you have told us I can tell that you wish a castle at Stockton."

"Aye my lord but I am not foolish enough to think we can abandon this one. It is past midsummer and we need a safe refuge for the farmers. We can look at Stockton in the next year or so. William has told me that it will take some time to finish his work here. Besides, we need our new men at arms training and equipping. The smith in Stockton may have a surly tongue but he can make us some armour."

I saw the nodding and the approving glances from Wulfstan and the others. For the first time in my life, I felt as though I had done something right.

Chapter 10

While my father, Ralph and a semi-recovered Garth set off to visit with our farmers we left for Stockton to collect our stones. Wulfstan wanted to use the journey to see how our new warriors worked together.

While the men loaded the stone onto the cart Wulfstan took me to visit Alf the Smith. I was reluctant for I did not like the man but Wulfstan could be very persuasive. "My lord Alfraed, here tells me you are a smith. Is it just horses that you shoe or can you make war gear?"

He looked up at Wulfstan. My father's oathsworn was so big that everyone had to look up at him. "I can make war gear." He looked at my armour. "But I have never seen armour like that and I would need to examine it first if you wished me to repair it."

I reddened, "It does not need repair!"

Wulfstan laughed, "Nothing so complicated, my friend. We need helmets for our men as well as arrowheads. Eventually, we would need mail armour but for the moment we would be happy with ten helmets."

"Closed or open?"

"Open will be fine. We have all the closed ones that we need."

"I can do them but there will be a price."

I wondered how Wulfstan would deal with this. "Of course, there will and we will gladly pay it. However, once Baron Ridley begins to collect his taxes then we will be getting some of our coins back. And then when young Alfraed builds his castle here then we will be much closer and able to refine our choices of the work we wish you to undertake for us."

That surprised the smith. "You would build a castle here?"

I decided to speak. After all, it would be my castle. "Eventually we will build a stone castle here. Remember that, Alf the Smith, the next time you speak with me."

Alf looked me up and down and nodded, "I may have misjudged you sir but it is early days yet. When the Scots come then we shall see your mettle."

I was about to speak when Wulfstan said, "If I were the Scots I would fear Lord Alfraed's sword. He has the fastest blade I have ever seen."

The blacksmith nodded. "I can have your helmets ready by harvest time."

Wulfstan shook his head, "That is not good enough. We will call once a week and pick up the ones you have made. We will pay for each one as they are produced so that you will not lose money."

He held out his hand and Alf grinned and clasped it, "I can see that you are English and not Norman. Good. The first will be ready in three days. I shall start on it now."

The next month went by so quickly that I barely had time to think. Harold now had mail and we had to fit it for him. Faren and Judith made the padded under tunic for him. Wulfstan showed him how to make a shield. Harold and Branton then showed the others and by the end of the month, the ten archers we had brought north were armed each with a shield and a spear. Most of them had a sword and, thanks to Alf and our captured helmets, half of them had a helmet too. Osric had shown them how to make a shield wall and how to defend their lord.

All would have been perfect but I still worried about the lack of horses and the total lack of skill they possessed as horsemen. Wulfstan, Harold and I were the only warriors who could fight on horseback and Harold was still learning. When our enemies came we would have to hide behind our walls. My dreams of meeting them lance to lance were just that, dreams.

William worked wonders. He finished the church first for that was my father's dream. Father Peter was delighted to have a stone floor in his church. It had been Father Egbert's dream. William also improved the somewhat shabby stonework of the buttresses of the church so that the building was more solid and could be used as a refuge in case of an attack.

The tower was begun just a couple of weeks before harvest time. "We will not finish it before the spring sowing but it will be a solid tower. We will have a refuge."

I was about to complain when my father spoke. "We need more labourers. Perhaps we should visit York and hire them."

Garth had totally recovered and he disagreed. "It is a four-day journey south, my lord and we cannot guarantee success. If we wait until after harvest then we can use all of our tenants to help us. It is in their interest to have a secure tower as a refuge for them."

We all saw the wisdom of that but I was still uncertain about the willingness of our people to work for us. As harvest time approached Wulfstan began to give orders related to the defence of the manor. I was less than happy to be taking orders from one of my father's men but I had yet to command men in battle and Wulfstan had. I went along with his decisions.

"We will take a conroi of ten men to our borders and watch for sign of the Scots. I would not have your father's farmers surprised by a sudden attack."

"Will they not flee if they see us?"

He laughed, "If they do flee without fighting then so much the better but I suspect they will come in enough numbers to fight if they are seen."

Norton was not a large manor. A knight could ride, as we discovered, all the way around it, in less than one day. Wulfstan impressed upon me the need to show those who looked to us for protection that we were capable of doing so. "They will remember the Scots and the Vikings raiding. They will look at us and be afeard because of our paltry numbers. I will talk to them but you must look the lord."

We had equipped the men with shields and they were well made. As a coat of arms, we had used the axe my father and Aelfraed had discovered in the Welsh forests when they were fighting the Welsh. It seemed appropriate and looked nothing like any of the other coats of arms we had seen. I insisted upon a blue background and no one argued with me. I used a plain blue Gonfanon which Harold proudly bore. He now looked the part of a squire with his new helmet and shield. One of the swords we had taken from our ambushers was a reasonably good broadsword and he bore that too.

We traversed the manor every three days. At first, the villagers and farmers had been both sceptical and wary but after our fourth visit, there was more warmth in their greeting. Wulfstan still spoke to them whilst I remained lordly and aloof. If I am to be honest I felt foolish but Wulfstan insisted that they would expect that. Olaf had more stones for us when we visited Stockton and, after paying him, I sent him back for more. The stone was stored in Stockton. It saved us having to store it at Norton which was already becoming crowded. I would have my castle started the following year by which time William would have finished with the defences of the caste at Norton. Wulfstan gave the same message to all of our people; at the first sign of danger, they were to head for the church at Norton. With Father Peter now holding services on Sunday we saw all of our people gathered under the one roof. They marvelled at the stone floor and the walls of the castle were increasingly imposing. After the church service, Osric would drill all the men. Most only had bill hooks or scythes as weapons but Branton promised he would have bows made for them by the spring. Once they were under his tutelage they would become the bowmen that the Scots would fear.

The spring was a long way off. I was just grateful when the fruits, crops and vegetables began to be harvested. All of us needed food for the winter. Our arrival had meant that the farmers had less for themselves; they had to provide for those of us within the fort. My father had decided that we would have our own vegetables the following year but man cannot fight nature. For the time being, we would be reliant upon our tenants.

"If I have to I will send this Captain Olaf of yours to buy food for us for the winter."

We had plenty of meat for Branton and the men of the woods were excellent hunters. They provided well. We also had fish and shellfish from the river. It was not the life I was used to but I was becoming accustomed to it. And then the Scots came.

Our patrols did not see them. It was Aelfric, one of Branton's hunters who spotted them. He was up by the woods close to Thorpe when he spied them. The deer there made fine eating and he had just felled a stag when he saw the column of riders. He saw no identification upon them but knew that they were a war band dressed in war gear. He galloped back as quickly as he could.

My father was calmness itself. He sent riders to the farms and villages which lay nearby and ordered them within our walls. The ones within a mile or so were there within the hour. Alf and the people of Stockton took a little longer to reach us. Wulfstan looked at the church. "If we had a bell we could signal them quicker." It was one of many ideas we had after that first attack and raid. We saw the deficiencies in our defences.

Those from the outlying settlements, close to Yarum and Egglescliffe were the last to reach us and they barely made it before the Scots arrived. We had our men on the walls. Father hoped that a show of strength might send them elsewhere. In my mind lurked the question of the direction of their approach. Coming from Thorpe they had to have passed through Durham. Why had the Seneschal's men not stopped their progress?

Aelfric stood next to Branton. I saw him frown as the fierce-looking Scots halted a mile from our walls. Branton came to my father and me. "My lord, Aelfric says that this is not the same number of men as he saw close by Thorpe. There were many more than those before us."

Wulfstan studied the land for a while and then said, "They are drawing our attention north so that they can attack across the swamps. Come, Alfraed, let us see if we can surprise them."

We had put a small sally gate in the wall near to the swampy and muddy ground. The autumn rains had made it even worse than when we had arrived in high summer. Under Osric's keen eye we had created more swampy areas and the Scots would have to tread very carefully to reach us.

Wulfstan took four of Branton's men with us. There were just seven of us and I wondered what Wulfstan hoped to achieve. We halted behind the gate. "They will attack here after dark. It is an old Viking trick and the Scots have learned well."

"Why not just shower them with arrows from the walls?"

"We would waste too many valuable arrows loosing blindly in the dark and besides there is nothing more terrifying than being attacked unseen in the dark." He put his hand on my cloak. "Your blue cloak makes a good disguise my lord and Branton's men here can hide in plain sight. We will sally forth and wait. No one attacks until I give the order and when I say fall back you all get inside the gate." He stared at me. "Especially our reckless English knight!"

I saw the grins on the faces of Harold and the rest of Branton's men. They all knew my reputation. I tried to maintain my dignity by donning my helmet to disguise my emotions. I remembered that first night attack on the way to England. I hoped that I had improved as a warrior since then. I nodded and hefted my shield around to my front. We waited until the sun dipped behind the hills to the west before we risked leaving the castle. The Scots would have men watching the walls. Darkness would be our ally.

There were just three of us armed with shields and the rest had their bows and spears. We slipped silently through the gate. We were like shadows. I glanced at the walls as we left. There were just four boys on the walls and they were armed with mere slingshots. If we failed then the castle would be taken despite our work and new defences. Much rested on our shoulders. Branton and the archers smeared mud on their faces so that they would not show up in the dark.

Wulfstan slipped out first. He was a huge man but he could move like a cat. I left next followed by Harold. I was reassured by both his weapons and his armour. His skills with a sword had improved during the last few weeks but they would soon be tested for the Scots were fierce warriors.

We crossed the small bridge over the ditch and descended the slope to the edge of the swampy area. Wulfstan's hand came up. I saw, in the gloom of the dark, the archers jamming their spears into the ground and nocking their bows. My sword was already drawn and I watched the darkness below. I knew that I would have to ask Wulfstan why the Scots had not raided the farms first. I could not understand this attack on a castle. My speculation was ended when I heard the sound of someone slipping in the mud and grunting.

Once we heard the noise we knew the direction from which they were coming and we realigned ourselves. Wulfstan was in the middle with me to his left and Harold to his right. The bowmen were behind us. I suddenly caught a glimpse of white. It was the face of a Scot. Then there were half a dozen faces and they were just thirty paces from us. I heard Wulfstan hiss, "Archers, loose!"

The four arrows sailed up and I saw two men fall, pierced by the deadly missiles. The leader of the raiders realised they had been seen. I saw a knight, with a kite shield, raise his sword as he looked at the walls for the archers who had struck so accurately. I only understood one or two of his words but his intention was clear. The warband rushed towards the silent walls. I knew that they had not seen us for there was no flesh to see amongst any of us. More arrows fell amongst them and they raised their shields whilst advancing towards the wooden ramparts. We had yet to lay traps in the ditch but it was still a better obstacle than they had met when they had raided before.

Wulfstan spoke quietly, "Right my lord, we go in quickly, kill as many as we can and step back."

My mouth felt dry. There were at least four knights advancing up the slope. My skills would be sorely tested. I glanced over at Harold. He seemed calm. I wondered if he knew the danger we were in.

"Now!"

Wulfstan stepped forward and smote a mighty blow at the leader of the Scots. He must have seen the blade at the last moment for he attempted to raise his shield but Wulfstan was too quick for him and the blade cleaved his helmet and his skull in two.

The knight to his right looked in horror at his leader and I lunged forward, my sword darted in the dark towards his head. I was lucky for it found his eye. He screamed and held his hands to his damaged face. It was a natural although fatal decision. I pulled back and stabbed into the knight's middle. His mail links broke as the razor-sharp sword sliced into him and he fell to the ground. I ignored him and stepped forward. A wild Scottish warrior hacked at me with his axe. I spun away from the blow. His axe head slid down my shield and I continued my spin and brought my sword across his back. He had a leather jerkin on and it did not even slow the blade down; I stopped when I smashed into his spine. He crumpled to the ground. My spin had taken me away from Wulfstan and two Scots ran to attack him. I was uphill and I hurled myself at them. The slope, my armour and my shield conspired to throw them both to the ground. I regained my feet first. I struck one in the groin with my sword while I jammed the tip of my shield into the throat of the second. He sighed his way to the next world.

"Back!"

I had seen how close we had come to disaster and I obeyed instantly. I began to turn until Wulfstan roared at me, "Face the enemy!"

I turned and was just in time to deflect the spear which was thrust at me. I hacked down with my sword and the spear shattered in two. The Scot looked at the broken haft and I could see, in the half-light, that he was considering using that as a weapon. I raised my sword and took one step forward. He turned and slipped his way down the slope as he fled my wrath.

Wulfstan was the last one through the sally gate. The first thing I did was to look for Harold. He was grinning at me but I could see that he had been cut across the cheek. It was bleeding profusely. Wulfstan saw it too. "You did well, Harold, now get to Faren and she will stitch it for you."

"But the Scots…"

"Will need time to regroup and reconsider. They will not be back for some time." Harold nodded and, holding his hand to his cheek, he ran to the hall. "You archers did well. Get to the ramparts and shout if you see danger. I doubt that they will venture into your killing zone. They have seen that you have knight killers for arrows."

"Aye, Wulfstan!"

"Come, we will see how your father fares."

Chapter 11

I could hear no sounds of battle as we hurried across the bailey. I saw my father and his men on the southern wall. Our banner still fluttered. He looked at us with relief when we climbed the ladder. "You are safe." He frowned, "Harold?"

"He needs a few stitches in his cheek. It is a wound to make maidens fall in love with him."

I looked over the walls and I could dimly make out some mounted shadows a couple of hundred paces from the walls. "Why have they not attacked?"

"I believe they are waiting for the attack on the northern wall to succeed."

"Then it has failed. We killed their leader and two other knights. Branton's archers struck five men at arms. They have withdrawn to lick their wounds."

I looked along the ramparts. The men, like Alf, and the farmers stood with their weapons ready to repulse an attack. If the Scots only knew how few men we had I am sure they would have attacked. We had barely ten effective warriors. Garth was still wounded and Branton's men were better at ambush than fighting from a rampart. Perhaps my father sensed my nervousness for he patted my arm and smiled. "It is no easy thing to assault walls; even wooden walls such as these. When you have your own stone castle you can hold an army off with twenty doughty men at arms. It is worth remembering."

There was no further fighting that night. Ralph ensured that everyone was fed and Osric even allowed half of the men to sleep. As dawn broke, three riders edged forward from the warriors who were now becoming clearer. They held their hands out in the sign for a truce. The leader had a full-face helmet. Their shields all bore the sign of the wild boar. They halted just fifty paces from the gate and they removed their helmets.

I saw that the leader had an enormous red beard; it was so big that, even when he lowered his ventail all that you could see were his eyes. "I see King Henry has put a cannier knight here in Norton."

My father said nothing. He had no need to. I noticed that the Scot spoke in Norman. That was interesting. The other two knights looked younger and were both clean-shaven. All three knights had mail which was covered by a red surcoat. I had seen these worn by those travelling to the Holy Land. They stopped armour from becoming too hot. I wondered why they needed them in Scotland. The only conclusion I could come to was that they had fought in a Crusade which would make them difficult opponents to defeat.

"You have not told me your name yet and so I will give you mine, "I am Tancred de Mamers," I remembered the name; it was a town in northern Maine. What was a Norman knight doing here?

"And I am Baron Ridley of Norton."

He nodded. "I have heard of you. You and your men were Housecarls to the Emperor." My father nodded. From his tone, I guessed this Tancred de Mamers was laughing as he said, "The Housecarls were trounced at Hastings." My father's men were so well trained that none reacted to the insult. I did not know how they could ignore it. "We will do you a favour, Baron Ridley. We will take half of your animals and your grain. In return, we will let you live."

My father nodded, "And that sounds like a typical Scottish offer. I will give you a piece of advice. If you wish to prey on the unwary then return to the Holy Land from which you have fled. Here we do not give in to such threats and my men are all sound warriors. I will count to five and if you have not withdrawn then you will leave your bones to mark where Scottish arrogance died. One, two."

Ralph said quietly, "Ready, Branton."

"Three, four, five." The knights did not move. Sir Tancred shook his head and began to turn to, presumably, order his men forward."

"Loose!"

I had seen Branton and his archers when they practised. They could send an arrow three hundred paces with pinpoint accuracy when they chose. They had arrows they called knight killers which could pierce any armour and they could release five arrows before the first struck the target. There were only five of them but one of the knight's horses was struck, the second knight took two arrows to his right shoulder and Sir Tancred only avoided injury by the deft use of his shield. He turned and galloped back to his men. The knight whose horse had been killed tried to grab the stirrup of his wounded companion and they began to retreat. An arrow struck him in the back and had he not been holding the stirrup then he would have fallen too. The arrows began to strike the advancing Scots. Every arrow struck a shield or flesh and they retreated with Sir Tancred.

We could now see their numbers. There were now just two knights other than Sir Tancred. We had wounded two. There seemed to be about twenty men at arms. Athelstan said, "I will check the north wall. If this is all they have…"

As he descended my father said, "It may be a trick. We are safe within these walls for a while."

My father constantly surprised me. He had a mind as sharp as a razor and he had deduced far more about the Scots than I would have ever dreamed possible. I glanced down the walls and saw that villagers and farmers were also looking at my father with admiration on their faces. Even Alf the Smith appeared impressed.

When Athelstan came back he said, "We counted just ten men at arms. They have been discouraged from advancing by Branton's bowmen."

It was time I asserted myself. "Let me take four men and the archers. We will clear these ten away and recover the mail and the weapons from the dead. That way we can concentrate on the men to our fore."

I noticed that my father glanced at me before he said, "Very well."

"Athelstan, Harold, Egbert, come with me." I hesitated. Wulfstan grinned at me, "I did not think that you would need an invite."

He laughed, "Aye well I like your enthusiasm but I shall lead when we leave the gate." I hurried down the ladders and they followed me.

When we reached the four archers Wulfstan waved them down. "We are going hunting and the Scots are our targets. If you can kill them then do so." He stared at them, "Try to avoid hitting us eh?"

They laughed. We had all seen their accuracy and knew that they would have no problem in the daylight. They were the men of the woods and they had survived for many years because of their accuracy with their longbows. Surprisingly the Scots had brought no archers. All of the warriors wore a helmet and carried a shield along with either a sword or an axe. I could see one knight with them. His shield and surcoat bore a golden star. I watched as he rallied his men into a rough shield wall. Although there were just six of us descending we were all dressed as he was. Even though three had old fashioned round shields my father's oathsworn looked like the veterans they were.

"Harold, protect your master, do not worry about us old dogs! We can handle ourselves."

Harold hurried to my left to protect my shield side. His wound looked red and angry but it did not appear to be bothering him. He grinned as he tucked his shield across his wound. I would see if I could secure him a mail ventail. It would prevent such injuries.

Wulfstan led us down the path between the swampy areas. It was just wide enough for three men and we followed Wulfstan. The Scots had chosen this side to attack because it was swampy. They would now find themselves at a disadvantage because of it. Behind me, the four archers began to aim at their targets. The Scots raiders had no choice but to raise their shields. All the time Wulfstan was leading us inexorably towards them.

I saw, fifty paces or so behind them, their horses. They were being tended by three squires on a small bank with a hedgerow running along it. There were three knight's horses but the rest were ponies. I had hoped for a better reward. As my foot slipped into the muddy water I chastised myself. First, kill your enemy and then take his horse! The Scots began to retreat to the drier ground where they could make their superior numbers count. It is never easy walking backwards in armour; especially when there are muddy hollows in which you could easily slip.

I wondered if they were making for their horses. Wulfstan must have had the same thought for he shouted, in Saxon, "Archers, kill the squires!"

If the squires were eliminated then the horses might run. We needed these ten out of the battle to give us a chance with Tancred and the others. One of the squires fell immediately, pierced by two arrows. A second was struck by an arrow while one of the horses was hit in the rump by a fourth arrow when the last squire ran. The wounded squire bravely tried to hold on to the destriers. The arrows and the whinnying of the horses made the Scots look nervously over their shoulders and we were able to close with them.

Wulfstan made for the knight and he brought his sword over his head in an attempt to end the skirmish quickly. This was a young knight and he brought his shield up to block the blow. He did so but I saw the shield shiver with the force of the strike. Egbert and Athelstan tried the same stroke but the men at arms they were fighting were neither as quick nor as skilled as the knight. They both died quickly. Leaving Wulfstan to fight the knight they charged the Scots before them.

"Norton!" I screamed my war cry for the first time and I lunged at a man at arms who tried to block the blow with his sword. He deflected the blade but I punched him in the face with my shield. As his head went back I brought my sword around and it hacked into his shoulder. He screamed as he dropped his shield. As he fell Harold ended his life.

I heard a cheer from my right and saw Wulfstan pulling his sword from the Scottish knight's dead body. With two more men killed by Egbert and Athelstan the remaining six ran. Egbert and Athelstan reached the three destriers before the men at arms who ran after the fleeing ponies. When we reached them Egbert was cradling the dying squire who had hung on to the horses. He spoke in Norman, "I did my duty. My father will be proud."

I could see that the arrow had gone through his stomach and out of his back. Egbert spoke kindly, "You did well. Your father would be proud. You would have made a fine knight."

"Thank you…" His eyes glazed over and he died.

"He was a brave laddie."

Wulfstan looked at me. "I think we have the three warhorses we sought. We had better get the arms, armour and horses inside and find out what your father wishes."

The Scots were still gathered out of arrow range where the valley dipped to the two farms. Osric grinned when he saw us all return. "Well, this should be interesting. If I was this Tancred de Mamers I think I would cut my losses and return north. He has lost a handful of knights and he has lost men at arms. We now outnumber him."

"But he still has more experienced men than we do. It might go ill for us." My father stretched. I suddenly realised he had been on his feet all night. It was too much for someone his age. I was about to suggest he retire when he spoke again, "I do not think these are Scots. So far they have only spoken Norman. Their arms and their livery suggest that they are from the east and yet if they were successful why did they not stay there? They have returned for a reason. I am curious as to what that is. This is not over yet." He turned to look in the bailey where Aiden tended the captured horses. "I see we have warhorses now. They may be needed soon."

"Wulfstan, take the men who had just fought and get some food from Faren. Ask Father Peter to minister to the women and children I fear they may become worried at the siege."

Osric laughed, "This is not a siege! I could sally forth and destroy these Norman cockerels."

"I know you could but they do not. Their last lord was slain and their animals all were taken." He spread a hand towards the animals they had brought in with them. "Do you notice what they do not have? Neither cattle nor cows. There are sheep, goats and a couple of pigs. How will they live through the winter? No, these people are worried and Peter can console them."

As Wulfstan led us away I found myself in awe of my father. He saw things with a clarity that was startling. He understood these people. Would I ever be able to do so once they became my charge?

As we headed towards the hall Wulfstan said, "Take your armour off and wash."

"But we may need to fight again."

"And that is why you take off your armour. It is light, Alfraed but it will slow you down unless you take it off for a while. Do not worry, we can put armour on in the time it takes to saddle a horse." He spread his arm around the bailey which was filled with people. "They can all help if necessary." He shouted up to Alf, "Smith, can you put an edge on these blades for us?" Alf cocked his head to one side. "There is a silver piece for you."

He rubbed his hands in anticipation of the profit and came down.

Wulfstan shook his head and said quietly. "It is not my coin. I took it from the dead Norman."

I suddenly felt foolish. I had only taken weapons. As I dropped my armour to the floor Wulfstan added, seeing my crestfallen look, "You will learn, Alfraed, to the victor go the spoils. You kill a man then search him."

Faren waved us over when we entered the hall. She shooed away the archers who were eating the broth she had made. "Here my lord, we have some of the game stew left. The meat is good for your liver and it will put strength in your sword."

I nodded my thanks and took the bowl she offered. I saw Aiden leaving, "Aiden, find me the best destrier. He will be mine."

He grinned, "Yes my lord."

Wulfstan laughed as he tore a piece of meat from the bone he was holding. "Now you are learning but it is right for you will be the one who needs the best horse. Aiden, choose the second-best for Harold here."

Harold looked in surprise, "Me?"

"I fight better on foot. I can fight on a horse but you two will fight on horseback."

Harold said, "Thank you", and grinned. When his wound began to drip blood he winced.

"You will have to smile less until it heals, my squire."

He nodded and began to sup the broth from the stew. "Why are the bigger horses so important, my lord? I did not like to ask."

"It means they can carry us in our armour and not tire during a battle. I will still ride Scout to war but when I ride to battle I shall ride my new horse."

I was excited. Only one of the warhorses looked to be a quality beast and he would now be mine. He was jet black with a white blaze. I had a mind to call him Star but I knew that the best horses, like Scout, named themselves. I would wait.

We had finished eating, drinking and washing when my father called down to us. "Better arm yourselves."

Wulfstan had been correct; it did not take long to arm. We raced up the ladder and I was amazed how refreshed I felt, even after a night without sleep. My father pointed to the Scots or, as we now believed them to be, Norman Crusaders.

"They are leaving."

"Then it is a good thing. We have won a great victory father."

"I am not so certain. Wulfstan, mount the men at arms. Just leave the villagers and Branton with me. Follow them and see where they go." He looked at me. "Take your lances. I would not have them get up to mischief until they have left our land."

As much as I wanted to ride my new horse I could not risk it. I had to get to know him and he had to learn about me. It would take time. God willing we would have the winter to learn each other's ways. I was not used to the lance which Wulfstan thrust into my hand and it felt a little awkward. I had to grip both my shield and my reins in my left hand and my lance in my right.

The Normans had disappeared into the woods by the time we galloped over the bridge from our castle. I felt happier having four of my father's warriors with us. Only my father and Garth remained at the castle.

We were outnumbered but they would be hungry, tired and they had been beaten. As we reached the woods I suddenly realised that they had not taken the Durham Road. They were heading up the valley.

"Wulfstan, these mean mischief. We should hurry."

He frowned, "Mischief?"

"There are two farms along this road. The farmers are with us but their homes are in danger."

"They are buildings and they can be rebuilt."

"And imagine the heartache of having to rebuild again. My father is right we owe a duty to our people. We must hurry."

He stared at me, "That is your command, my lord?"

I knew that this was a test. I went with my heart, "It is."

He grinned and clapped me on my back. "We will make a knight of you yet, young Lord Alfraed. Ride!"

Unlike the Normans our horses were fresh as were we and we galloped hard up the lane. We also knew the land. The farms were on a high ridge on the other side of the valley. Like the land to the north of the castle, the valley bottom was boggy and we kept to the road riding in a tight column. Wulfstan led flanked by Osric. Osric did not have a spear or a lance. Instead, he hefted a mighty war axe. He could do as much damage with that as a lance.

We saw the flames beginning to lick around the wooden roof of the first building. However, the Normans had not expected pursuit and we caught them unawares. Only the handful of knights was mounted. The others were all on foot. I saw Sir Tancred shout an order and his men hurried to their horses. He and his knights galloped north down the valley. Our priority was saving the buildings. As we were on the rising slope we were able to spread out and I found myself riding next to Athelstan. I shouted, "The rest of you men douse the flames and save what you can! We will deal with these animals!"

One of the men at arms had managed to mount his horse but Scout was pounding towards him quickly and his horse was not under control. I pulled my arm back as I had been trained to do and I punched the lance, as though with my fist. The head of the lance punctured his armour and his chest. My blow was so hard that it threw him from his horses. I saw Osric swing his axe. It split the man at arms who had yet to mount his horse in two. They were too concerned with an escape to fight but now there were but six of us.

I wheeled Scout around to follow the knights north. I found myself alone until I heard Wulfstan's voice shout. "Slow down my lord. Keep a steady pace."

He was right, of course. The blood was coursing through my veins and the joy of battle filled my head. I needed to focus. The others joined me and I rode at the head of the small column of oathsworn with Wulfstan. We could clearly see our enemies as they began to climb the ridge of Billing. They were not heading for Durham, or if they were they were taking a long and circuitous route. I realised that they were not extending their lead and yet our horses were not exerting themselves. Wulfstan had been right. We could catch them when the time was right.

"That was a good thrust with the lance. I could never do that as well as you did." I looked at Wulfstan in surprise. "I told you I fight on foot. You must teach Harold that skill."

After another couple of miles, I knew that they were taking the road north. It ran close by Hartness. We had yet to meet De Brus. Would he aid us or the Normans? I noticed that the sun was past its zenith. Wulfstan seemed to read my thoughts. "We are now in the land of Hartness. Soon they will become the problem of De Brus but we will follow them a little further."

I saw a large wood ahead and I became immediately wary. It looked ominously tempting. I did not wish to be ambushed again. "We will halt here. There is little point in courting danger."

Wulfstan laughed, "You have grown today. Where is the reckless fire eater we all know and love? We had better dismount and rest the horses before we ride back."

We had barely stepped down when we found ourselves surrounded. A Norman voice said, "Who are you intruders to trespass on the land of Baron Robert De Brus and to risk his wrath?"

Chapter 12

We realised later that they had been waiting for us. There were four knights and ten men at arms. The men at arms had crossbows pointed at us. The quarrels they used could punch through any armour. Resistance would be futile. The man who spoke was completely mailed; his age and features were hidden. He, like me, wore a full-face helmet.

Wulfstan spoke, "We serve Baron Ridley of Norton and we were pursuing Scots raiders who attempted to storm our castle yesterday."

"We saw no Scots."

"And yet we pursued them. They were but a short way ahead of us." Wulfstan pointed into the forest, "You can see where they passed by the broken branches and leaves."

The knight who spoke first ignored Wulfstan's words. "You will have to accompany me to Hartness and await judgement by my master. Hand over your weapons."

No one moved and Wulfstan's voice took on a more powerful note. "We cannot do that for we have not broken any law. We did not leave the king's road which merely crosses the land of Hartness and we have neither hunted nor taken from your master. We must decline your offer."

"I have eight crossbows aimed at you, Housecarl, you would all be dead in an instant if I so commanded."

Wulfstan actually laughed, "If we so chose we could be upon your crossbowmen before they could raise their machines and the bolts would be as likely to hit one of you as us. You have us surrounded." He shook his head, "A good leader would have had his crossbowmen on one side. We will not go with you, at least, not peacefully."

The crossbowmen raised their crossbows again. It made me smile for a crossbow is a heavy weapon and hard to aim whilst on a horse. Wulfstan had been very clever. He had forced the men at arms to continue aiming them. He was tiring them.

"Who are you, Housecarl?"

"I am Wulfstan of the Varangian Guard." There was silence. The men of Hartness who surrounded us looked intent upon mischief and I had this uneasy feeling that this had all been planned. I worried that the Normans we had pursued would return to join these men of De Brus. I saw Wulfstan glance towards the woods and he edged his horse away from the threat and towards the knight. It seems he had the same thought. "Will you let us go or will blood be spilt this day?"

Once again the knights maintained their threatening silence. Osric lifted his helmet and ran his hands through his lion-like mane. "This knight you see before you, Alfraed of Norton, saved the life of King Henry in Normandy. King Henry is your master too. Allow us to pass or you may suffer his majesty's displeasure."

For the first time, we had said something which disconcerted them. "He is a mere stripling and he does not even own a warhorse!"

"Then you should be even more impressed that he fought on a palfrey and defeated two knights who would have slain our liege."

"I do not believe you."

Osric's face darkened, "Are you calling me a liar?"

"Let us put your word to a trial by combat. If your young knight here is as good as you say then he should easily be able to unhorse one of my knights."

Wulfstan shook his head, "Your knights all ride destriers."

I heard the sarcastic, mocking laugh in the voice of the hidden knight. "Your red-headed friend here said he managed to defeat two knights on his palfrey."

I could see that we would either be cut down by bolts or I would have to fight. "It is fine, Wulfstan. I am bored listening to this arrogant Norman's rants. The sooner we fight the sooner we can get home." Just then Scout decided to open his legs and unload a pile of stinking dung in front of the knight. I laughed, "And my horse agrees!" I drew my sword.

Wulfstan rode next to me. "Be careful Alfraed; they mean to kill you. This whole pretence of unhorsing you is just that, a ruse so that they can legitimately kill the heir to Norton."

"I know."

"Watch for their horses. A good warhorse is trained to fight just like its master."

I nodded. I was aware of that too. I moved my shield around so that it completely covered my left side. I saw their leader nod to one of his men. It was the one I would have expected. He was as big as Wulfstan and his horse was at least five hands bigger than Scout. I had seen smaller bulls! I slipped a dagger into my left hand. I had a feeling that I would need all the help I could give myself.

The men of Hartness formed a circle around us. There was a gap of just thirty paces between us. I saw Wulfstan smile and nod. They had made a mistake. The smaller circle suited the nimble Scout. Then my heart sank when I saw that the knight wielded an axe and not a sword. They did intend my death. The leader of the knights said loudly, "May God's will be done."

The men of Hartness all crossed themselves and their champion charged at me. I trotted towards him and, as he swung his axe I raised my shield and spurred Scout who leapt past. The axe whistled through fresh air and I whipped Scout's head around and chased after the Norman who was trying to turn his own horse. He was travelling too fast and in danger of crashing into his fellows. I swung my sword as I drew level with him. He managed to bring his axe up to block the blow but I had the satisfaction of seeing slivers of wood shaved from the haft. I had to pull Scout to the right to avoid the men at arms.

I leaned forward, "Good boy. Let us show this carthorse what you can do eh?" His ears pricked and he whinnied.

I had upset the knight's plans. He had thought to cow me with a fast charge and a quick blow. He moved more cautiously towards me. I knew that I had to rely on my speed of hand and Scout's gait if I was to survive. This time he moved towards me with purpose. I kept him to my left so that I could use my shield. My sword had a longer reach than his axe and I did not wish to risk the axe striking Scout.

He brought the axe over his head and I braced myself for the blow. At the same time, his horse opened his jaws as he tried to bite Scout. I had to use my sword hand to yank the reins and move his head from the teeth. The axe blow struck my shield and numbed my arm. I spurred Scout and used my left hand to wheel him around so that I could use my sword. I rode parallel to the knight who tried to turn the mighty warhorse. I had the chance to strike with my sword and, once again, I saw slivers of wood sliced from the haft of his axe as he blocked it. His axe was becoming weaker. I could not see his face for he had a full-face helmet but he wheeled away from me which showed that he was wary of me.

"Good lad, Scout. You keep away from those teeth, eh boy?"

The knight would get lucky unless I ended the contest quickly. The question was how to do it. I decided to use speed. I kicked on and went for the left side of the Norman. I saw him readying to strike me and, at the last moment, I jerked Scout's head to the left and brought my sword down towards his head. He was too busy trying to adjust his horse and he failed to bring his shield up in time. He had a good helmet but I dented it and I saw him stagger in his saddle. Only the cantle and the pommel of his saddle kept him on his horse.

I continued my wheel around his back and while he was still disorientated struck him with the flat of my blade on his side. He could not keep his balance and he tumbled to the ground. I leapt from Scout's back and had my sword at his throat as he fought to get his breath. "Do you yield?"

His helmet had fallen from his head and I saw the anger on his bloody face. My blow had scarred his features. It had been a good one. He said nothing and so I moved my sword between his legs and cut the thongs holding the mail hose on one leg. "Unless you yield you will lose part of your manhood." I laughed as I added, "It is only a small target but I am accurate."

"I yield."

I sheathed my sword and took off my helmet. I picked up his damaged war axe and snapped it in two across my knee. It had been badly weakened by my blows. Wulfstan brought Scout over and nodded his approval. "Neatly done my lord, but I would have had his bollocks anyway."

I mounted and Osric said, "Your name, sir knight, for you and I will have words again. I remember insults. I am Osric War Axe!"

The leader took off his helmet and I saw that he was an older knight, of an age with Wulfstan. "And I am Geoffrey Guiscard and we will meet again. I had thought that we had rid the world of your type at Hastings."

Osric laughed, "You will never rid the world of our type for we are Englishmen and this is our land that you have borrowed."

I saw crossbows raised and Wulfstan snapped, "Would you be foresworn, Geoffrey Guiscard? You said a trial by combat and my lord won. God watches." Geoffrey Guiscard nodded and the crossbows were lowered. "And I would prefer you to leave first."

They helped the downed knight to his horse. "And what is your name sir knight? You are the first knight I have defeated and not killed."

"I am Richard d'Oilli and I will remember you, Alfraed of Norton."

"Of course, you will, you have a scar to remember me by and you will need a new haft for your axe."

We watched them leave and then we headed south. "That was planned Wulfstan. They are in league with Tancred."

"As I think, are those who live in Durham. There is much treachery here. I wonder if the choice of this manor was so accidental."

Osric stared at Wulfstan. "What do you mean?"

"The king and Brother John found this manor remarkably quickly. We were in Normandy and not England yet a manor close to such danger and treachery was found. He even had the seal ready to give to us. I believe that he had someone in mind for this manor; someone in Normandy but our arrival allowed him to use us. We were disposable. He could trust us but he owed us little. King Henry managed to wrest a kingdom from his brother I am sure he does not give away manors lightly. I think we need more men and better defences quickly."

When we reached Norton and told my father he concurred. "But the raiders have gone? The people can return home?"

Wulfstan nodded, "Aye but we will need to rebuild Osbert's farm. Part of it was burned."

"The men have already begun to do so." My father put his arm around my shoulder. "I am sorry to have brought you into such danger, my son. Perhaps I should have died peacefully in the east and allowed you to continue your studies."

"No father, I was destined to come here. I can feel it and, besides, I am still alive despite the Normans' best efforts!"

Wulfstan laughed, "Aye, my lord but you have only so much luck. We need to work on your skills and train you to use your new warhorse."

"That reminds me, where is Aiden and my new mount?"

Aiden was grooming the black beast. I led Scout into the stall next to him. They had to get along. The black stallion stamped his hooves and Scout whinnied. They sniffed each other and then went to their pails to drink. They would get on.

Aiden nodded at the stallion. "It is a fine horse, sir. I have seen few as good or as powerful." He gave me a worried look. "Can you ride him?"

I did not take offence. I had not yet fully grown and I looked too slight to master such a horse. "I hope so but between you, me and Harold we will learn eh?" Both of them nodded. "We need his name."

Aiden smiled, "The best names come from the horse, my lord." He rubbed the white blaze, "This one will tell you. He has a star."

The stallion seemed to nod and all three of us looked at each other. Aiden nodded to me. "Is your name Star then boy?"

This time he whinnied. In the days of my father, they would have said this was *wyrd*. Now we said it was God's will. I believed that it was *wyrd*!

Chapter 13

Surprisingly the attack and the raid worked wonders for our people. When we went to Stockton, we were greeted with smiles. The church in Norton was full each Sunday and the men of the fyrd set to training with enthusiasm As Branton and his men made bows so they were able to use them. This was where Branton and his skill came into their own. He had been Aelfraed's Sergeant of Archers and what he did not know about archery was not worth knowing.

Garth's wound had healed but he was not the warrior he was and my father made him steward of the manor. He was reluctant at first but we needed someone to deal with the tenants. A manor was like a huge estate back home in Constantinople. We were lucky in that there were few disputes which my father needed to settle but that was because we had so few farmers. He would soon have to hold a court for the minor disputes which might arise. We had come to a world that was totally different to the Empire. Here each manor was like a small kingdom and the lord of the manor had great power. Although I spent much of my time either hunting or training with Harold and Branton's men I attended the weekly council meeting which father held.

The council consisted of father, Garth, Father Peter, William the Mason, Wulfstan and me. At the first meeting, my father made it clear that he wanted representation from the farmers. This was not to make decisions but so that he could consult them. Father Peter was our link to the tenants. They trusted and liked him despite his youth. He worked tirelessly to visit each tenant during the week. He held classes to teach some of the young how to read. I discovered that this was unusual. The king and the Normans wished the people to be kept in the dark. Perhaps my father was more enlightened but it suited Father Peter who went from strength to strength and proved an invaluable ally for my father.

A week or so after the bone fires we held our meeting and Garth rose. He had obviously had instruction from my father. "We are coming towards the end of the year and we need to make decisions." He looked directly at me. "This manor is a poor one and until now your father has used his own coin to keep it going. It is your inheritance he is spending. Unless we can find a way of making an income from the land then we will run out of money in five to ten years."

I saw my father smile as my mouth dropped open. "Do not worry yet son, just listen to the steward."

"We will need to invest coin in animals. When the markets open in the spring we will travel to Yorkshire to buy cows and cattle. We will also hire drovers and herdsmen to watch over them."

"How does that create an income?" This was all new to me. I was a knight. Why did I need to worry about cows?

"We can use their meat. Their milk we can drink and use to make cheese and butter. Their hides we can tan. Their young we can sell. Your father does not tax the tenants heavily; in fact, he barely taxes them. Father Peter has told us that they would be able to buy cows and cattle from us if we had them for sale. Once they have the beasts then we can tax them more heavily and generate an income. We are investing for your future, my lord."

I nodded, "We need men too. If the Norman raiders come again we need to be stronger."

My father shook his head, "We need an income first. If we hire men then they must be paid. When you stop paying them they become a problem."

"But Branton and his men do not receive pay."

"They are oathsworn. They are the most valuable of men, my son. You have just Harold at the moment but eventually, your name will attract others who wish to serve you."

I was not certain I could be that patient.

Garth coughed and continued, "And we need a mill. In the spring we will buy wheat seed although we have been told it will not grow here Father Peter seems to think it will. With a mill, we can sell our surplus flour to our neighbours."

Wulfstan spoke for the first time, "Neighbours is a word which suggests friends. I have seen little friendliness from our so-called neighbours."

"You may be right but I am hopeful that we may discover friends to the south. We all believe that King Henry put us here for a purpose. One day we may discover what that purpose is." My father was a patient man; I was less so. "And we will try to encourage those who pass through our lands to stay. There are many trades which we need in addition to a miller; we also need a moneyer as well. I dare say we can buy slaves to make cheese and butter."

"I need a falconer!"

For some reason that made them all laugh. Wulfstan shook his head, "That is probably the last thing that we need. I suggest you send Aiden, in the spring, to see if he can get you a hawk chick. He has a way with animals and he may be able to train one."

William spoke too, "We now have enough stone at Stockton. We could lay the foundations for your castle before it becomes too cold for the mortar."

I became excited. "We should make a start then?"

Garth nodded, "After the services on Sunday I will find out which men are available for labour." I gave him a quizzical look. "Each of your father's tenants has to provide a certain number of days labour depending upon their holding. The ones who live in Stockton, such as Alf may well give more time as it is in their interest for a castle to be built."

I looked at William. "And how long will it take for it to be built?"

In my mind, I envisaged weeks or months and I was disappointed when he said, "It will take years before it is fully completed but it should be defensible within a year." He spread his arm around the hall. "It will certainly be stronger than this."

"Good, then we will go tomorrow and lay the foundations out."

My father nodded to Ralph, "Ralph will go with you. He helped to construct some of the forts on the borders when we served the Emperor."

It was a cold and damp day when we reached Stockton. William did not seem put out by the weather. "We just need to peg out the lines of the walls and the tower. But I need to know both the shape and the size."

I looked at Ralph and Wulfstan for help. I had seen other castles but I had neither served in one nor attacked one. Wulfstan said, "A large square tower in a bailey with a curtain wall would be my suggestion."

Garth nodded. "There is plenty of room here and the wall can surround the smith and the other buildings. The river means that one wall does not need to be big. We could get away with one large gate."

William nodded, "That will save stone. And how big would you want the tower?"

"Not too big; we will not have enough men to defend a large one." Wulfstan was always a realist.

William wandered to the river and waved Ralph over. They spoke for a while. When they returned Ralph said, "William has had a good idea. If we build the castle yonder in the bend of the river then we only need a curtain wall across the neck of land. We would dig a channel for the river so that the castle would be protected by water. That would save much stone and speed up the building process. He thinks that we could have a ground floor for the animals, a first floor for your hall and your quarters on the third floor."

"And the kitchens and servant's quarters?"

"Separate from the hall." I gave him a questioning look. "You do not want fire near to your home."

I was so engrossed in the laying out of the castle that I did not notice it was drawing on to dark. I reluctantly mounted my horse and followed the others back to Norton. It was on the journey back, with the wind and rain howling around my shoulders that I realised how much I had changed. The cold and the wet did not bother me. I no longer yearned to be with the rich and spoiled aristocrats of Constantinople. I was happy living in a hall with an earth floor and no hot baths. I had become English.

The long, cold winter passed faster than I would have possibly imagined. This was mainly due to my days being filled with training, hunting and building. I also spent as much time as I could with Wulfstan building up my body. I had, as Wulfstan said, been lucky. My combats had been short but I had been exhausted by them. I knew that more testing encounters would come and so I also toiled with the huge stones which William used to build my castle. He had a crane built to lift the stones and I joined the others to haul and lift the massive stones into place. Wulfstan told me, one night as we headed back to Norton, that I had gained the respect of not only the men at arms but villagers too. I was not a pampered knight and they liked that.

One side effect, however, was that my armour became tighter and I was forced to visit Alf one cold morning around Candlemas. I went in my heaviest cloak to keep out the biting wind which whistled in from the east. He smiled more these days.

"What can I do for you, my lord?"

"I am afraid my armour is a little tight. I could just loosen the ties but that would mean it would no longer be a tight, protective fit. Could you add some scales?"

He held his hand out and examined the armour. He nodded his approval. "This is well-made war gear, my lord. It is far superior to the mail armour I have made before."

"Are you saying you cannot repair it?"

He stared at me, "My lord I am a good smith and if it is made of metal then I can fashion it. I just need to examine it and work out how to fit it. Could I have it for a couple of days?"

I smiled, "So long as the Scots do not raid then aye."

He looked seriously at me, "My lord, it is not the Scots who are the problem."

"What do you mean?"

He put the armour down and came closer to me. "I hear things. Riders passing through assume that the blacksmith is either deaf or stupid and I am neither. Olaf hears things and we talk each evening. The men of Hartness sheltered those raiders who came last harvest time. They did not come from Scotland. They landed at St Hild's and took shelter with Baron De Brus. He is their kinsman." He saw the look on my face. "Aye my lord, the sooner you get this castle finished the happier we shall be."

"William the mason is working as hard as he can."

"I know my lord and he is doing a fine job." He hesitated; now that he had begun to talk to me he seemed to have much to say. "Will you abandon Norton?"

I shook my head, "My father is happy there and that is where the church is. No, I will come here and live."

"Will you have enough men to guard it, sir? No disrespect meant."

I was less prickly these days. I smiled, "None taken. No, I will not but the castle will not need a garrison for another year. Until then it will serve as another refuge in addition to Norton."

"Then we shall have to find souls who wish to live here and to fight for you, sir."

"Are there such men?"

He held up the armour. "This has given me an idea, my lord. There are iron workings south of the river. With the extra coins we have from your father, God bless him, I can afford to take on more workers. If I can make armour like this I can charge more than I can for mail. Those workers will be tough men and they can fight too."

"Good then I will tell my father of your good offices and if you hear of other craftsmen we can employ them too."

I looked at the river. "It is a shame that someone has not had the idea of building a ferry and transporting men across. It would save a long journey down to the ferry at Yarum or the bridge at Persebrig."

It was as though a light had been lit in his eyes for he rubbed his hands together. "And I know the very man for that, my lord." Enigmatically he left it at that.

When I told my father my news he did not seem surprised. "We have much to do in the spring, my son. I have written a letter to King Henry to tell him of our progress and to inform him that we are building a second castle at Stockton."

"You have not accused De Brus have you?"

He laughed, "I have an old head on my shoulders, Alfraed, it may not be wise but it has experience. No, I have merely pointed out certain events and left it to the king to make a judgement. He struck me as a clever man." He patted me on the back. "And I like your ideas for Stockton. Perhaps when you are there you can charge the ships for landing. Even a few pennies each landing would pay for men at arms and that is what we will need."

"Have you heard something, father?" We did not have many visitors who passed through our lands but enough to keep us informed of events outside our manor. I was rarely there and so I had to get my knowledge second hand.

"There are rumours that many of the barons to the north of us are unhappy with King Henry spending so much time in Normandy. No one has said anything which is tangible. It will be interesting when the king's tax collectors come north. We will pay but I am not certain about some of the other barons."

"What will the king do?"

He shrugged, "I know the king is a clever man but I do not know if he is as ruthless as his father. William the Bastard would have slaughtered them all and sent loyal barons north. I hated William but I had to admire his strength."

"What was Harold Godwinson like? Would he have made a better king?"

He nodded and his eyes looked watery, albeit briefly. "He was a hard man but he knew how to laugh and to live. His problem was that he lived amongst treacherous men. Even his own brother, Tostig turned against him. And he did not have the castles which now cover the land. You have shown a greater wisdom than I could ever have imagined in deciding to build a bigger castle to the south of here. You are a new kind of knight. You are an English knight but you have brought ideas that are fresh. That is how this land will be tamed and controlled. That and a strong right arm."

That evening as I lay in the hall listening to Osric snore I reflected on that. My father was a Saxon but I was not. I was English and that was different from all the other knights who surrounded us. I would have to make them all remember me.

Chapter 14

By the time the early flowers risked the chill cold of the northeast, we had a tower built that was as tall as Wulfstan. William began to build the gate and once that was completed then the villagers would have a refuge. I was desperate to move in but I knew that it would still be under construction for another year. Of course, the work would be a little slower from now on as the men who had worked on it would be needed on their land. It was, however, a start.

Leaving Garth with Branton and his men my father took the rest of us south to Yorkshire to visit the markets. We took spare horses and plenty of coins. None of us liked leaving Norton so barely defended but there were many things we needed to buy. Once across the river Egbert and Athelstan took the road to York. They had a letter to send and they would see what could be purchased there.

We headed towards Northallerton which was just a few hours journey down the old Roman Road. Alf's older brother, Ethelred, now operated a ferry and for a couple of pennies, we had saved an hour's travel. We now all bore the same coat of arms on our shields but, remembering Sir Tancred, I regretted not having surcoats to match. The Gonfanon which fluttered above us was held by Harold. It told all we encountered who we were. We would need squires too.

The hills rose steeply to the east as we headed southwest. Northallerton nestled in the fine farmland of Yorkshire. This was good wheat land and the manors hereabouts were rich ones. We expected to see fine castles and well-armed knights. However, we saw comfortable manor houses and prosperous farmers only. We did not see any castles as we headed south but we saw a deserted motte and bailey at Brompton. It showed that this part of the land was peaceful. It was a mere twenty miles from our manor and yet there was a world of difference. We saw many farms and they were built of stone rather than wood. Prosperity was evident everywhere.

It had been the font of all knowledge, Alf, who had told us when the market was being held. Olaf was his brother in law and, between them, they knew all that was necessary.

There was just an old wooden wall around Northallerton and no castle. While Ralph and my father headed for the animal auctions Wulfstan and Osric took the rest of us to the place where slaves and hired men were congregated. Wulfstan had an eye for slaves and Osric and I just watched. Poor Harold had been left with the horses and was missing the excitement of a market day in Northallerton. My father bought six female slaves. That seemed a great deal to me but he did not pay much. I would ask him later about his choices. Three were under twenty while one had some grey hairs. There must have been something about her that my father recognised as a talent that would be useful to us. He had spent some time with Faren and Father Peter before we had left Norton. He knew what skills we needed.

We found six herders, all of whom were younger than I was and we hired them too. Things were going well. While Osric took them back to Harold, Wulfstan and I cast our eye over the unemployed soldiers. They were just gathered around the table which was serving ale. I noticed that few of them had full beakers and they sipped carefully. The exceptions were two who were roaring drunk. I did not need Wulfstan to tell me to avoid those two.

We stood for a while and studied the rest of them. I beckoned over the girl who was serving drinks and asked for two barley beers. When they came I asked, quietly, what Wulfstan was looking for.

"I am not bothered about a man's clothes. He can fall upon hard times through no fault of his own. I do not mind a man with scars on his face. It shows he has faced danger but anyone who carries an injury is no good to me but the first thing I look at is a man's weapons. They should be the best thing about him. A warrior who does not care for his weapons is no warrior. I have already whittled down our choices to four."

He finished his ale. "Come I have seen enough." He gave me his serious look and wagged his finger. "Just watch and listen, my lord." We wandered over to them. I noticed that they did not talk but looked in the bottom of the ever emptying beakers. He stood facing five men who were seated at a roughly hewn log table. "Would you men like a drink?"

One looked up eagerly and said, "Aye sir."

"And the rest of you?"

One, who had a badly scarred cheek nodded and said, "I can always use a drink but I only accept if I know the man or what I have to do to earn it."

The other three all nodded too. "Good. You need only listen to me to earn the beer." Wulfstan nodded to the girl. He took a coin from his purse and handed it to the girl. "Bring these men beers." When she had gone he said, "I am Wulfstan and I fight for Baron Ridley of Norton. It is a small manor north of the Tees. I am seeking men to serve in the castle and to fight for the Baron."

Even I could see that Wulfstan's words had struck home. Their eyes brightened and they leaned forward. Their spokesman smiled. He pointed to the three men closest to him. "I am Edward of Derby, this is Alan my brother's son, Scanlan of Doncaster and Richard of Whitby."

The warrior eager for ale piped up, "And I am Wulfric of Colchester."

Wulfstan smiled and shook his head, "I am not offering you work."

"Why not? I can fight as well as they can."

"You might but I hire no man whose sword is rusty and lies at his feet like a discarded bone. Have a drink on me but if you wish work then look to your tools. You are either a warrior or a drunk."

Anger flashed across his face and he looked to be ready to fight for he was drunk. However, he was not drunk enough to risk the wrath of the giant who towered over him.

The ale came and Edward asked, "How much are you paying, sir, and what about weapons?"

"Good questions. We will provide all your food and a penny a week for the first six months. After that, if you have satisfied the baron then it will be two pennies a week. We will provide shields, armour and any other weapons you might need. Can you ride?"

Edward smiled, "We can stay on a horse but we do not fight on horses."

"That is fair enough. As you can see I am not like my lord here, I am a Housecarl and I like my feet on the ground when I fight. What say you?"

Edward looked to the others who all nodded and said, "We are your men."

"Good, then finish your ale and we will return for you when we have completed our purchases."

We found my father and Ralph still at the animal pens. Osric had joined him. They looked as we approached. Wulfstan nodded and held up four fingers; my father smiled and continued looking at the animals.

Osric sidled over. "We have bought some cows and some cattle but your father is now looking at the bulls. He has found that there are some horses to be had further south. We will leave that for another day. The animals are expensive. The Scottish raids along the borders have pushed the prices of horses too high." He shook his head. "Had we more men then we could go cattle raiding."

"Men are more valuable than cattle. It is not worth the effort. We would have a two-day journey north and then have to try to get them back. This is a better way. We are warriors and not cattle thieves."

"You are right, my friend."

There were three bulls for sale. My father was outbid on the first. He did not seem concerned. As the next two were paraded I knew which one I would choose. Of the two one had much longer horns and had an aggressive demeanour. That would be a bull to sire fine young. Surprisingly my father did not bid for that one but the other, more docile looking beast which had barely any horns at all. He paid the least for it. As we were going back to collect the rest of our party I asked him why.

"If I was to leave the bull wandering our land then I would get the aggressive one but we will keep our bull within our walls. We do not need aggression. We need a compliant animal that will sire animals. We are seeking animals which have weight and meat. He was the biggest bull. He will do.

When we had collected our herders, slaves, men at arms and our horses we returned to the animal pens and, with our bull led by Osric, we drove our animals north. It would be a good test of Ethelred's new ferry.

I rode with Wulfstan and the new men at arms. These would be fighting with us and we needed to discover their backgrounds.

"We all fought in the Welsh Marches with our Lord, Geoffrey of Hereford. We were betrayed by his brother and the four of us were the only ones to escape the ambush. We have fled as far from Wales as we could."

I could not resist asking, "Why?"

"His brother is a marcher lord and has great power. We were witnesses to his treachery."

Even Wulfstan was intrigued, "But why should the lord of the Welsh Marches have his brother ambushed and killed. Surely that would weaken him?"

Edward laughed wryly. "Our lord had a pretty young wife whom his brother coveted. In addition, he had suborned many of the men of the household. My brother was the sergeant at arms and neither he nor we could be seduced by gold. When our lord and my brother were dead those who had remained true fled. There were six of us but two succumbed to their wounds."

"A sad story."

Edward nodded and put his arm around his nephew. "Aye, but my brother died well and with honour. That is all a warrior can ask."

I looked north towards our home and thought about his words. Treachery appeared as common here as in the east. For some reason, I had thought it to be different. And what of the king to whom we had pledged allegiance? He had no more male heirs and his daughter was a young girl married to the Holy Roman Emperor. Had my father made a mistake in coming here?

Behind me, I heard Edward questioning Wulfstan. "We were offered work in the north by some Norman knights who were seeking men at arms."

"You chose not to go with them?"

I heard a wry laugh, "The pay was not as good but there was a promise of plunder. It did not sound like dependable work. If our lord had not been betrayed then we would still be in the Welsh Marches." There was a pause, "How many men at arms are we?"

"We have eleven more at the castle and two of my fellows are in York on the Baron's business."

"And we would be the garrison for Norton?"

"My lord?" I turned, "Would you join us? Needs must you should answer the sergeant's questions." I reined Scout back and rode next to Wulfstan. "You will be serving this knight, Sir Alfraed. He is building a castle some five miles from Norton; at Stockton."

"Stockton?"

"Aye Stockton. It is on the river." I looked at the man. "I am having a stone tower built. By this time next year, it will be finished."

Wulfstan saw the doubt creep into Edward's cheeks. "Do not let his youth deceive you. This knight has killed many knights including one who was trying to kill King Henry. I serve him happily."

I felt proud when I heard those words from a warrior as fine as Wulfstan.

Edward knuckled his forehead, "I am sorry for any disrespect sir. Had I not seen you in armour I would have taken you for a priest."

I laughed, "Well that is a first. There were many matrons in Constantinople who wished that I been a priest! We are small in number, Edward, but my mason, William, is building a solid stone castle and the river will help to defend us. We will enjoy success there, I promise you."

It was late afternoon when we reached the river. Ethelred did not seem bothered when he saw the animals."I will carry your lordship and the female slaves first. I can bring the animals across in two journeys." He rubbed his hands. "I am grateful to Alf for suggesting this. I will soon be a rich man."

As we boarded my father smiled, "And I look forward to the taxes you shall pay!"

As he pulled us across he said, "You have to earn the money to pay the taxes. I am happy enough, my lord."

It took some time to cross and it was dark by the time all the animals had been transported. "I will travel back with Wulfstan, Osric and Ralph. You can spend the night in your half-built castle, my son."

I was more than happy about that. "I will guard our animals with my life and bring them in the morning."

"Good. We will have pens built by then."

Sarah, the alewife, did a healthy business that night. Edward and his men had coin for ale and I paid her for some food for us. The slaves and herders looked surprised at my generosity. They had expected water only.

There were no houses built yet but there was some shelter against one of the external walls. I wandered around my walls with Harold. In my mind, I was imagining it finished. Edward joined us.

"What do you think?"

"It is good, my lord. The river will provide defence, however…"

I frowned. Was my new man criticising me already? "Speak."

"The gate looks a little wide to me; in my experience the narrower the gate the better."

"But what if we have to bring wagons or carts inside?"

He gave me a patient look, "This is a tower, my lord. If you have stables on the ground floor then that is all you need; protection for your horses. Everything else can be carried inside by your slaves. If this was my castle I would have the gateway big enough just for a horse to be led through."

I went to the gate entrance. There was no wooden barrier yet and I could see what he meant. If you only had a narrow entrance then only one man at a time could come through. "You are right. I will see William in the morning. Any other suggestions?"

"I assume you will be building a curtain wall and a moat too?"

"Aye."

"Then this will be a hard castle to take."

The next day I left our four new men to help William continue his building. William liked the suggestions about the narrower door and I left the masons and my men at arms toiling away. We had been away but a couple of days and yet Norton looked small and inconsequential. It looked as though a strong breeze would demolish the walls. I bit my tongue. It would not do to upset the others.

Now that we were back we were able to send some of Branton's men to help build the castle. As my father and Garth were busy with the allocation of animals and slaves I took Aiden and Harold. It was spring and a good time to hunt. We took both bows and boar spears. We did not know what we would encounter.

The boggy bottoms were still too wet to cross and so we headed up the track towards Wulfestun. There was but one farm here, Thomas Two Toes, his sons and his hardy wife eked out a parlous existence close to the forest. They seemed to survive. I called at their hut on the way north.

Thomas gave a slight bow. "Good morning my lord. Going hunting?"

"Yes, Thomas. Yesterday we were at the market and I need the hunt. Have you seen any hawks this spring?"

"No, my lord, my sons are watching out for you as you asked." I nodded my thanks. "A word of warning sir, there is a family of wild pigs come to live not far from here and the sow has had young 'uns. They are protective and dangerous. The boars are nasty buggers!" He hesitated, "I wasn't certain if you would know coming from foreign parts."

I laughed, "I knew but I thank you for your advice. And we now have cows and cattle at Norton. My father is keen to let farmers graze them in return for a share in the bounty."

Thomas grinned, "That'll be good news for the wife sir. She is keen to be making cheese and butter. Sheep's milk butter is not as fine as that made from cow's milk."

I nodded, "I shall tell him you are interested." Before I put spurs to Scout I asked, "Any sign of any visitors?"

"No, my lord and the ground is still wet enough to show the tracks. I will send young Tom if we see aught."

I knew that there were a couple of ponds in the forest and they attracted game. As we entered the thick forest I checked on the wind. It came from the north and worked in our favour. We would smell the animals before they smelled us. I had Aiden to the fore; this was not because he was a slave but because he was most at home with animals. He loved training dogs and horses. He rarely washed and smelled more like a horse than a horse. That said he could detect an animal with his nose. He would be as good as any dog.

We went slowly. We were in no hurry and I wanted to go back carrying a dead animal. I wanted to prove to my new men that I was a skilled hunter. I was young in those days. If we rushed we might scare them and they would be gone forever. Suddenly Aiden slipped silently from his rouncy. He dropped to the ground and picked something up which he rubbed between his fingers and then sniffed. He came close to me and said quietly. "Deer were here less than an hour ago. There were five of them."

He led his mount and I strung my bow as Scout followed his rouncy. I knew that Harold would do the same. I could guarantee that if we saw any animals then Harold would make a kill; he was that good. When it was strung I chose the straightest arrow I had and nocked it. I would be ready.

After a short while, Aiden held up his hand and, after examining the ground, waved us to the path. I dismounted and tied Scout's reins, loosely, to a branch. Our quarry was close. Aiden had no bow; he was a slave after all but I had given him a dagger. He drew that as he led us off the path and through the trees. We had to watch where we put our feet for we did not wish to startle the animals. I caught the pungent smell of a deer and knew that they were close. I realised that we had been descending for some time. We were heading for water.

Aiden's hand came up and he slowly squatted. There, some fifty paces away was a small herd of deer. They were not large but I saw that there were at least seven young. They made the best eating; they would be tender and succulent. I did not need to tell Harold when to release he would choose his own target but he would wait until I had released my arrow. I took aim at the largest of the young and pulled the bow back. They had no idea we were there. I released my hunting arrow and it flew straight and true. It struck the young animal just behind the ear. As the herd started to scatter Harold's arrow flew past my ear and took the young hind which had leapt over the dying one I had hit.

We moved forward quickly. By the time we reached the water the herd had vanished as though they had never been there. Aiden set to work to gut the animals. The sooner he did that the better. He had a sack in which he put the guts. Some would be discarded but some would be used by Faren. Even the bowels could be used. If they were emptied and washed they could be used to make bait traps for foxes and rats. We wasted nothing.

Harold helped Aiden. This was familiar work for him. We had brought our spears with us and we used these to carry the two dead deer to our horses. I followed the two of them back to where we had tied Scout and the others with an arrow nocked in my bow in case we saw anything else worth hunting. I was feeling pleased with myself. It almost led to disaster. The wind was now carrying our scent and masking the scent of the animals before us. It hid the smell of the huge wild boar which hurtled towards us.

"Down!" Aiden and Harold dived to the side and I released my arrow and then dropped the bow. I hit the tusker in the chest from no more than twenty paces but it did not even slow it down. It was lucky that I had such fast hands. I drew my sword and spun as it tried to rip my stomach open with its wickedly sharp tusks. As it was one of its tusks ripped open my leggings. I brought my blade around and felt it slice across the pig's rump. It would neither slow it down nor hurt it. It turned remarkably quickly and its feet scrabbled for purchase on the leafy, muddy ground. That gave me the chance to plant my feet apart. This time it would go for the kill and I had to treat it as though it was another knight.

Its tiny red eyes seemed to glow as it launched itself at me. I swung from right to left as hard as I could. I had gained much strength over the winter but, even so, this was a powerful boar. The blade of my sword bit into the side of the boar's head; blood spattered from the screaming animal's jaw. Its shoulder struck me and, even though I had a wide stance it knocked me to the ground. I was now in the gravest danger for the enraged beast turned to come back and finish me off. I barely had time to turn and brace myself on one knee. It vaulted towards me and I jabbed my sword forward. The boar seemed to eat the sword. It disappeared down its yawning gullet. Only the hilt was left. I was forced to drop it and use my hands to grab the two tusks which were coming directly for my eyes. By holding his tusks I stopped his teeth from closing on me as did the hilt of my sword but I was now trapped by the huge boar which crashed on top of me. I heard something in my side crack. I could barely breathe. Then I saw Aiden and his dagger ripped across the boar's throat as Harold thrust his sword through the ear and skull of the boar. I was showered in warm pig's blood.

My two companions pushed the dead boar from me and Harold looked terrified as he asked, "My lord! Are you hurt?"

I laughed and then winced as my cracked ribs sent spasms of pain through my body. "No Harold, but I thank you both for God smiled on us today."

Aiden's eyes widened. "That is a huge boar, my lord!"

"Aye, and there will be at least one angry sow nearby. We have pushed our luck enough. Bring the horses here and we will take our bounty back to Norton."

We slung the boar on Aiden's rouncy and the two deer across the necks of our horses. Aiden led his mount. When we reached Thomas Two Toes' farm they came out. "Good lord! What has happened, my lord?"

I looked down at my tunic. It was almost black with the boar's blood. "It is the boar's," I shouted to Aiden. Aiden had taken the heart, kidneys and liver from the boar. He handed them to Thomas. "Thank you for the warning. Here is a present from the forest."

Thomas grinned, "We will eat well tonight. Thank you, my lord."

We were spied from some way off and my father was waiting. He looked concerned but his voice did not betray his inner fears. "Good hunting, my son?"

When we had dismounted and told him our tale he did something unusual, he crossed himself. Then he embraced me. "What is it, father?"

"Your namesake, Aelfraed did much the same thing save he had a boar spear. You have done something I never expected, you have outshone Aelfraed!"

Chapter 15

I went up in the estimation of all of the warriors. To face a wild boar with just a sword was seen as a mark of a great warrior. I was not sure. I felt I had just been lucky. It made me glad to be alive and I threw myself into the building of the castle. However, I had to do one thing, as soon as the blood had been cleaned from my clothes and Faren had tended to my ribs.

"Father I wish to free Aiden."

"Why?"

"If he and Harold had not been so prompt then I might be dead." He nodded and said nothing, "Besides he seems more than a slave. I do not think he will leave us."

"You would pay him." He pointed to my purse and repeated, emphasising the 'you', "You would pay him?"

"Aye, I would. He would be my freeman."

His face broke and he threw his arms around me. "You are becoming a man my son and I am proud of you. Your mother will be looking down from heaven and she will be smiling too. Let us go and do it now."

My father told Aiden, in front of the men at arms that he was free and then he stepped back. I stepped forward smiling at the shock on Aiden's face. "And I would have you as my freeman to look after my animals. What say you?"

In answer, he dropped to his knees, took my hand and kissed it. Tears were coursing down his cheeks. Wulfstan said quietly, "I would take that as a yes."

I gave him a rouncy to use and one of the short swords we had captured the previous year. I asked him to keep an eye out for some dogs. There were many strays; they were all that was left of their owners who had died. They tended to gather around the farms and settlements to beg for food. I was convinced that Aiden could train them. The experience with the boar had shown me that we needed animals to smell out the danger.

Edward and the others had worked hard and the ground floor of the castle was completed. William had narrowed the entrance and I tried it with Scout. I stripped to the waist and began to help. Judith, William's wife, saw my bandaged ribs, "My lord you are injured. Should you be working?"

"Injured or not this is my castle and I will work as hard as any to complete it."

I spent a week there and we saw a massive change. We had a wall on the second floor which came to my waist. I ascended the ladder and looked out across the river. I imagined when it was finished and I would have a view of the hills in the south. This would be a fine castle. It was as I stood there with Harold and Edward that we spied the two riders leading a third horse, approaching the southern bank from the west. I was not worried; it was, after all, just two riders. Ethelred took the ferry over for he was ever keen to make a profit.

"What do you make of it Harold?"

"It looks like a knight and a squire."

"Can you make out the coat of arms?"

I knew which ones I had to be wary of and I had learned caution.

"It looks to be a plain blue shield and he wears no surcoat."

I was intrigued. He had approached from the west. We had had little contact with the west. When we had visited the quarries the land had been empty. Had he come from the west coast? My speculation was pointless. He would soon be here.

We kept on working. I actually enjoyed pulling on the rope as the crane hoisted the huge stone blocks into place. I would soon have to visit Alf and have my armour repaired once more. I was still broadening out. I heard Edward laugh, "My lord, haul slower, we cannot position it if you pull so fast."

"I should have hired stronger men at arms."

"My lord, you should have employed Titans!"

I could see that William was pleased with the progress. He had worked on a carved stone over the gate. It was my father's axe and I was pleased. It was a reminder of our past and our connection to Harold Godwin and the Housecarls.

I caught sight, out of the corner of my eye, the knight, his squire and his horses as they left the ferry. They would have to travel a hundred or so paces to reach me or they could head directly north for Norton. They headed for the castle. Edward had just tied the stone to the crane and waved to Harold and me. We began to haul. The stone was halfway up when I heard a Norman voice ask Edward, "How do I reach Baron Ridley of Norton?"

Edward ignored him as he was continuing to hold the rope taut. If he had let go then we might have lost a valuable piece of stone.

"I am talking to you; fellow with the rope. Do you not understand Norman?"

I kept pulling but shouted down, in Norman, "He understands you but he is busy. Just wait!"

Harold grinned and kept pulling. I heard the knight curse and say to his squire, "Impudent serfs. They should be whipped!"

I shook my head and hauled on the rope. As William pulled it into place and began to smooth the mortar I grabbed the rope and slid down to the ground. I landed next to his horse.

"Now then! What is it you wish to know?"

The knight had taken off his helmet and lowered his mail coif. I could see that he was only a little older than I was but he was a little thin, as though he had not eaten well lately. His squire was much older and looked like a skeleton in mail.

The knight looked imperiously down his nose at me. I waved to Harold to bring a drying sheet for I was sweating heavily. "I wish to know how to get to your master, Baron Ridley. And be quick about it, my man. I already have some bad reports to make about his serfs. Do not exacerbate the problem. Tell me quickly how do I get to the Baron?"

Edward, Aiden, Harold, everyone was grinning at the knight's mistake. As Harold brought me the drying sheet I winked at him. After I had dried my face I dropped to one knee, "Oh I pray sir that you give no bad reports of me. I cannot stand another whipping."

He nodded, "Very well but be quick. How do I reach Norton?"

I stood and pointed to the north. "Well sir, if you keep on this track for a couple of miles you will see his castle at Norton."

"That is better. And what is your name so that I might tell him of your assistance?"

I smiled and said, "I am Sir Alfraed of Norton, Baron Ridley's son."

If a silence could be said to echo then this one did. I nodded to Harold, "Harold, get dressed and escort...."

The knight recovered his composure and said, "Sir Richard Fitzherbert."

"To my father, tell him I will join him for the meal tonight. I am sure it will be interesting!"

It did not take Harold long to throw on his tunic and mount his palfrey. After the knight had gone Edward and his men fell about laughing.

"What did you make of his war gear, Edward?"

He stopped laughing and composed himself, "Old fashioned mail. It must date from the invasion but it is well cared for. He has a good squire. He has a good palfrey but the destrier is old. His shield is old fashioned and bears no mark. He has no lord. His squire is a little like me, my lord, his face shows that he has been on the wrong side of an argument." He laughed, "I quite like that. They have not eaten well lately but they are close."

I was intrigued, "How do you know?"

"When you mocked him his squire's hand went to his sword. He is oathsworn. He is no hired man."

"Thank you, Edward. We will finish for the day. I shall go back to Norton. You can come with me if you wish."

Edward grinned and began to rub himself dry. "No thank you, my lord. We can stay here and get an early start."

William laughed, "Do not worry, my lord, he and the alewife have become quite close since he arrived. It is the lure of her bed which is attractive."

Edward shrugged, "What can I say, my lord? My needs are small." His nephew was about to say something and Edward, laughing, pointed at him and said, "And that is all that is small, nephew!"

I stripped off and dived into the river to clean off the sweat, stone dust and dirt of the day. It was no hot bath but it sufficed to make me feel cleaner. I had clean hose and my tunic had lain in the sun all day. Aiden and I rode back towards Norton feeling replete. There was something satisfying in physical work. As I looked back and saw another course on the castle I saw progress; in every shape and form.

It was approaching dusk when we saw the gates of Norton. After the stone gate of Stockton, it seemed a little flimsy but I knew that its ditches were sown with traps and it would be well defended. Branton and his archers would rain death on any attacker.

I saw the horses of the knight with his squire watching them. The knight was nowhere to be seen. William's son had begun to build new structures to house the new men who had arrived and although they were as yet unfinished I was sure that the knight and his squire could be accommodated. The rules of hospitality meant we had to offer the impoverished warrior shelter for the night.

Aiden took the horses away. He had captured a couple of dogs a few days earlier and I heard them howling their welcome as they scented him. I heard him shout to them, "I'll be with you in a moment you noisy buggers!" Aiden now had a complete life and was as happy as any within Norton's wooden walls.

The knight was seated with my father at the table. Faren had served them some ale. I held out my hand and she poured me a beaker.

"I hear you have met our new knight, Sir Richard?"

I smiled, "Aye although he took me for a serf!"

Sir Richard flushed and saw an irritated look flicker across my father's face, "You must excuse my son, Sir Richard. He has a wicked sense of humour."

Sir Richard forced a smile onto his face. "I can remember when I had a sense of humour but then my father died and I was forced from my own land by my own brother to make a living. You are lucky Sir Alfraed, you have no brothers and you will inherit this fine manor."

I toasted Sir Richard, "In which case I apologise for my jest but we were in good spirits. The castle is coming on apace."

The new knight nodded, "It is well situated. When do you move in, Sir Ridley?"

"I do not. It is my son's castle. He and my mason have designed it and he and his men at arms build it."

"But you only have four men at arms!"

It was my turn to flush. "At the moment, aye but Wulfstan serves me too and he is a mighty knight." I looked around. "Where is he, by the way?"

"He and my oathsworn heard reports from Thomas Two Toes of strangers on our borders. He has gone to investigate."

It was getting on towards summer and our land burgeoned with young animals and growing crops. If someone was going to raid then this would be the opportunity. "In which case, I will take my men from the castle building and we will join Wulfstan to hunt down these intruders."

"They may be a figment of the old man's imagination."

I pointed to my ribs, "That old man has sharp senses, father, if he says there are intruders then we should be worried." I looked at Sir Richard.

My father saw my look and nodded, "So, Sir Richard, will you serve under my son?"

He stared at me and then smiling, bobbed his head, "It will be an honour my lord but I should warn you that I stay only to make my fortune."

"Then I am afraid it will be a brief stay for enemies travel here in hope and their bones and riches remain here in Norton."

My father shook his head and touched the hammer of Thor he wore alongside his crucifix. He still spoke of the weird sisters who wove their webs. I did not believe such nonsense but he had been brought up in a different time.

We were about to sit down to eat when a weary Wulfstan and the others entered. They sat at the table and downed their ales in one. "I was ready for that." Wulfstan briefly looked at Sir Richard before addressing my father. "The old man is right. There were tracks north of the forest. There were no hoof prints but the marks of men. Someone has been scouting our land. We followed them west to the Durham Road. They crossed the road."

My father looked at Sir Richard. "Did you cross the Durham Road, Sir Richard?"

"We came along the south bank of the Tees and we saw no one. My squire, Carl, had begun to think that no-one lived in these parts."

My father nodded to Wulfstan who continued, "We rode down to Edward at the castle and warned them to be on the lookout for enemies."

I frowned, "I will send Harold to bring them back here. William can stop work on the castle for a while and work here. We need to quash this raid before it begins."

Sir Richard put down the piece of bread he had been eating, "Would it not be better to wait behind these walls and see where they strike?"

The comment was addressed to my father who began to open his mouth to speak but I forestalled him, "We are a small manor, Sir Richard, and we are well mounted. We can patrol the borders to the north and the west. Better to destroy them before they hurt our people."

I was pleased to see a nod and a smile from Wulfstan. Sir Richard picked up his bread and began to chew. I could see that he was thinking. "My son is impetuous and speaks before his elders and betters but he is correct. "

Osric belched and swallowed some ale. "And I do not think it is those Normans we had trouble with last year. I think that this will be the Scots."

"What makes you say that?"

He reached into his purse and pulled out a feather. It was the feather of a golden eagle. "Unless I miss my guess, this came from one of the scouts. I have never seen a golden eagle in these parts but they have them in Scotland and they like to adorn their hair with them." He nodded to Egbert, "Remember those lads who came to join the Varangians? They had tattoos, limed hair and these hung from their pigtails." Egbert nodded his agreement.

"Then it is a slave raid. You are right my son. Send Harold to Stock's ton. Tomorrow you go hunting Scotsmen."

Chapter 16

Thanks to the earlier raids we had plenty of horses and ponies. We left Ralph, Branton and four archers to help my father defend the castle while the rest of us, all nineteen of us, including Aiden, set off to hunt that most dangerous of game, man. My ribs were a reminder of how dangerous wild animals could be and man could be even more fatal.

Aiden said as we left the castle, "I have brought Wolf, sir. He is almost trained."

I looked around at the huge hound which Aiden had saved during the winter. He had come half-starved with a damaged paw and Aiden had brought him back to life. The huge wolf-like beast now growled threateningly at the men at arms as they passed him.

"Almost?"

Aiden shrugged, "He only bites those I tell him to."

I laughed, "Very well then but remember our avowed aim is to find these raiders."

"I know, my lord, and we will find them."

"Then take your beast and head for Thorpe. That is the last place Wulfstan saw them."

He kicked his rouncy on and the wild dog led him northwest.

Wulfstan nudged his horse next to mine. "So, young Alfraed, you need no advice?"

"Of course I do but you did say the tracks began near Thorpe did you not? And the farm which is furthest from the manor is that of Grim son of Aelfric." He had a farm far to the west. He had been one of the few farmers who had had cattle before my father had bought some. He now had a healthy, although small herd. He and his three sons were clearing the forest. He had ambitions to make a much bigger farm. When I had visited him he had told me that there was land that could be cleared for farms for his sons. If the Scots were raiding he was a prime target.

"You are learning. How will we deal with the raiders, should we find them?"

I knew Wulfstan well enough now to know that he was doing my father's bidding and asking me leading questions to test me. "We need to do more than stop them. We must make pay such a price that they choose other manors."

"Grim and his sons may pay the price."

I set my face. "I know and I will try to do all that I can to minimise the damage but we have the whole manor to think of and not just one farmer."

He nodded, "I agree but it is good that you are aware of the consequences of failure."

I looked at him, as sternly as I could. "We will not fail."

Our route took us past Thomas Two Toes farm. He and his sons waved. I noticed that they were armed and his animals were within his enclosure. If we were wrong then it might be Thomas who would pay the price. I was gambling that the Scots would strike as far away from the manor as they could. I had no doubt that the Normans who had raided us would have spread the word about the new teeth on the old dog that was my father. The land dipped below Thorpe and then rose to the small ridge. Aiden waited there. He was on the ground, examining the tracks.

He pointed to the hoof prints. "These are the prints of the hooves of the raider's horses. They have four of them. See how they are much deeper than those of my rouncy. They carry mailed warriors. It is hard to estimate the numbers of those on foot but I would say there are at least twenty."

"Good. And where are they?"

He pointed to the west. "They are heading for Grim's farm."

The farm was less than two miles away. The track twisted, turned, climbed and fell. The raiders would have to tread warily. I needed them all inside a trap. "Wulfstan, you take the oathsworn and the archers. Approach from the north. I will take Edward's men and our new knight. We will approach from the south. We should trap them between us."

"We will keep the same road for a mile anyway, Alfraed."

"I know but once we are close I shall move quickly. We take no prisoners but let one live."

Osric had been listening and he cocked his head to one side, "One?"

"I would have a message go back to the north. Find easier pickings than Norton!"

We were a mile away when we heard the sounds of screams. I kicked Scout on. Sir Richard rode his destrier. I did not know why. This would not be a battle. Wulfstan and his column disappeared through the woods. I shouted to Aiden, "Keep out of the battle. Use your bow to stop any mischief."

"Aye my lord."

I rode knee to knee with Sir Richard as we thundered along the track which led to the southern entrance to the farm. I smelled smoke.

Grim had built a wall. It was mainly to keep his animals in but it had served to slow down the Scots. I saw one half-naked dead warrior at the gate. It was a heavily tattooed body. It was a Scot. A slave's body lay close by. Sir Richard had a lance but I had a long spear. As we galloped through I saw that the Scots were hacking at the door of the large hut and they had fired it to make those inside leave. One warrior, at the rear of the band, turned as he heard us. I punched my spear into his chest and flicked the body to one side. I stabbed at a second warrior but the man dived to the side and I merely scored his ribs. The three mailed warriors had dismounted and were organising a ram. I held my spear aloft and I hurled it towards them. A warrior called a warning and an enormous Scot turned just in time to have the spear plunge into his chest. He was such a large man that he fell amongst his comrades and knocked some of them to the ground.

As I drew my sword I saw Sir Richard still using his lance. I leaned to the side as Scout galloped towards a knot of warriors I swung it horizontally and it cracked and crashed into the side of the skull of a man at arms. His falling body jerked my blade from his head. A warrior with a spear lunged at Scout and I whipped his head to the left. The spearhead rose over my pommel and I smashed down with my sword. The head broke from the haft. I backhanded the man and my sword ripped across his face.

I saw two of the raiders fall at my feet, their backs pierced with arrows and I knew that Wulfstan had arrived. The three mailed warriors now advanced towards Sir Richard and me. I galloped Scout towards them. He was a brave horse but he would not charge their wall of shields. I reined him in and leapt from his back. Harold grabbed his reins and took him away from the fray. The three knights advanced menacingly towards me. I was not worried. Edward and his men were already dismounted and rushing to my aid. I just had to hold them off until they arrived and Harold returned.

I had time to work out which was the most dangerous of my opponents. They all had mail with a ventail and they wore helmets with a nasal. They all bore swords and held shields but two of them were the old fashioned longer shields. They were difficult to use on foot. I brought my sword over and swung at the knight with the better shield. He deflected the blow and he and a second knight struck at my shield. I dropped to one knee and supported my shield with my left leg. At the same time, I swept my sword at knee height. None of them wore greaves and I felt my sword slice into the shins of one of them who screamed and dropped to the ground. I stood and leapt into the gap he had created. The move took the other two by surprise. I saw, through my visor, Edward and my men at arms rushing to reach me but they had to fight their way through half-naked Scotsmen who were laying about them with two handed swords. Sir Richard was still mounted! The man whose legs I had hacked was out of the fray and he was writhing on the ground. The two remaining knights were warier now.

I did not give them the chance to outflank me. I darted forward with my sword and the tip went for the eye of the one to my right. His head jerked back and I flicked the sword to the left. It caught the nasal of the second knight. I stepped back quickly as the first knight hacked at the space my head had just occupied. My move took my head away from the body of the blade but the end of the sword cracked into my helmet. It made my head ring but my helmet was well made and my padding prevented injury. I stepped forward and punched at the knight whose nasal I had caught. My shield caught him full in the face and he fell to the floor.

It was the last knight who was the most dangerous. He had managed to strike my helmet. His sword arced towards me and I met it with my sword. It rang like a church bell. I had quick hands and I brought my sword around faster than he did. He barely had time to block the blow and he stepped back. I saw that there were no Scots behind him and he was backing towards the hut. Bodies littered the ground before us. I feinted towards his eye again and, as his head jerked back I stabbed down towards his knee. Although covered by hose it was not good mail hose and the tip tore through the links. I twisted as I pulled the sword from it. He suddenly dropped his sword and yelled, "I yield! I am your prisoner! Mercy!"

I was suddenly aware that Edward and his men, along with Harold were now standing at my back. I saw the other two knights behind me, lying dead. My men had finished them off. We had won. I took off my helmet and felt the cool air wash over me and I struggled to get my breath. All I could hear were the cheers of my men and the sound of their swords on their shields as they chanted, "Alfraed! Alfraed!" Over and over.

I looked up and saw that Sir Richard had taken off his helmet and he was grinning too. He saluted me with his sword. "I can see that I will make my fortune with you, Sir Alfraed." He shook his head. "By God sir but you are fearless!"

Wulfstan walked over to us, "He has been ever thus Sir Richard. Next time I would recommend that you dismount or else you risk losing the lord who will bring you that fortune." There was heavy censure in his words. He nodded to Edward, "And you need to be a little nimbler on your feet too!"

Edward looked a little shamefaced. "It will not happen again, my lord. Sir Alfraed is a mighty warrior and we will become better."

I had regained my breath and I took the sword of the knight. "What is your name, sir?"

"I am William of Jedburgh."

"And can your family afford a ransom or should I have your throat slit here and now?"

He looked shocked. I saw that he was my age. This was his first loss. "But I surrendered my sword!"

I pointed my sword at the hut. "And you tried to kill my people. I ask again, can your family afford a ransom?"

He nodded, "Aye sir, they can."

I turned to Wulfstan, "Are there any of his men left alive?"

Osric laughed, "We left one as you requested Sir Alfraed."

"Good. Then give him a rouncy and send him back for the ransom." They brought the man forward and gave him a horse. He had a slight wound to the head but he would survive. "Tell your master's family that they have one month to send the ransom or he dies."

The warrior looked at William of Jedburgh who asked, "How much is the ransom to be?"

"I laughed, "Whatever they think you are worth so you had better pray, William of Jedburgh, that it is enough." I slapped the rump of the rouncy which galloped off.

Grim and his family came out. He was nursing a wounded arm but he was smiling. "Thank you for coming to our aid, my lord."

"I am sorry we were so tardy. Take any weapons you wish from the dead. We will dispose of the bodies."

He nodded, "Thank you, my lord. That is kind."

"Did you lose anything?"

He shook his head, "Two slaves and my son has a cut to his coxcomb but we were lucky." He pointed to his hut. "I built my hut big enough for the animals too."

"Perhaps you should use stone next time. It does not burn!"

As we stripped the bodies and piled them up I noticed that there had been casualties. Scanlan had a wound to the leg and he would limp for the rest of his life but, more seriously Big Tom, one of Branton's archers had suffered a wound to the shoulder. He tried to struggle to his feet as I approached. His son, Little Tom was bandaging him. I waved them both down.

"Well, Tom how is it?"

He looked up at Harold and shook his head, "I'll never pull a bow again, my lord. I am useless as an archer."

I saw, from Harold's face, just what a devastating piece of news that was. Young Tom, too, was upset. "Fear not, we will not abandon you. We will devise something."

As we rode back to Norton, leaving a pall of smoke marking the dead Scots, I spoke with Wulfstan and Harold. "What can we do for him? He is a doughty warrior."

Harold spoke up, "I know him. He could not bear to watch others using their bows and him unable to help."

Wulfstan nodded, "He can still work though. He could farm." Harold shot a look of surprise at Wulfstan. "We need farmers and farmers who can fight are even more valuable than ordinary ones."

"What about his son Tom?"

Tom and Harold were of an age.

"He could join his father on the farm."

I found myself agreeing with Wulfstan. "It is time we trained our own men to be archers. If it had not been for Branton and the rest of you we would not have survived. We owe you all a debt we can never repay. Have you a plot of land in mind?"

Wulfstan nodded, "When we came back the other day we passed by the burn where the deer congregate. It looks to be a pleasant little plot of land and no one lives there yet. It will need clearing but Tom could hunt for us while the land was being cleared. It is just a mile or so from the castle. They would have a safe refuge."

"Good, then they can have the land at Hart Burn. I shall speak with my father." I glanced over my shoulder and saw Sir Richard watching us. "Well, Sir Richard, what say you?"

"Your men are brave and loyal and we have had a good day." He hesitated, "But tell me, how do we divide up the spoils?"

I laughed, "This is the largest haul we have yet made. We will decide when we get home."

Although the raiders from Scotland had had few coins about their person there was enough to give every one of my men some silver. I gave one of the knight's horses to Sir Richard as well as one of the suits of mail. The other suit of mail I gave to Edward and he was grateful. The swords were of dubious quality. The better ones were given to those who lacked one and the rest of the weapons were given to Alf to make into new ones. The whole community prospered and there was a joyous atmosphere that evening. My father, of course, agreed to give the land around the Hart Burn to Tom and his son. Branton nodded his grateful approval. They had gambled much when they had followed us north and he was relieved that we looked after his men.

Father Peter and Faren saw to the wound of William of Jedburgh. Having given his word he was allowed to wander the castle freely although we kept an eye upon him. That evening as we ate my father questioned him.

"Why on earth did you come all the way from Jedburgh to raid my small manor?"

"The ones further north are too well defended. We could go west but it is a short road down to here. The Romans built well. And we heard you had cattle." He shrugged, "The news of prosperity travels far in this poor land."

"It will cost your family I think." My father looked at me, "What ransom did you ask?"

"I asked them to decide. If it is not enough we can send them back his ears."

I thought Ralph was going to choke on his food. My father laughed, "I think William of Jedburgh, that I will decide if the ransom is enough."

I shrugged, "If this is the quality of Scottish knights then we will have more when others seek to rob us"

My father frowned as he stared at me. He hated rudeness more than anything and I had never learned to curb my tongue.

Sir Richard said, "Before you censure him my lord you should know that he took on three knights, on foot and defeated them all. I have never seen such speed in a sword. Sir William and his fellows were brave but they were no match for your son. Is that not right, Sir William?"

Our guest nodded. "Sadly I must agree. I am used to fighting knights who fight on horses. Your son used a spear as a lance and then managed to kill one of my best men with a single throw." He waved a hand at Wulfstan and the others. "Had I known that there were two knights and five Varangians then I might have tried elsewhere."

"A costly lesson, but at least you are alive to learn it. We will try to make your stay as comfortable as we can."

"I hope that it is not too long, Baron Ridley. I will have to seek my fortune in the Holy Land. It is said that a man can make a fortune there."

"Perhaps or you could just run your manor well." My father was a kind man. I am not so certain we would have experienced the same hospitality had the roles been reversed.

Chapter 17

I could not wait to get back to the castle. Scanlan refused to stay at the hall and he came with us to Stockton. He mixed the mortar whilst we laboured. We also had William's son for his work at Norton was done. Wulfstan came with us as he wanted to see the progress we had made. He stood with me by the river and looked up at the tower. "There will be three floors?"

"Aye and a small tower at each corner." I pointed to the river. "The river will protect us yonder and with a moat, a curtain and a drawbridge we could laugh away a siege."

"It would be strong I grant you. Well, I will join you in work today my young apprentice. I cannot have you becoming bigger and stronger than me."

The addition of Wulfstan meant that the building raced on. He was both strong and hard working. A week before midsummer saw us ready to begin the final floor and the four towers. The shell would soon be finished. Scanlan was on the second floor helping William with the mortar when he shouted, "Armed men on the southern bank my lord."

Each of us grabbed our arms. Ethelred hurried from his ferry. "Should I fetch them, my lord, or send to Norton?"

Wulfstan peered across. "They are not knights and there are but five of them. Edward, take your weapons and Alan; accompany Ethelred. Do not set foot on land until you know their intentions."

We watched the ferry as the three men hauled it across to the other bank. Surprisingly Edward allowed it to land directly. The five armed men boarded and they pulled across.

I put on my tunic to greet them. I did not see them approach. When I did, finally see them, I had a surprise. One of them was the fellow who had drunk too much and had a rusty weapon in Northallerton. Wulfstan was talking to them when I emerged. He was grinning. "It seems that Wulfric here took offence at my words. I saw the man blush. "He became sober, cleaned his weapons and decided to become a warrior once more." Wulfstan nodded at the others, "These fellows fought alongside Edward. All seek service with you, Lord Alfraed."

I looked at them one by one. All had a leather jerkin. Two had bows and all carried a sword. One had a poleaxe. "Take out your swords." I saw that they were all sharp and rust-free. I glanced surreptitiously at

Edward who gave the slightest of nods. "Very well, if you will swear allegiance you are my men." They all knelt and offered their sword hilts to me.

"Welcome to your new home."

I looked up at the tower. William leaned out. "That is all that we can do, my lord until we get more stone."

"Then we will all travel back to Norton and I can introduce you to my father and the rest of the garrison."

As we rode back we were able to discover all the latest news. Although they had all spent the last couple of months in Northallerton it was close enough to York to hear the gossip. The most interesting news was that King Henry was back in England. The disturbing news was that his tax collectors were in the south part of Yorkshire and were rigorously enforcing their lord's wishes for money. We would soon need money from our tenants. I did not look forward to collecting it. They were not well off.

We spent the next week preparing for the midsummer holiday. My father had decided to hold a market on that day. Many of the farmers and their wives had spent the winter and the spring making clothes, pots and items carved from bone. The market would give everyone the chance to buy and sell their surplus as well as give us the chance to celebrate a year since we had come. My father paid for a barrel of beer from Sarah Ale Wife and had Tom, and his son, hunt some of the deer from their land. He made sure that the two were recompensed.

Poor Sir Richard felt out of the celebrations. Everyone, even the five new men at arms, was familiar to someone in the castle. He ended up talking to our hostage. William of Jedburgh's leg had healed well and he now only had a slight limp. He and Sir Richard had enjoyed some practice with weapons and so they sat away from the rest of the community and chatted.

For everyone else, it became the ancient ceremony of courtship. The farmers brought their daughters to the castle and they had garlands of summer flowers in their hair. The men at arms had been celibate since arriving and the sight of so many pretty young girls sparked many a romance. We already had a long-standing romance of our own. Wulfstan and Faren often spent the night together. My father had told me privately that as soon as Wulfstan wished he would free Faren and they would marry. I could not understand why Wulfstan had not asked for her freedom and her hand.

I thoroughly enjoyed the day. I just sat back and watched the games that were played and listened to the music. These were my people. These were the farmers and workers of the manor. I looked over to my father and saw the joy on his face. He was remembering such days before the Normans came. The ale flowed freely although I did not drink much. I was more used to eastern wines than English ale but I drank and I toasted sociably. I also ate sparingly of the food. That was not because I was not enjoying it; it was delicious. It was more that I wanted no one to go hungry. Many of those who enjoyed the festivities struggled to have enough to eat. This was their opportunity to fill themselves with well-cooked food. The spices we had brought from the east made all our food special.

I found myself smiling as various couples came and asked my father's permission to wed. The red flushed cheeks bespoke sudden passion in some. Sir Richard and Sir William seemed bemused by it all. As twilight settled and people looked as though they were ready to depart, my father stood.

Everyone applauded and was then silent. "My friends; this is our first Midsummer feast. It will not be the last," There was huge applause at that. "I am pleased that many couples have decided to marry. Father Peter will know the marriage ceremony without the book soon!" There was laughter at that. "For myself, I have to say that I am happy that Good King Henry gave me this manor for it is all that I hoped it would be and now before you all depart, I have an announcement to make." Everyone went silent in anticipation. "My son Alfraed has shown himself to be a great knight and a worthy leader. It goes without saying that I am proud of him but he is young. There are many who are older than he is and are yet to be knighted, however today I confer on my son the title of knight. Come forward Alfraed."

I stood before him, really pleased that I was almost sober.

"Kneel." I knelt. He dubbed me on both sides of my head. "Rise Sir Alfraed of Stockton." Ralph handed me my spurs and gave me an intricate silver ring, my new seal.

And so I became a knight. In an instant, my father had created a new manor. I hoped that this was legal but I would worry about that later on. I stood and everyone applauded. I was amazed to see Sir William and Sir Richard applauding and cheering as loudly as any. When the cheering died Wulfstan stepped forward, "And now, my lord, that my apprentice is spurred I would like to buy the freedom of Faren and take her to wife."

This had obviously been planned for my father said, "I give Faren her freedom and welcome."

The midsummer feasted ended as joyfully as any could have imagined.

When I awoke I did not feel any different. I knew that something important had happened but I was the same warrior I had always been. I woke Harold and the two of us left for my castle. My father had deliberately named it the manor of Stockton, for me. I knew that was important. This marked it as mine to hold for my father. I wanted to get there as soon as I could.

Alf and the villagers were within the walls when we arrived. The children were up and many of the women but the men were still drunk from the excesses of the feast. I rode through an open gate. There was no danger but this would all change when I moved in with my men at arms. Then we would keep a secure watch on the gate and the river.

Although there was no gate on the tower we could still gain entrance that way. The lower level would be the stables and we allowed our horses to rest in the cool of the stone tower. Whilst Harold fetched water and hay I ascended the tower. We needed more stone but Olaf had promised me fresh supplies by the end of the week. I was a realist. The quarried stones which remained were few in number. We had enough for the tower and the gate through the curtain wall but that was all. The curtain wall itself would require stones from a different source or we would have to quarry them ourselves.

I looked at the hills to the south and east. One day I would have to visit those lands; apart from Hartness, they were our nearest neighbours. I knew that there was a priory and I had heard the land around Guisborough was also owned by the De Brus family. I wondered if it was the same man who owned Hartness. I doubted it for Guisborough was a rich manor yielding wheat. I rubbed my hand along the stone of the wall. It came away dirty. This castle would need finishing first.

One advantage of my tower was that you could see all of those who wished to use Ethelred's ferry. Word had spread and many travellers saved time when heading for the north by coming directly across our river. Ethelred had begun to employ men to help him. It was a well-made ferry. He now had a rail running along two sides and the first rope he had used to haul the ferry across had been augmented by a second. It was a swift passage even at high tide. Ethelred himself now dressed in finer clothes. He also showed himself to be a clever man by becoming a trader. He had his men travel to York and Northallerton to buy goods that he resold. Norton held a market each Saturday and Ethelred built up his fortune. He made profits. I knew that my father would become richer as a result. Ethelred had more monies for us to tax. We now made our own money and my father produced copper coins which we used to pay for small services. We were still on the lookout for a miller. The women of the farms and Norton had to grind by hand. It took hours each day. A mill could change all that. I knew that, once my castle was finished he would have a mill and mill pond built. That would supply us with fish all year round.

When my reverie was ended I wandered around my new manor. I was greeted by smiles. A weary Alf bobbed his head when I passed his smithy. "A grand party, my lord. It had been a good year."

"It has."

"And we were spared Vikings this year too."

I was surprised, "Vikings?"

"They still raid although not as frequently as they used to. Sometimes six months go by without a raid. This last year is the longest anyone has ever known without a visit from the dragon ships."

"What do they come for?"

"Slaves and animals." He pointed to the north. "We just head as far north as we can when we know they are coming. They don't like to stray too far from the river. Olaf and the fishermen were usually fortunate enough to spot them at sea. Ten years ago the bastards came out of a fog and they took many on that raid." He nodded towards the tower. "When you are here, sir, we will be safe."

I had thought Vikings were a thing of the past. The ones who travelled through the Rus to Miklagård seemed to me the last remnants of the Viking raider. Apparently, I was wrong.

I used our walk around the village to plan what it would look like when I ruled there. We already knew where the ditch and moat would be. They were marked by a line of river sand which William had used as a marker. The moat would run along the other side. Even if we were short of stone we could still build a moat and, with the stone of the tower for protection, we would be safe there.

We had a leisurely ride back to Norton. We went the long way, through the Hart Burn. I was anxious to see how the two Toms had settled. They were not where I had expected. There was a piece of flat land close to the burn but they had not built there. Harold pointed to the reason. "Look, sir. The land close to the river is very verdant. This burn bursts its banks when it rains heavily and the land is flat here. Any house would be flooded every time it rained. Tom is no fool. If we climb this bank I am sure we will find him."

He was right. At the top of the bank, they had cleared trees and were making a wooden hall. Despite having only one good arm to use effectively Old Tom was still doing his share. They stopped working when we arrived. Tying our animals to the trees Harold and I helped them to move some logs. The extra hands made light work of it. "We can bring the men to help you, Tom, if you desire? It would not take us long."

Old Tom shook his head. "No sir, you and your father have done enough. Besides I want our blood and sweat to be here. We have had no home since the Normans destroyed our old one. This will be my last home. I shall die here. I would rather build it myself."

I understood. They were almost exactly the same words as used by my father. Both my father and Tom had lived much longer than most men. They were unusual. They were seeing old age.

Four days after the feast the ransom arrived. William's younger brother arrived with an escort of four men at arms. I saw the worried look on his face. He thought he had not brought enough. He looked at my father who shook his head, "It is not mine to collect. My son was the victor." He stepped aside.

Robert Fitzjedburgh lifted a small chest from the sumpter. He handed it to me. "My father says that this is all the gold he can raise and hopes that my brother can keep his ears."

I caught sight of William who coloured. I think he knew at that point that I would let him go no matter what the ransom was. I opened it and saw that it contained gold. I was about to count when Robert said, "There are thirty-four gold pieces, my lord although some are smaller than others."

I feigned deliberation. I lifted the gold pieces and examined them. Some were familiar and I recognised the face of King David but others appeared to show other rulers. The men of Jedburgh raided far and wide.

Finally, I nodded, "The ransom is paid. Sir William, you may take your destrier and return to your family."

That surprised him. "You are letting me keep my horse?" Such animals were valuable; a good one was worth more than the ransom I had just received.

I smiled, "I would not deprive you of your livelihood but I would choose easier pickings next time if I were you."

He grinned, "The lesson is learned." He clasped my arm. "Thank you for your hospitality. I have learned much here."

The goodbyes took some time. I noticed that he and Sir Richard had a long farewell. They had become friends. I took the chest into the hall and began to divide the coins. It was mine to divide. I was the master. I knew, however, that it would be foolish to lose the goodwill of my men.

I summoned Richard, Wulfstan, Egbert, Osric and Athelstan. I chose the five largest coins and then five smaller ones. I gave one of each to them. They nodded and smiled. Only Sir Richard looked slightly disappointed. When my father's oathsworn had gone I asked, "Disappointed, Richard?"

"Not with my pay but with the size of the ransom. From what Sir William said I thought his family had more money than this."

"Then perhaps they are wise for they have not impoverished their manor for one reckless son."

He nodded and left. I summoned Edward and his men along with Dick and John, the two archers who had come with us. I gave each of them a gold coin. "You have done well. Dick and John here are the coins for the two Toms. Take them to them."

Dick grinned, "They will be both pleased and surprised. This is more gold than I have ever seen in my life."

"You fight for me now. There will be more." Then I summoned Harold and Aiden.

To Harold, I gave one gold coin and Aiden, to his surprise, received a smaller one. "But my lord I did no fighting!"

"You are my man, Aiden, and you will benefit like the others."

I took some coins from the box and then replaced it under my bed. I had more than half left yet. Father Peter was at the church. It showed the effects of the feast and he was tidying. I gave him a gold coin. "Here, father. This is for you and the church. Use it as you see fit." I looked at his vestments which were quite plain.

He saw my look and shook his head, "The last thing I need, my lord, are fine clothes. I am a priest. I will use some of this to commission a bell from Alf and I will ask William to build a small vestry for me."

I knew that he slept in the church. It was a cold existence in winter.

Finally, I found William and gave him five coins. "What is this for, my lord?"

"For the building of the castle. I pay you now so that when I am not here the work will continue apace."

"Not here? You are going somewhere?"

I nodded, "I will need to take my men and visit with our neighbours. It is time that they knew there was a new knight in this land. I would not have any confusion over it."

Chapter 18

Two weeks later we heard rumours of the imminent arrival of the king's tax collectors. Some had fled north to avoid paying and Ethelred learned of the unwelcome visit. They were the merchants who could carry their riches with them surrounded by armed guards. Ethelred profited. We saw them all as we toiled in my castle. I virtually lived there now. I lived in what would be the hall with Harold and my men at arms. The top floor was still under construction and was too dirty but the room we used was adequate. We had yet to put in internal walls. The pillars which supported the ceiling were the only encumbrance in the huge space.

It was Wulfric who saw the tax collector. "My lord, there is a mighty host across the river. I think it is the tax collector."

I leaned over the battlements, "Aiden, ride to my father and warn him that the tax collectors are here." I turned to William. "Keep my men working, Harold, and I will take them to my father."

I cleaned myself up as best I could and donned my tunic and sword. By the time I reached the river the heavily laden ferry was almost across. I frowned. The ferry was full and yet there were as many men and horses on the other side. How many tax collectors did King Henry need?

I strode down to meet them. I noticed that there were knights disembarking. This was my first experience of tax collection in England; did they need knights to enforce the collection? I was twenty paces from them when they stopped and parted. It was not just the tax collector. It was King Henry himself. I bowed and stammered, "Your majesty! We were not expecting you!"

He came over and raised me up. "I know. Walk with me." He spoke quietly. "Your father's letter, along with news I received from elsewhere made me fear for the north. I thought I would come with my tax collector and see for myself."

His equerry brought his horse and he mounted. As he did so I saw his glance flick to the castle but he said nothing. "Ride with me to Norton and we can talk."

Harold had anticipated well and he brought Scout over.

"I will stay only briefly for I wish to reach Durham by this evening." He turned and looked at the ferry. "That is a good idea. Whose was it?

Yours?" I nodded. "You are an enthusiastic young man I can see that. Tell me all."

I told him of the raid by Sir Tancred and our encounter with the De Brus family. I mentioned the Scots raid but not the ransom. "You have been busy. And is your father well?"

"He seems to get younger the longer he lives in this land. He is grateful that you gave him this manor."

He flashed me a look and examined my face for a lie. He had given us this manor because he knew it was dangerous. I had grown up in Constantinople and I could keep a stoic look upon my face easily. He seemed satisfied and grunted, "Aye well, I could have done worse with my gift."

We rode into the castle and the king turned to the leader of his retinue. "Keep the men out here. I shall be safe within these walls. Water the beasts for we leave within the hour."

We were followed by the tax collector and his clerks. Ominously they carried large books with them. King Henry strode up to the hall as though he owned it; which, of course, he did. He saw my father bob and bow, "Baron Ridley, have your steward give the details of your farmers and your holdings to my tax collector."

"Yes my liege, Garth."

Garth nodded and took the tax collector and clerks off. Faren appeared with some ale and we all sat at the large table. King Henry toasted us. "A fine castle. You have done well to survive here."

It was as we had suspected King Henry had had his suspicions and we had been the sacrificial goat. Had we been consumed we would have proved to him beyond any doubt that there was treachery. As it was he still had the manor and we had given evidence of treachery.

"I have spoken with the Bishop of Durham. He is still indisposed and wishes to stay in London for a while longer. However, I have persuaded him that the manor of Norton should no longer form part of his holdings. You just pay tax to me." He smiled but there was no warmth in the smile, "My tax collector will tell you how much you owe me." I think this was a double punishment. He was taking money from his Bishop while building better defences south of the Bishop's holdings. This was complicated politics.

He finished his beer. "This is good ale but do you not have any wine? Beer is for peasants and wine is for nobles."

"I am sorry my liege, we held a midsummer festival and we have yet to replenish our stocks."

He grunted, "Aye well I can see that. Now, what about this castle you have built upon the river? Did you ask permission for that?"

He darted the question at my father like a strike with a sword. My father began to speak but I interrupted. I would not allow my father to take the blame for my decision. "I thought, my liege, that you had given permission for a castle to be built. When we reached here we found a castle already in place and just built a new one to guard the river crossing you used today."

He stared at me and I saw my father shake his head then the king roared with laughter. "My God, sir but you know how to defend an impossible position! Deftly done." He shook his head, "I could order you to pull it down stone by stone, you know that?"

I raised my head resolutely, "Aye my lord."

He considered. "What is the name of that settlement?"

Before I could speak my father said, "It is Stockton, sire. I gave it to my son to hold." He went on hurriedly, "It is part of the manor of Norton."

"So now you make lords of the manor too? Should I worry about your search for power Baron Ridley of Norton?"

My father did not rise to the bait, "I am an old man, my liege and if you fear an old man like me then I fear for England. When I met you I told you that I came here to die and I am not a man who is foresworn."

King Henry's face softened. "I can see that and all that I have heard confirms that you are a good lord of the manor." His words told me that he had spies but who were they? "I am happy to confirm your son as baron of Stockton and to allow the erection of the castle, however," he paused and I discovered the real reason for his visit, "in return I require the services of two knights and ten men at arms for a campaign in Wales. The Welsh have attacked Chester and are causing no end of trouble rampaging through Cheshire." His reptilian smile told us both that he wanted me to serve him and fight his battles with him.

I had little choice in the matter and I nodded. "I would be honoured, sire."

"Excellent then we will see how much tax you owe and I will return from Durham in a few days." An ashen-faced Garth came in with the tax collector. "Ah, Master Jocelyn, how much does Baron Ridley owe us for the year?"

The cleric was a hatchet-faced man and his words sounded like blows as he said, "Twenty gold pieces, your majesty!"

My father showed his shock. "My liege, we are a poor manor! Where would my people get such gold from?"

The king shrugged, "I have been told, Baron Ridley that you are a rich man and brought much gold from the east. My men can collect the gold in the form of animals from your farmers if you wish."

I stood. "That will not be necessary, your majesty." I went to my bed and brought out the small chest. I handed it to the tax collector. "I believe the amount you require is in here."

I saw the look of relief and gratitude on the face of Garth and a frown appear on my father's face. The tax collector counted out the coin and nodded to the king. "You are a resourceful fellow, Alfraed of Stockton. I look forward to learning more about you as we travel south." He stood. "I will take my leave." With that, he strode from the hall.

The tax collector picked up the chest. I laid my dagger across it. "A receipt is in order, I believe."

I am a big man and I had learned the intimidating stare. The tax collector, Jocelyn, actually shook as he waved his clerks over and began to write out the receipt.

The hall seemed almost silent when they had gone. My father said, "I had the gold, my son."

"I know but you may need it. Besides those weird sisters you go on about meant I was given the ransom for a purpose. I will get more. I am just worried that with Sir Richard and I gone as well as ten men at arms we leave you vulnerable to attack."

"We can get more men but tell me why Sir Richard and not Wulfstan?"

"Wulfstan will be more useful here and besides he has just married. He and Faren need time together."

He shook his head, "It is but two years since we left our home in the east and I now see the man grown from the boy."

The good news was that I had had my title and my castle confirmed. I would have to leave it in the hands of the villagers of Stockton but that was a small price to pay. We had two days of frenetic activity as we had horses shoed and clothes prepared. I had to pick ten men at arms to accompany us. I picked Edward and his men first. I chose Dick and John as my archers and finally Wilfred and Edgar from my new men. Wulfric was upset. "Why not me my lord? Have I displeased you?"

"No Wulfric. Until I return I want you as constable of my castle. I would like that and my village kept safe while I am away. Can you hold it for me and keep my people safe?"

He seemed to grow taller. "Aye my lord."

I was determined to spend my last night in my castle and I took leave of my father as I led my men to Stockton. It was not only my father but his oathsworn, Aiden and Faren who were all tearful as we parted.

"My son, take care. You are a mighty knight but do not allow the king to throw the lives of you and your men away lightly."

"I will not and I know that Wulfstan will look after you."

"I can come with you, my lord"

"I know you could, Wulfstan, but this is a journey I must make as a leader. This is a quest to see the world and to find out what kind of knight I am. I will return and I will be a better knight for it. I know that when I return my manor and its people will have prospered and I will bring back riches, father."

As he embraced me he said, "The only riches I need are you, returned to me healthy. God speed."

The joy of a night alone in my castle was spoiled by the late arrival in the night of the king and his retinue. My men had to sleep on the top floor which had no roof although Sir Richard and I were not ejected from our own hall. It proved a propitious happenstance.

We were awoken before dawn by Alf who banged on the door of the castle. "Vikings, my lord! Vikings!"

I grabbed my armour and began to dress. King Henry was already awake. "What is it, Sir Alfraed?"

"One of my people has seen a Viking ship in the river." He looked at me as though I had spoken a foreign language. "They still raid apparently."

His squire began to dress him and he laughed, "Then I am more than happy that you chose to build a stone castle."

We clambered the stairs to the top of the tower. We could see, peering above the mist the mast of the dragon ship as it rowed towards the ferry and the village. I saw no lookout on the mast and so I assumed that they did not know we now had a tower.

"Edward, bring the men. Sir Richard!"

Leaving a bemused king to dress and follow with his household knights we raced down to the river. My people were being shepherded by Ethelred and Alf towards the sanctuary of the castle. Alf had told me that there could be more than sixty Vikings on a single raider. We would need the help of the king. However, we had enough men to slow them down.

Sir Richard and I had drawn swords and Carl and Harold watched our backs. Dick and John had arrows already nocked and ready to loose. The last stragglers from the village were screaming their way along the river bank fearful of the depredations of the Norsemen. And suddenly the mist cleared and we saw the Vikings. Half had mail but most were almost naked with a large round shield and either a sword or an axe. They saw us and raced towards us. There was no order to their attack. They saw a handful of warriors and assumed they could kill us and have their way with the villagers. They would learn to their cost that we were not to be knocked aside like wheat. The bank was narrow and we had the advantage that the river was to our left.

The first reckless warrior almost hurled himself at me. He swung his axe from far behind his head. I stepped back and swung backhand. My sword sliced into his back as his swing took him beyond me and threw him into the river. Sir Richard had despatched a second and their leader must have realised that we knew our business. He halted his men and they formed a small shield wall. That suited me for we had reinforcements coming.

The leader led from the front. He had mail armour and a spear. He stabbed at my shield with his spear. He punched, as much as I might have done from a horse. It deflected along the boss of my shield. I did not hack, I jabbed quickly and sharply. He barely had time to bring his shield up. I felt a blow hit my helmet as one of his men stabbed at me with a spear. Edgar's pole axe came swooping down from behind me and I heard a gurgled scream as the spearman was killed. The warrior on the other side of the leader fell. The pressure from the front diminished and I took the opportunity of punching with my shield into the face of the mailed warrior. He grunted as blood spattered from his broken nose. I stabbed forward into the press of warriors and felt my sword sink into flesh. Sir Richard hacked sideways at the chief of the Vikings and he lurched across my front. I stabbed blindly a second time and this time the sword went into his side. He was a big brave man and he stepped backwards into the protection of a wall of shields.

Behind me, I heard a cheer as King Henry's household knights ran down the bank towards us. This was our chance! "Charge!"

My small band hurled themselves at the shield wall. They were in the process of carrying their leader aboard and in the confusion we broke into their wall. Swords and axes rained down on my shield and helmet but they were too close to hurt me. Two Vikings fell into the river and the departure allowed me to swing my sword. It bit into the side of a half-naked warrior. I twisted as I pulled and stepped over his body to cleave the helmet and skull of another.

The Vikings had had enough and they poured back aboard their dragon ship. John and Dick rained arrows as fast as they could nock them. The wooden jetty was slippery with blood and I halted. I did not want any of my men to slip and fall to a stray spear or arrow. Even as they pulled away from the shore Dick and John continued to score hits. This was one Viking raider who would not return.

King Henry arrived in time to see the dragon ship turn and head east. "That was impressive with just twelve men. I look forward to seeing how well you do on a horse."

We searched the bodies and removed all weapons and treasure before returning the Vikings to the sea where they would feed the fishes. I gave the weapons and armour to Alf as compensation for any damage and as a reward for the warning.

We merely had to wait for Ethelred to repair the ferry and we would be ready to cross the river. The King said, "There is no hurry. We are waiting for more knights."

He said no more. At noon I saw a conroi of armed and mailed men coming from the east. The king nodded, "Ah, we can now load the ferry. Here is Sir Robert De Brus and the knights of Hartness. Our army of the north is complete"

Chapter 19

King Henry's voice was silky. He was watching me and seeing how I would react. I smiled. I was from the east. I could be as two-faced as the next man if I chose. The next man happened to be the king and he was, as I soon discovered, extremely devious.

Sir Robert had brought five knights and thirty men at arms. I did not recognise them as the knights I had encountered previously. That worried me for it meant my home and my father were both in danger. Sir Robert was at least ten years older than I was and had a hint of grey in his beard. He bowed to the king and then smiled at me. "Ah Sir Alfraed, I have been looking forward to meeting with you. It has been remiss of me not to invite you over as a neighbour."

I bowed and smiled back, "I met with some of your knights and enjoyed their hospitality and a bout with blades."

He nodded, "Ah yes, I have heard you are good. That was an unfortunate encounter and there was a great deal of misunderstanding. The men concerned have been punished. It is one reason why I did not bring them with me. Such failure will not be tolerated in the future."

I listened to his words. What he meant was that the next time his men would carry out his orders and there would be no survivors. I was not worried. So long as we were with the king and his household knights then Sir Robert would have to behave himself. As we were ferried to the south bank I wondered at his inclusion. Was the king keeping his enemies closer than his friends and if so how did he view me?

On the journey to Wales, I came to know some of the household knights and the entourage of the king. We were the lowly end of the entourage and given the job of guarding the pack animals. Sir Richard felt slighted, especially as we rode in the dust of the others but I was happy as it allowed me to listen to the chatter and gossip of the squires who led the animals. My father had taught me to listen, always. He had advised me that just because a person was low born did not mean that they were stupid. As much as I could I treated all of them with respect. It was something Sir Richard could never quite manage.

I learned that King Henry relied heavily upon his illegitimate son, Robert of Gloucester. He was an able general. Ranulf le Meschin was also a fine warrior and well respected by the household knights. We saw little of them while we travelled as they formed the bodyguard around the king. Some men at arms and knights had been detached to escort the tax collector back to London. Although they would meet us again, closer to Wales we were a small force, certainly by Eastern standards. We had just over a hundred knights and six hundred men at arms. We had a small force of archers; there were only one hundred of them including my two who had impressed the king in the skirmish with the Vikings.

Poor Harold found himself with his hands full. He had his own horse, Star, a rouncy and a sumpter to contend with. He was learning to be a horseman. This was the first time Star had left the Tees since I had captured him. He behaved well enough. I was relieved that he looked as good as any of the other destriers being led by their squires. They were, however, an aggressive breed. The squires had to work hard to stop them from biting and kicking each other. The work I had done over the winter had made me confident that I could not only ride him I could control him and make him do my bidding. That was no mean feat.

The king pushed hard and we rode almost fifty miles each day. We passed over the high, bleak centre of the country. No one lived there and all we saw were birds flying high and looking for their next meal. It was desolate but once we dropped down to the western side it became not only warmer but we could see the fields of ripening wheat. I could see why the king was addressing this issue of the Welsh. This land was too valuable to risk.

I had never campaigned before but it was a similar experience to our journey from the east. Each night we camped and every conroi was expected to fend for itself. The influence of each knight could be measured in their proximity to the king. We were on the periphery. I did not mind. Our position at the end of the column meant I could send Dick and John off hunting as we travelled the road. We ate well. I have no doubt we broke many laws as we hunted on the lands of other lords. However, I felt certain that the presence of the king worked in our favour. The desolate high lands only resulted in a few game birds but they made a pleasant change to our diet.

We halted on the banks of the Mearsey. There was an old Roman bridge hard by Wilderspool. There the King sent for each conroi leader. Although I only had one knight serving me that meant I was included amongst the great and the good.

"Since Richard Earl of Chester drowned with my son on the White Ship, Maredudd ap Bleddyn has begun privations against our lands here in Cheshire. He has retreated from Cheshire but as I intend to travel to

Normandy in the autumn I will crush this rebellion and extract such a price that the Welsh will hide in the hills with their sheep. I will have these borders safe and secure at least." He waved his arm around us all. "The Welsh have few knights and none as skilled as we. Our men at arms will secure our bases and we will spread death and destruction throughout this land."

There was much cheering before Baron Robert De Brus asked. "The land of the Welsh is not good for destriers. Will your majesty compensate us for any losses?"

Henry stared at the knight until he sat down. Sir Richard murmured. "He is right to ask. This is not the country for fine horses."

"Then we shall ride with care!" I hissed. I did not want to be associated with such carping comments.

Robert of Gloucester stood. "We will divide into three battles. I will lead one, Lord Ranulf a second and King Henry the third. The men at arms will all march with the king and they will guard the animals and supplies but each knight will bring their mounted archers with them."

We were then allocated a battle. Sir Richard and I were to be with Robert of Gloucester. I smiled when I saw that Robert de Brus was to be with the king. He had made a mistake in asking his question. The king would keep him under close scrutiny. There were just thirty knights with Richard. He gathered us around him. He had a map of the area before him. "We are going down the southern side of the Clwyd Valley. The squires will be banded together under my squire Roger Tancerville. Their job will be to find the Welsh and draw them on to our lances. Ranulf will proceed down the northern side of the valley while the king will travel along the coast road. Our aim is to defeat any horsemen they send against us. Hopefully, we will catch them in a trap with my father waiting for them with the bulk of the knights and the men at arms. You should regard yourselves as the beaters who will drive the game into the traps." He stared belligerently around the tent. "Any questions?"

No one had any and we began to leave. His voice suddenly called, "Sir Alfraed, a moment if you please."

I waited and the tent emptied. "The king tells me that you fight as well on foot as on a horse."

"My father and his oathsworn were Varangians. It was their natural way of fighting. I was taught well by the best from an early age."

"Good, for Sir Robert was correct. This is not a good horse country. If we have to go on foot and winkle out these Welshmen I want you to lead a small conroi. Can you do that?"

"Aye my lord."

He laughed, "Good, he said that nothing would surprise you. You may be young but I can see the steel in your eyes."

"I hope so, my lord."

I saw that Harold was nervous as he and the other squires followed Robert of Gloucester's man. "Fear nothing Harold. You are as worthy as any of them and remember that you have Dick and John with you too."

Edward took Scout with the other horses and all of the equipment. "Fear not my lord; not a hair of your steed will be harmed. You have my word."

I smiled, "Ride him, Edward, he has a good nose and ears. He will smell out the Welsh."

I had my Gonfanon on my lance as did Richard. It marked for who we were. I had never ridden with so many knights. We were not at the rear this time. Robert of Gloucester had us four knights lead from the front. I took that as a compliment. We headed south towards the head of the Clwyd. The ground was not as rough as it might have been; there was an ancient stone road, but I was wary of riding Star to war for the first time. Aiden had given me a few tips and I had slipped an apple or two into my saddlebags. Star liked them, apparently. I decided to keep on his good side. It might save my life.

It took us half a day to reach the southern side of the valley. We knew that our thirty odd squires and twenty or so archers were ahead, tormenting and teasing the Welsh. We were the hammer waiting to strike. I was aware that this was excellent ambush country. Arrows could fly from cover. I was confident in my armour but I remembered that my archers used knight killers. I hoped and prayed that the Welsh did not possess them.

I was not worried about either my men or my horses. They were both well trained. However, I did close my eyes and offer a silent prayer that they might survive the day. I had too few to risk loss. We rested at the head of the valley. Richard and I checked our stirrups and our girths. I worried that many of the young knights did not and seemed happy and jovial. War was not something to be taken lightly.

When we were ready we remounted. We were about to continue our westward march when we heard the thunder of hooves. We saw, less than half a mile away, the squires and mounted archers. They were falling back up the centre of the valley pursued by an untidy mob of Welsh. There appeared to be no order in the pursuit. There were horsemen and knights but there were also many soldiers on foot.

Robert of Gloucester turned to us, "We will charge on my command. There will be two lines. God be with you!"

I found myself and my companion four knights from Robert of Gloucester. We were knee to knee. Our shields hung from our shoulders which allowed us to use our left hand to guide the reins although once we were in action I would use my knees to direct my horse. Star stamped his hoof impatiently. "Steady boy! We will go soon enough!"

The squires were cleverly leading the enemy up the valley. We rode obliquely down the gentle side of the upper Clwyd. We trotted to keep the line. I saw Robert of Gloucester as he kept glancing to his left and right to watch for any errant knight. There were none. We kept a perfect formation. The first of the Welsh spotted us and a wail went up as some of them tried to halt. Robert of Gloucester increased the speed of our charge. Star was coping magnificently. It seemed effortless for the huge warhorse. We were now cantering down the slope and we were like two walls of steel. I did not risk turning but I knew that there was an identical line of knights behind me. Roger of Tames, who led the second line, would choose his target once we had struck their line.

The Welsh were attempting to face us with their own knights. They had the disadvantage that they had halted and were charging uphill. Arrows showered down upon us. They had been released hurriedly and did little damage. I heard Robert of Gloucester shout, "Charge for King Henry!" and we spurred our horses. I pulled my right hand back in preparation for the blow. I had trained to do this many times but this would be the first charge against knights for me. I had speared men at arms on foot, not knights who were armed as I was. The handful of knights who had managed to turn tried to charge uphill. They had no speed and they were not in a line. I punched with my lance at the knight who tried to wheel to face me. The head of my lance powered into his chest forcing the mail into his flesh. He was thrown from his horse with an ugly tear in the centre of his chest. His dying hand dragged his horse to crash amongst the archers who were trying to hit us at close range.

As Star galloped down I heard a crack and a crunch as his hooves crushed skulls and shattered bones. My lance was intact although there was now a gap between my right side and the next knight. I saw a warrior rallying the men around him. He saw my approach and hefted his shield for protection. I pulled my arm back again and this time I aimed at the top of his shield. I punched hard. As I had expected he pulled his shield up but he merely succeeded in guiding the lance into his throat. It came out of the rear but the weight of his body pulled the lance from my hand and broke the head.

I risked a glance along the line. It was no longer straight and many lances were missing. Sir Richard still rode next to me and his lance was intact. I drew my sword and in one motion swung it sideways across the head of the spearman who tried to stab Star. I felt the spearhead slide off my armour and strike the girth then my arm jarred as my blade bit across the top of his skull.

Two men, sheltering behind one shield stepped before Star and tried to jab him with their spears. It was brave but foolish. I leaned forward, stood in my stirrups and pulled back Star's head. His mighty hooves rose high in the air and crashed down on the two brave Welshmen. I heard their brief screams before they were crushed into the ground. We had stopped and I reined in, the better to survey the scene. I saw that the Welsh were fleeing. Ranulf had brought his knights from the southern side and we had trapped them between us. Although vastly outnumbered our surprise attack and our superior skills had turned the tide. I saw the squires flooding back down the valley with the mounted archers to support us.

Sir Richard's voice carried across the field, "Pursue them to the sea. Slaughter them all!"

We did not have enough men to take prisoners for ransom. All we met would be put to the sword. Star was rested and I spurred him again. We soon caught up with the stragglers. These were not the knights or the mounted men. Most of those lay dead at the head of the valley or were leading the rout. These were the heavier armed and mailed Welshmen who could not outrun us. Their own archers tried to stop us by gathering in knots and releasing their arrows but our own mounted archers would stop and deliver a more deadly shower of their own each time they tried to rally.

I had to lean to one side of Star to slice down at the men who tried to make themselves as small a target as possible. Sometimes their mail and their helmets saved their life as my sword failed to find a vital organ but each one I struck was out of the battle. I had a powerful arm, lifting blocks of stone had ensured that and my sword was a powerful and well-made weapon. If I hit them they went down and stayed down. My descent down the valley was marked by a trail of dead and wounded Welshmen.

We were no longer galloping. Even Star was tiring but I could see the sea ahead. With any luck, there would be a line of men at arms and King Henry waiting for them. I saw the brilliance of his plan. We had been the beaters driving the prey into the trap that was the men at arms. They would be a solid line of shields bristling with a variety of weapons. The Welsh had nowhere to go. They would break themselves upon King Henry's steel.

I watched them slow as the line of men at arms appeared from valley side to valley side. Sir Richard shouted, "Leave those and bear left! Follow those knights!" I glanced to where he pointed. There were twenty or thirty knights and men at arms riding hard to the south. They were trying to escape. Their fluttering Gonfanon showed that there were a number of Barons amongst them.

I wheeled Star to the left and with Sir Richard close by we joined Robert of Gloucester. I found myself riding to his left. He turned his head. "Still with me eh? That is a fine warhorse." He had no lance but his sword dripped with blood and gore. There were just twenty of us. Others were either engaged upon the field or one or two had suffered wounds to their horses. Twenty knights would be more than enough to deal with the threat which remained.

"Ride in a column of four!"

The land was climbing and it was hard to maintain a line twenty knights abreast. The others pulled in behind us. It was a trot rather than a gallop. The Welsh knights ahead made the mistake of trying to whip their horses up the slope. They were blown and we watched as the fleeing knights became an extended line. Robert of Gloucester stood in his stirrups and, leaning forward, brought his sword down across the back of the last Welsh man at arms in the line. Robert of Gloucester was a hugely powerful knight. The blow split the man at arm's back open to the bone and he tumbled from the horse. His dying cry made the next four knights turn and when they saw us approach the four of them held up their hands and shouted, "We surrender! Quarter!"

It was lucky for them that Robert of Gloucester led us for he was able to rescind his earlier order. "Sir Guy, secure our prisoners!"

One of his knights reined in to watch those who had surrendered and the rest of us carried on.

The land spread out in a small plateau before rising to sharp rocks, cliffs and gullies. Three knights darted to our left.

"Sir Alfraed, fetch them!"

I wheeled left, taking Sir Richard with me. Star seemed to be coping well with the difficult terrain and the land was flatter. I urged him on and began to outstrip Sir Richard. I angled my attack so that I came at the last knight from his shield side. He would feel protected. I noticed that he was riding a palfrey and not a destrier. I stood in my stirrups and leaned forward. Star did not falter as he crashed into the knight's horse and I brought my blade down hard upon his shield and his shoulder. Our joint attack threw both horse and rider to the ground where he remained stunned.

I wheeled Star around and Sir Richard and I came up alongside the second knight. We were on both sides of his him and he threw his sword to the ground, "Quarter!" I was becoming tired but there was still one knight relentlessly trying to evade us. God must have been with us for the knight tried to jump over a small stream and his horsed faltered. He flew from its back and his head was crushed against the small rocky cliff which rose to our right.

I reined in Star. The battle was over.

Chapter 20

Sir Richard searched the body of the dead knight and secured the horse. I returned to the knight who had surrendered. He bowed and held his sword, hilt first towards me, "I am Cynwrig ap Cynan and I am your prisoner…"

"Alfraed of Stockton. Bring your horse and we will see to your companion."

"That is my elder brother Gruffyd ap Cynan."

"Then I hope that your family has gold or you will rot in Chester castle."

The young man gave me a worried look. The stunned warrior stood as we approached. My prisoner asked, "Are you hurt brother?"

He took off his helmet and shook his head. His expression showed that he regretted the action immediately. "I have a bloodied head. That is all."

Sir Richard arrived with the last knight's body draped over the saddle of the horse. Cynwrig bowed his head, "Well Gruffyd you are head of the family now, our father is dead."

There were no tears and the two brothers led their father's horse and carried his body back to the battlefield. We walked back for there was no need to rush and Star deserved the rest. The squires and the archers covered the valley sides. They looked like a flock of crows picking over the dead. They sought anything of value. By nightfall, it would be the turn of the foxes and the rats to begin to rid the field of the bodies.

Robert of Gloucester waited for us. There were six sad-looking knights surrounded by our companions. Our leader grinned at us. "You have done well." He spread an arm around the prisoners. "We have all done well. We share the ransom!"

It was not a request it was a command but I understood. For the day we had fought beneath his banner. He was entitled to determine the spoils. Sir Richard and I would not make as much as we might have done but we would have enough and we had won the favour of the king's son. I was learning that such trades were worth making. I also knew that Harold, Dick and John would have gathered a great deal of booty from the dead. They were my men and they fought for me.

By the time we reached the mouth of the valley, we saw the huge number of prisoners who had been captured. It had been a great victory. King Henry greeted his son with a huge grin and a bear-like embrace. He winced a little and I saw the bandage on his arm. He had been struck by an arrow. He dismissed the wound as nothing. "It is like the Welsh king, a little prick!" Everyone laughed. He put his good arm around Robert of Gloucester. "What a son! You have done well Robert." He was close enough for me to hear his words. "Maredudd ap Bleddyn has fled towards Anglesey. Tomorrow morning take your battle and demand his surrender. If he does not then tell him I will put his hand to the sword and make Powys a wasteland. I would go but I have a pinprick of a wound. I am not in a good humour. Your words might be kinder."

"Aye father." He nodded at me. "You were right about this cockerel. He is a fast blade!"

"I know. He is one we should watch!"

Although he was smiling I felt a threat in his words. However that night I was happy. I had fought in my first battle as a knight and I had acquitted myself well. None of my men had been hurt and all had profited from the day. It did not get any better. As we ate around our campfire Robert of Gloucester sought us out. "We will not need our destrier tomorrow. Speed is of the essence. Bring your archers, Sir Alfraed, my squire told me they did well today."

I nodded, "They are the best archers in England."

He looked at them, "As good as the outlaws of the woods?"

I smiled and said, enigmatically, "Their equal, at least."

Robert of Gloucester burst out laughing. "You are no spoiled aristocrat I can see that!"

Edward and the others had had a good day. They brought out their spoils and divided them up. They were going to include Sir Richard and me but I shook my head. "We have ransom coming. You deserve the victory."

Harold was full of the battle. It was the first time he had fought without me by his side. His experiences both with me and in the woods had stood him in good stead. He, along with Dick and John, had used their arrows well and brought down two knights. I discovered later that they had killed a local leader and it had precipitated the headlong pursuit of the archers. My conroi was held in high esteem by our comrades.

As we galloped along the coast road the next day I found that Sir Robert de Brus had fared less well. His squires and men at arms had been too busy looting and it had allowed the Welsh king to escape. His men had also allowed the enemy archer to close with the king and to wound him. King Henry was not a forgiving man. He had De Brus and his knights sent back to Hartness without any ransom as a punishment. I later wondered if this contributed to the treachery of De Brus. Our campaign was not over but the king had broken the hearts of the opposition and we could mop up the last vestiges of resistance with those that remained.

"Will, the king not wish to conquer Wales?"

Robert of Gloucester swept his hand around the mountains which surrounded us. "What in God's name for? You cannot grow grain here. Anglesey is the only prize worth having and it is preyed upon by the Irish pirates. No, my father will fine this Maredudd ap Bleddyn harshly and we will go to Maine."

"Is there trouble there?"

He leaned in to me. "Count Fulk of Anjou promised his daughter Matilda to my half brother, William, who drowned on the White Ship. He wants the dowry back he gave and my father is loath to return it. Count Fulk has come from Outremer, the Holy Land. He is a rich man now and a more dangerous enemy than he was. Like all rich men, he is never content with the riches he has and seeks more. The men of Anjou will prove a harder nut to crack than these Welsh."

Ahead we saw a stone tower surrounded by a curtain wall. The castle was well sited for the mountains rose on one side and the sea was on the other. I wondered what Robert of Gloucester would do. It looked too difficult for us to assault. He did not seem worried. We halted out of bow range. Robert rode forward to address the castle. "I am Robert of Gloucester, the emissary of King Henry of England and Normandy. I have a message for King Maredudd ap Bleddyn. Is he within?"

There was no reply. All that we could hear was the crash of the waves on the beach and the cries of the gulls. All within the tower were silent. "Come, make haste. We have much ransom to collect and we have little enough time to waste on a beaten king who ran with his tail between his legs."

A figure appeared at the gatehouse, "I am King Maredudd ap Bleddyn; what does your king require of me?"

Robert of Gloucester laughed, "Why, your surrender of course. Your knights are dead or captured and we have a mighty host ready to tear your land apart should you refuse our kind and generous offer."

"Fine words for someone who is beyond my walls whilst we are safe within."

Robert of Gloucester laughed, "This is not a castle! This is a pile of stones gathered from the beach and if I so chose I could take it with my battle of knights." He began to jerk his horse's head around, "If that is your answer then I will find my king and he will bring the full force of his army upon you. I, for one, would fear his wrath!"

"Stay!" The voice sounded resigned, "What are your terms?"

Robert of Gloucester turned his horse around, "Terms? I told you, total surrender. My father will determine the size of the fine for your destruction and rampage in Cheshire. You are beaten and you know it. You are wasting my time. What say you?"

There was a brief silence, "Very well. I agree. Open the gates."

Robert of Gloucester turned to me, "Return to my father and tell him that King Maredudd ap Bleddyn has surrendered."

I led my warriors back to the main camp. The king was delighted with the result. He turned to Ranulf. "You command here. I will take Alfraed and my household knights. Send for the ransoms. I would have us away from here before the end of the month!"

I felt honoured to be riding with the leading knights of the land. All wore armour as good, if not better than mine and they were from the noblest families in the land. It was sad to realise that within twenty years they would be fighting each other and picking over the corpse that would be England but on that glorious day, we rode with Gonfanon flying and armour gleaming. We saw not a single Welshmen. They fled in fear at the sight of the mighty host. Robert of Gloucester had secured all the prisoners and the Welsh king dropped to his knees when King Henry sat on his temporary throne.

"You have been a foolish king, Maredudd ap Bleddyn. You have dared to attack my lands. Your knights have paid a fearful price and now you shall pay an even greater one. I fine you and your people ten thousand head of cattle! They shall be delivered before we leave!"

"But my liege, that is too great a number."

"Nonetheless that is the number that you will provide and we will hold you and your family prisoner here until they are delivered." He leaned forward and said, threateningly, "I leave you your sheep but my men will eat mutton until the cattle are here. Unless you wish your people to both starve and freeze this winter then deliver my cattle sooner rather than later. You have fourteen nights to do so."

He was a beaten man. He sent out his riders to begin to collect the cattle. I could not begin to conceive of the size of a herd of ten thousand cattle. As we made camp in the valley close to the castle I asked Robert of Gloucester what the king would do with the cattle when he had them.

He laughed, "I can see that you are new to this. The king will take half. Ranulf and I will each take half of the ones who remain and the remaining half will be divided between the knights who fought for the king. Sir Robert has returned to his home in Hartness and so that means there are one hundred and sixty knights who will share the bounty. You represent one-fiftieth of the knights and so your share will be fifty cattle."

We were rich. With the ransom from the captured knights and the cattle, we would return to Norton with enough cattle and gold to pay our taxes for years to come. My father had been right to come to England. This was indeed a land of opportunity. If all my campaigns were as easy and successful as this one then I could build an even bigger and better castle than the one I had.

It was late September when we left with our cattle and our gold to return north to Norton. The king requested that I provide three knights and thirty men at arms in April the following year for a campaign in Maine. I was to be at Caen before the start of spring. I knew that there was little point in protesting and, to be honest, I was looking forward to more loot and spoils of war. Even dour Sir Richard seemed happy as we headed slowly north leading our fifty cattle. We had also managed to acquire some sheep. They were, ostensibly, food for the journey home but I knew that we could use them to induce people to farm our land. We had captured some five palfreys and a rouncy. They carried the chest with the forty gold pieces of the ransom which were mine. My men and Sir Richard had their share of ransoms. There would be many impoverished Welsh families and King Maredudd ap Bleddyn would not go to war so quickly again. His knights would need to recover their fortune. My men could not believe the riches they were taking back. Edward and Sarah the Alewife would be wed and I knew that Edward had plans for an inn in the town. Others had similar dreams. What Sir Richard would do with his money I had no idea. He never seemed to spend anything. I still found him too cold and distant to be a friend.

Each time we halted in a town, on the way home, we attracted attention. Out of workmen at arms sought employment with me. I let Edward pick the best. He knew his men. It was close to Harrogate, however, that we had our stroke of fortune. We were passing the stocks and I saw a man with a white apron being pelted with rotten fruit. This had been a familiar sight as we had passed north for it was a common punishment. There was, however, something about this man that attracted my attention. He did not look cowed but he stared each person who passed in the eye. He had pride despite the indignity he was suffering. I waved my men forward and dismounted.

"What is your crime, sir?"

He shook his head defiantly, "No crime, sir, I am innocent."

I shook my head. It was ever thus with criminals. The gaols and prisons were full of innocent men. I half-turned to leave. "Then you deserve your punishment."

"Sir, you look like a kind man. You are the first to stop and not to punish me. Will you not hear me out?"

I thought of my father and knew that he would have listened. "Speak." I was aware that while I stood there no one threw anything at him. I was not a fool. The man was getting some respite from the abuse but I would hear him out. I had given my word.

"I am William of Knaresborough and I was the miller there. I left my father's mill and came here with my wife. We found success. I took on a young apprentice and taught him all that I knew about grinding grain. What I did not know was that they were making free behind my back. I worked too hard and spent longer at the mill than in my hearth. They enjoyed themselves in my absence. Stone and chalk were found in my bread. I was accused by the village of trying to defraud them. My wife and my apprentice also accused me and I was thrown from my home. She and my apprentice now have my mill and I am punished for working too hard and being blind to the deceit under my roof."

My father had the gift of knowing when a man spoke the truth and I had inherited it. I knew that this man spoke the truth. "You swear that you are a good miller and are innocent of the charges."

"I swear!"

"Then when you are released seek me out. We will be camped to the east of the town. I am Alfraed of Stockton and my father, Ridley of Norton requires a miller. At the very least we will feed you and shelter you. What say you?"

"I am your man, sir for you are the only one to share kind words and not to judge me." He shook his head, "And there is nothing left for me here now."

And so we found our miller. It was another example of what my father's oathsworn would call *wyrd*. I was coming to see that God was not alone in changing the destiny of men. By the time we passed through Northallerton we had twenty-six men at arms as well as William the Miller and Leofric the Moneyer whom we had met on the road. His story had been as sad as William's. His downfall had been caused by an Irish raid. His family had been enslaved and he had fled from Lancaster across the Pennines to forget his loss. He too wished to ply his trade again. We were a huge caravan as we headed towards the river and the ferry.

I confess that I felt a lump in my throat when I saw the yellow tower rising across the river. This was my home. We had seen the stone building growing from the river for some miles. Our long campaign had made us all, even Sir Richard, closer and the men sang as we marched. I hoped that there would be enough maidens for them all. They were lusty men and they were victorious. More than that they had coins in their purses and they were keen to spend. The markets we had visited on our way home had done well out of my conroi. Each man at arms was better dressed and armed than he had been. They knew that war was their trade and they all had the finest tools that money could buy. This was what a victorious army looked and sounded like.

Ethelred looked pleased to see us. I noticed he was even more rotund. He had prospered. "Welcome back from the wars my lord. Were they profitable?"

I laughed, "You will get your coin, you old rogue!"

As we led our horses to the castle I saw William and his son toiling away at the curtain wall. Our departure had delayed the building of the moat but he had worked hard to complete more of the wall. With the new men at arms, we would have them both finished before winter. The castle would be finished well ahead of schedule. That was another result of our victory. God was smiling upon us.

I knew that I could not enjoy the comfort of my home yet. Taking Harold with me to escort Leofric and William the Miller to their new home I left Sir Richard in charge of the cattle. "Give five head to the village as a reward from me." As I rode north I determined that at least half of our cattle and all of the sheep would be given to the tenants. It would inspire loyalty and also result in more taxes for us. I had learned much when talking to the other knights. We all enjoyed combat but each of them knew that it was the farmers at home who allowed them the freedom to do what they loved. I would be on campaign the next year. I needed the manor to be safe and secure.

William the Miller became more nervous and worried as we approached Norton. "Suppose your father has employed a miller, my lord?"

I had told him of the building of the mill. "Then I shall build a mill at Stockton. You will be employed William; I gave my word and I am never foresworn."

My joy at my return was short-lived. As soon as we entered the gates a worried Wulfstan sought me out. "Sir Alfraed, your father is ill!"

Chapter 21

I was more worried that Wulfstan was so concerned than anything else. He never looked frightened but that day, as I dismounted and ran to the hall, he did. I took in nothing. It was as though my senses had deserted me. The greetings were ignored as I ran to his chamber. He looked very grey and very old. He smiled wanly at me as I approached. "Ah, the warrior is returned. Were you victorious?"

Suddenly the cattle, the victories and the gold seemed hollow. "Father, what ails you?"

"Old age. I have lived longer than any of those with whom I fought. I should have been like Aelfraed and died with a sword in my hand."

"I will not hear such nonsense. I forbid you to die!"

He laughed, "And I will try to obey but do not expect miracles. I will say that I feel better now having seen you hale and hearty. Sit and tell me all." He nodded to the slave, "Fetch me Faren's broth I have a mind to eat while I listen to my son's stories."

I took off my cloak and threw it to the floor. I laid my sword and scabbard on the table. Before I could begin my tale a pregnant Faren came in with a bowl of broth. She gave me the most wonderful smile. It showed she was glad to see me. She put the bowl and the bread on the table and helped my father into a seated position and then, as with a child, she put the bowl of broth and soup before him. "It is about time you began to eat!"

She turned and snapped, "And what are you doing throwing your good clothes on the floor!" She picked up the cloak and as she came close to me whispered, "It is good that you have returned. He pined for you. I pray you stay longer and he will improve. God bless you, sir."

The force of nature departed and I resumed my seat and told him all. It took some time and he finished both the bread and the broth. I saw colour reappear in his cheeks and I kept talking. I told him of the miller and the moneyer. I told him of the spring campaign and I told him of Sir Robert De Brus and his disgrace. His eyes were growing heavy when I had finished. He patted my hand. "I could not be more proud of you, my son. And I confess that I feel better now than in many a moon. Send a slave for the bowl, I am ready to sleep." A worried look must have flickered across my face for he smiled, "I will sleep only. I am under orders am I not? I cannot die until you give permission. Now go and see the others. They have missed you too."

I took the bowl and spoon with me and my sword. The others were waiting in the hall. Poor Ralph looked beside himself with worry. "How is he, my lord?"

"He is sleeping. How long has he been like this?"

"A month. He had a chill and it became worse. He hid the symptoms. Poor Faren had the medicine to cure him but he took it too late for it to be effective. Had you not returned then Father Peter would have given him his last rites. He told us to prepare his tomb."

"Well, I am back now. Fear not. I will stay here until he is well enough to walk around the manor." Ralph looked doubtful. "I promise you, Ralph, that he will walk around the manor again. I will make sure that he does."

When I saw belief fill their faces I told them all that I had told my father. Garth said, "I will see to the moneyer and the miller. Both are needed. You have done well, my lord."

It took much to impress Garth and I felt even more pleased with myself. I nodded, "I will have the cattle distributed on the morrow. I want all in the two manors to benefit. We must build pens inside the bailey to protect them" I paused, "We are requested to campaign next spring in Normandy. I want both estates secure and better defended before then."

They nodded. Wulfstan asked, "Will you need me on the campaign, my lord?"

"Want you? Yes. Need you? I think I need you here to watch over both estates and besides, you are to be a father are you not? What kind of lord would I be if I took you away from your son?"

They all laughed and he replied, "You have changed Alfraed. I cannot teach you anymore."

"But I am what I am because of all that each of you has taught me. I am your son as much as my father's and I thank you all. The campaign against the Welsh has shown me how well you have prepared me."

I spent a hectic three weeks at Norton seeing to the needs of my father and distributing the animals. I left Sir Richard and Edward to complete my castle. At the back of my mind, I had the worry that we were still not safe. King Henry would now be back in Normandy. He had cracked his whip but I still worried about my neighbours. Once my father took his first faltering steps in the bailey I took Wulfstan, Harold, Egbert, Osric and Athelstan to visit with Sir Robert de Brus. I did not know why I had to go but I knew that if I did not then I might come to regret it.

I rode Scout when we went the ten miles to Hartness. I did not want to go armed and ready for war but we did go in armour, helmed and with shields. There were dangerous marshes to cross and I knew that Sir Robert had outlaws who lived close to his land preying on travellers.

His castle was well positioned on a narrow neck of land overlooking the harbour. He had a solid gate that was protected by a wall as high as two men. I was recognised by the men at arms; they had been on campaign with us and we were admitted.

Sir Robert came down the steps to greet us. He had the false smile he always wore. I had only seen it disappear when he had been chastised by King Henry and sent back from the wars.

"Ah Sir Alfraed, how is Good King Henry? Has he recovered from his wound?"

"He has Sir Robert and the campaign is over."

"So I hear and our king has returned to Normandy. Come into my hall. Let us not stay out here. There is a chill wind. I hear your father is not well. Has he improved since your return?"

I heard Osric suck his teeth in annoyance. I agreed with my father's oathsworn. This knight took an unhealthy interest in my business.

"He had a slight chill but he is recovered. Living in the east did not prepare him for these northern climes."

As we entered his hall my eyes had to become accustomed to the gloom. I saw that it was full. When my eyes adjusted I saw that they were all knights.

"I believe you have met Sir Tancred de Mamers before."

The knights who had raided us were in the home of Robert de Brus! I flashed a look of warning at my comrades and I smiled. "I did not expect you here. I would have thought you would have gone back to Outremer."

"So long as Count Fulk is in Anjou I will enjoy the company of my friends."

Here was treachery. Count Fulk was the enemy of my king and here was one of his barons in this nest of vipers that was Hartness. I knew then that I had been right to come here. I had to draw on all my experiences in Constantinople. I smiled and played the game of the hypocrite. It did not sit well but it was necessary. I did not need to tell the others to be wary. They had taught me the rules of this game. I would let them identify the knights and the banners. I would concentrate on the words of the two leaders.

All were keen to hear of our exploits in Wales. I told them, simply, and without exaggeration of our capture of the Welsh king.

"And King Henry only chose cattle? He did not wish to conquer the country?"

"He appears to have no ambition in that direction. I think I agree with him. The land is fit for sheep. Our horses liked it not."

Robert de Brus nodded his agreement. "We lost two destriers when we charged them. Still, I think I would have taken hostages for their good behaviour."

I said nothing. We had had much ransom from the families. That would deter them from rising again. The knights in the hall began to question me and to court me. Their words told me that they wished me to join them. They were oblique in their approach and never once spoke directly but only an idiot would have misunderstood their intentions. I smiled a country bumpkin's smile and pretended that I was foolish. I was dismissed from their minds.

"We should be getting back. Night is falling and the swamps between our lands are treacherous."

Robert de Brus smiled. "You are right, we need no wall there. But be careful. There are bandits and outlaws who eke out a parlous existence between the land and the sea. I would hate to think of you being ambushed on the way home."

"Do not worry we have learned to be vigilant." I smiled at Tancred de Mamers. "And it was good to see you again. I had thought you might have returned to the warmer east. I know that I miss both the clime and the life there."

The smile from Tancred was a genuine one, "You are right. The food, the warmth, the baths and the women are all sadly lacking here in this wild and cold land. One day I shall return."

We rode in a tight formation as we headed south. When we were out of earshot they told me all that they had gleaned. "They are planning something. De Mamers and his men are waiting here for a reason. They are the men of Count Fulk." Wulfstan had a sharp mind. "I spoke with some of the squires. De Brus wants your cattle. He knows nothing of the ransoms we collected, my lord, but he knows of the cattle. His men say he was unhappy about being sent home before the fine was delivered. He feels cheated by the king."

"Then we will keep a close watch upon them." We were close to the sea at this point. I reined my horse in. "We could collect salt there could we not?"

"We could. What have you in mind?"

"We need salt anyway, Wulfstan, but we have too many cattle to keep them safe from raids. I would slaughter the old and weak cattle. Our men will benefit from beef each week anyway. Our surplus we can salt and store in barrels. If we breed from the younger animals we can make up those we eat in the spring."

Osric chuckled, "And that is a fine plan. It stops them being stolen and I like my beef."

Once we reached Norton and I had told Ralph and Garth of my plan we set to prepare secure pens within the walls to protect the cattle. I kept my father ignorant of the plotting of our neighbours. I needed him well again. He would be kept as free from worry as it was possible. I briefly returned to Stockton to fetch Edward and some of my men at arms. We kept a constant patrol of archers and men at arms along our borders. They hunted while they watched but every man knew the dangers.

I also introduced some eastern ideas to the two castles. We began to have more hides to tan. I had communal amphorae places around the castles. All were invited to use them; at first, they could not understand the need for 'piss pots' but when the tanner began to use them to cure the hides they did. Wulfstan explained to Faren how the liquid could also be used to bleach and clean clothes. Once she began to use it the rest of the two communities did so too. We soon had leather and cleaner laundry. Finally William the Miller began to produce flour. It was of a much better quality and finer than the hand-ground variety we were used to. Once we grew wheat we would be truly civilised.

Winter drew on but we were even more comfortable than we had been. We ate well and we all had purpose. More importantly, my father was well and all who lived in Norton felt the benefit. It was as though the heart of the manor was recovering too.

The outlaws came with the first frost. I received a message from Sir Richard that Old Tom and his son had been attacked at Hart Burn. My father was recovered enough to send me away. "Go, you have stayed and watched an old man long enough. I am becoming well again. You and your men are needed to purge your land of these vagabonds."

I pointed to Branton, "Do not be so quick to judge father. Branton was an outlaw but he was no vagabond."

Wulfstan laughed, "What a change we have here. I will come with you, my lord and I will bring my wife. She is keen to give a woman's touch to your castle."

In truth it needed it. William had finished the building but it was empty. We slept on straw like the horses and the dogs, and our food was cooked by the men at arms. It was neither comfortable nor homely. Richard did not regard it as his home and I had been over long at Norton. It seemed a good idea. My father gave us three female slaves and we returned to Stockton.

It still looked new but the winter would age it a little. I left Faren and the slaves tut-tutting about the lack of tables, chairs, beds, pots.... everything. Faren, the former slave, wagged a finger at her husband. "You have let Lord Alfraed live like this. I will need four of your men who are handy and I will see those in the village! When you return, I hope that you see a change! I will get some decent furniture made and we will send to the cities to get other furnishings. He is a lord and not a bandit!"

I led my men west along the river. There were a number of farms now which filled the land from the Hart Burn to the walls of my castle but the land between Hart Burn and the river was wooded and wild. They would be a perfect hiding place for outlaws. I let Harold lead Dick and John as scouts. They went with Aiden and his two dogs. The rest of us were armed as for the hunt. We did not wear armour but we took our shields.

The autumn rains had swollen the river and its waters covered the path at times. It ebbed and flowed by the roots of the mighty trees which lined it. We soon found evidence of occupation. There were the remnants of old fires. It was hard to work out when they had been used. Aiden found tracks heading east towards Tom's farm. I sent John and half a dozen men at arms to check on the two Toms. Wulfstan thought the tracks might be old ones.

We headed deeper into the woods. The land rose steeply and we had to dismount to climb the slopes. I doubted that any outlaws would choose to live in this particular part of my land. Wulfstan always told me that hunting needs great concentration. My mind had wandered as I climbed. I was ignoring danger and that is always perilous.

The arrow thudded into the arm of Padraigh who spun to the ground clutching the shaft of the missile. Edgar covered him with a shield and my archers nocked arrows. I held my shield above my head. It saved both me and Scout. Two arrows struck the leather covering. One skittered off into the woods and the other hung ominously from the top. That could have been my head.

I tied Scout to a tree and, hiding behind my shield, rushed up the slope with a drawn sword. The outlaws had the higher ground. The angle of their arrows told me that. I used the boles of the trees for protection as I ran up the leaf-covered slope. I had no armour and that made my journey both easier and quicker. Even so, arrows still rained down upon me. I took satisfaction in that. They could not loose at both me and my men at the same time. I heard a grunt from behind me and saw Wulfstan as he struggled up the hill. It made me feel better.

I caught sight of a movement ahead. It was a white face in a green and brown world. I found it remarkably easy to run quickly without my armour. In those days I was young and had lightning reactions. I saw the arrow as it sped towards me. I punched it away with my shield without breaking stride. The archer was already trying to nock an arrow when I fell upon him. I ran him through almost without thinking and I turned quickly as another outlaw ran at me with a spear. I held my shield before me and continued my turn so that my shield caught his spear and he tumbled down the slope. Wulfstan stabbed down as he fell close to the huge warrior. I faced uphill again. I saw the outlaws as they fled. They had set a trap and we had sprung it. I knew from Harold that outlaws only survived if they avoided superior numbers. We now outnumbered them and they ran.

I began to leave Wulfstan and the others behind. As I neared the knot of outlaws who had paused for breath at the top of the ridge I suddenly realised that they were better dressed than I might have expected outlaws to be. They wore leather and they had boots on their feet. They were well fed. I stored the information as I covered the last twenty paces to reach the six men. They were not outlaws!

When they drew swords I knew that these were not what they seemed. They had good swords. They were not as long as mine but they were the swords of soldiers. This was a trap for me and I had not walked into it. I had run. They had led me to the top of the ridge to be beyond the help of my men. I faced six of them alone.

I had two advantages: I had a shield and I was far better trained than they were. They spread out in a half-circle. If I stood and waited I was dead and so I lunged forward, holding my shield for protection. I felt a blade smash upon it as my sword penetrated the defence of the man before me and tore into his stomach. I had no time for self-congratulation as I sensed a sword coming from behind. The momentum of my killing stroke had carried me forward and I dived and rolled away from the blow. I felt the blade strike the heel of my boot but there was no pain.

As I came up I held my shield above me and managed to catch two swords upon it. I was resting on one knee and I swept my sword before me. It slashed into a bare knee and the soldier went to the ground screaming as deep purple blood gushed from it. Using my knee I pushed upwards against the two swords and the men holding them fell backwards. I brought my blade around and swung hard in the direction of the two men. Its extra length made them both recoil and I found I had a breathing space. I now faced four of them. One had a wound to his arm but they were warier now. They would not rush me. They circled me. They would try to attack from four sides at once.

I saw Wulfstan and the rest struggling up the slope to reach me. I smiled as I thought of the words with which Wulfstan would berate me. For some reason that smile seemed to intimidate the men I faced; they hesitated. I used that hesitation to strike. I punched with my shield at the man to my left as I stabbed at the sword to my right. I took them both by surprise and one soldier fell to the ground while the other recoiled holding a bleeding knuckle. I spun and waved my blade blindly behind me. I heard the clank of metal on metal as I managed to block the blow which was heading for my unprotected back. I turned and flicked my wrist. The move took the blade to my right and I slashed to the left. My sword opened his face and his chest. He fell screaming.

Then Wulfstan fell upon them. He was angry and his mighty sword took the head of one in a single blow. I brought my sword down on a second warrior who blocked it. I punched with my shield and heard his nose crack. Before he could recover I stabbed him in the chest and kicked his body from my sword. Suddenly two arrows plunged down on the last warrior and he fell dead. Harold and Dick sat on their horses just forty paces from us.

The rest of my men reached us. I heard a couple of screams from deeper in the woods and then John appeared on his horse. I bent over to catch my breath. Wulfstan could scarcely breathe either. When he could I received the chastisement I was expecting. "What in God's name did you think you were doing? Trying to beat them all on your own!"

"I was trying to catch them." I paused to allow my next words to sink in. "I did not know it was a trap until I reached the top."

Wulfstan's eyes narrowed. "A trap?"

Harold dismounted and walked over. "Aye my lord. Old Tom and Young Tom recognised one of the bodies they found after the initial attack. It was one of Tancred de Mamers' men."

He turned over the body pierced by two arrows. "And this fellow was with the De Brus men in Wales."

"So they meant to get you. This attack on Thomas was to draw us off."

"It failed."

Wulfstan nodded but I could see that he was not convinced. Their identity was confirmed when we found their horses. Outlaws would not possess such fine horses. We took their weapons and the two bodies we recognised and headed back to Stockton.

It was getting towards dark when we reached the safety of the walls. Nights were drawing in. I was hot and I was sweaty. I took off my clothes and jumped in the newly finished moat. The guards on the gate seemed bemused. I did not care for it felt good to let the water wash over me. The moat was new enough that the water was relatively clear and clean. I would not try this the following year.

Faren came out with a tunic. "Do you wish to catch your death of cold, my lord? Summer is the time for baths. I do not know what you are thinking! Come get dried. Your father would not be happy!"

I lay in the water ignoring her words. Why the trap now? Surely it would have been easier to wait until I returned to Stockton and then draw me into the ambush. They had wanted me away from Norton along with my men but why? It came to me with sudden clarity. Faren had told me without knowing; '*my father would not be happy*'! Tancred and De Brus were intending to attack Norton. The trap was intended for my father. I would have been the gilding.

I leapt from the moat and grabbed the tunic. "To horse! To horse! We ride tonight!"

"My lord, have you gone mad? You have just fought this day."

As I rubbed myself dry I said, "Faren, "Norton and my father are in danger! They are under attack."

Faren might love Wulfstan but the man she revered most was my father. Her hand went to her mouth and she murmured, "God protect him!"

Chapter 22

I explained to Wulfstan and Richard my suspicions as I dressed. They concurred. "You will need to leave guards here, Alfraed, in case this is a double trap."

"We need to anyway. I want the freshest men and horses. I will take Star. Scout will need rest. Aiden!"

My scout appeared, "Ride to Norton. I need to know if it is under attack. If it is, then return and tell me if not then warn my father that he is to be attacked."

Aiden deigned to use a saddle. He rode bareback and he and his dogs galloped across the drawbridge. The noise and the alarum had roused the villagers from their homes. I mounted Star and did not wait for the rest of my men. I would risk the wrath of Wulfstan again. I saw Alf, "I believe that we may be attacked. Bring your folk and the cattle within the bailey. I go to my father."

He nodded, "Aye, my lord. Take care!"

It was the enemy who needed to take care for I was angry. I hoped that Edward and his patrol had been close enough to Norton to go to my father's side. I heard the hooves of Wulfstan and the others as they hurried to be at my side. This time they would not allow me to venture alone into danger. Harold rode next to me. He had spurned his bow and now held his spear. I would have to make do with my sword. It needed an edge but I would wield a bar of iron if needs be. There were just ten of us in all. The rest would have to guard Stockton.

We were less than a mile from Norton when Aiden returned. "The gate has fallen. It is Tancred and his men who are attacking. They are stealing the cattle."

"Ride to Tom Two Toes and rouse him and his sons. You can cut off their escape north." In all honesty, I was unconcerned about the cattle. They had proved a curse as they had drawn our enemies upon us. Aiden wheeled his horse away north.

Knowing that my father was in danger added impetus to my ride. Star had not been ridden for some days and was full of running. Four soldiers came along the track herding six cattle. I drew my sword and as Star trampled one of them I brought my sword across the neck of a second severing it in one blow. Harold and Wulfstan ensured that these four would raid no more. I saw bodies around the shattered gate but did not slow down. I saw Branton's head staring sightlessly at the skies. He had guarded the gate with his body. My father's oathsworn had finally fulfilled his oath. Inside the castle, there were two knots of warriors. Our warriors were still fighting but they had been separated. Between them was a sea of Normans. Edward and his men were hard-pressed against the wall of the church while my father and his oathsworn held the door to the hall. I believed I had come in time until I saw that Garth lay dead and, even as we galloped through the gate Ralph had his life ended by the mace of Tancred de Mamers. My father was fighting his last battle. Osric guarded one side whilst a wounded Athelstan held two knights off on the other. Of Egbert, I saw no sign.

I smashed Star through the men at arms who turned to face the new foe who came at them. I was oblivious to their strikes and Star and I laid about us with hooves and blade. The press of bodies was too great and I leapt from his back. I smashed the end of my shield into the skull of one man while I ripped my blade across the throat of a second. I began to fight my way to my father. I saw that he was fighting bareheaded but he held his old shield as he had done for the Emperor and for King Harold. This was the last stand of Harold's housecarls and they were holding their own against knights and men at arms who were half their age. Of course, it could not last. Osric was felled by a blow to his helmet by Tancred. My father sliced his sword into the side of the knight who attempted to finish off Osric. It cost my father his life. Tancred smashed his mace against my father's shield and the old man fell to the floor. Tancred stood over him and he raised his mace. He glanced over at me. I could not see his face for his ventail covered it but I knew that he was laughing. He brought the mace down. My father's sword came up and slowed down the blow but it still made contact with his head. The cowardly Norman then mounted his horse and he and his knights galloped towards the wall.

I despatched the man at arms who had slowed me down and ran after Tancred. As I reached the end of the hall I saw that they had gained entry through the wall. They had pulled down a section and were galloping away through the newly made gap.

I turned and ran to my father. His face was a bloody mess. I threw down my sword and helmet and cradled him in my arms. "Father it is Alfraed!"

He opened one weak eye and a smile started to appear. A tendril of blood dripped from the corner of his mouth. "I knew you would come.

My oathsworn died well and so did I. I can meet Aelfraed and Harold Godwinson in heaven now and face them." I could not help the tears which dripped down my face. "Do not grieve for me, my son. I have seen you grow into a knight and a man. I could not be prouder of you. You will be a greater warrior than I could ever have dreamed of becoming. My only regret is that I have not had a grandchild but I shall watch from…"

And then he died. Ridley of Norton, the last of King Harold's housecarls died, slain by a Norman but with his honour intact.

I stood and looked up at the sky. "I swear that I shall have my revenge and I will avenge your death." I donned my helmet and grabbed Star. "Wulfstan, look to the wounded. Harold, Edward, we ride!"

Wulfstan grabbed my reins. "Do not do this in hot blood! Your father would not wish you to throw your life away."

"I am cold as ice, Wulfstan. I intend to kill these treacherous knights and when I am done I will scotch the snake that is De Brus. My sword has been sheathed too long."

I led my handful of men through the gap in the walls. I knew the route they would take. They would ride through the woods and then head around the marshes to reach Hartness and safety. "Edward, find us a way through the marshes! We will cut him off before he reaches safety." I did not want to have to winkle him out of Hartness.

It was a risk but Edward and Harold were familiar with the marshes and it would save us time. He spurred his horse past me. As he came next to me he said, "I am sorry my lord, we came too late from our patrol to save them!"

"But you came and that is all that is important."

Even though night was falling Edward managed to keep a good speed. We soon found firmer ground as we headed towards the farms around Cowpen. Harold suddenly shouted. "There, my lord, I see them!"

They had made the mistake of trying to take four head of cattle with them. Their greed would prove costly. I counted five knights and six men at arms. There were just eight of us. As soon as they heard the hooves following them they deserted the cattle and spurred their horses towards the safety of Hartness. They had neither honour nor courage. I can only assume that they thought we had more men than we actually had.

Star was in his element. He ate the ground up. The men at arms had either a rouncy or a palfrey between their legs. They were no match for Star. I did not even unsling my shield I held the reins in my left hand as I approached the rearmost soldier. As Star's head turned to bite at his horse I stood in the saddle and brought my sword to shatter his back. The blade almost cut him in two. Harold had overtaken me and I watched as he pulled back his spear to punch the next man at arms in the back. We now almost had parity of numbers.

Edward and the others were keen to redeem themselves and as three men at arms suddenly jerked their horses to the left Edward and Scanlan veered to follow them. Three knights were far ahead now but I saw that Tancred's horse had been injured and he and another knight were falling behind. The last man at arms made the mistake of looking over his shoulder at the wrong time. His horse tripped over a tree root and the rider flew over his head to crash into the bole of a tree. Tancred and the last knight saw that they could not outrun us and they halted. "Richard, take the men and pursue the last knights. I would know where they go." And there were just the four of us. I realised, from his shield, that the second knight was Tancred's son, Geoffrey. I recognised his livery. I hoped that Harold could deal with him for I would make sure that Tancred de Mamers ended his treacherous life this night.

My father's killer made the mistake of trying to fight me on horseback. He had an injured horse and Star's blood was up. He charged at me and approached shield to shield. He swung his mace at my shield. I struck at his head. Star did what he could by trying to take a chunk from his destrier's neck. My left arm felt the force of the mace and he then flicked it at my head and I saw stars but the blow from my sword almost unhorsed him.

I heard the clash of arms as Harold fought Geoffrey de Mamers but I could not watch. I wheeled Star who came around far quicker than the injured destrier of Tancred de Mamers. Speed is all-important in such contests and I was able to ride Star towards the side of the injured destrier. As Star bowled into him I brought down my sword. Tancred managed to half deflect the sword with his mace but his horse was already falling. As Tancred was knocked back in his saddle he pulled on the reins and the two of them tumbled to the ground. I leapt from Star and approached Tancred as he dragged himself from under his horse.

I saw that he did not stand easily. His leg was damaged. He dropped his ventail. "I yield! Quarter!"

I took off my helmet so that he could see my face. "No quarter! You do not deserve quarter. You are treacherous and killed the finest man I have ever known. The most noble and honourable of all knights. You gave my father no quarter and you will die, slowly!"

He laughed, "I have fought greater warriors than you. You will regret your decision."

He thought to catch me napping and lunged at me with his mace. He hoped to take advantage of the fact that I had no helmet. He was fast but his damaged leg and my speed took me out of range of his bloody mace. I swung my sword at his head and his helmet flew from it. I saw that his head was bleeding from my earlier strike. He suddenly hurled the mace at me as he drew his sword. I dodged the deadly club easily. His sword would be sharper; I had taken the edge off mine already.

He made the mistake of swinging at my shield rather than my unprotected head. Perhaps he thought he had weakened my arm. I deflected the blow easily. I feinted at his head and as his shield came up I slashed at his already damaged leg. I was in no mood to finish this quickly. He screamed in pain as the mail hose was ripped and blood started to ooze from the knee. He glanced over to his son who lay prostrate on the ground. I heard Harold as he shouted, "Do I give quarter, my lord?"

"For the moment. I may want to end the young snake's life myself when I have slain his father."

As I had expected, that enraged Tancred who tried to come at me with a flurry of blows. I halted them all with quick ripostes and the blows only served to tire him. "Your master, Count Fulk, will be disappointed that your plot has failed. You have not fermented rebellion in these northern lands. When I have finished with you then De Brus will feel both my sword and my wrath."

Tancred pointed the sword at me. He spoke in gasps for he was out of breath. "Count Fulk has not finished with you. He knows your name and it is marked for death."

"Then I hope he has a better assassin than you in mind or he will have wasted his gold."

He came at me again but he was losing too much blood. I feinted at his knee again and, when he lowered his shield, I sliced backhand across his left shoulder. My blade had lost its edge but it was still sharp enough to slice through the leather strap and into his arm. His shield fell at his feet and I saw resignation on his face. He knew then that death was inevitable. He may have had more experience but I had fast hands and a strong arm. I punched him in the face with my own shield and he fell to the floor. I ripped my blade across the mail covering his chest. Links broke. I stamped on his right hand and heard the bones break. "End it now I beg of you!"

I ripped my sword back across the already torn mail and saw my sword penetrate his padded tunic and his stomach. I heard horses behind as Edward and Alan arrived. I did not turn around. His eyes pleaded with me, "You will not take ransom?"

"If I need ransom then I have your son but I want you to die. I cannot make it as slow as I would like but I swear I will rid the world of your name and your seed."

I said it slowly so that he would know that I meant what I said. His eyes widened as he took in the words I spat at him. His eyes tried to move to his son but the tip of my sword was at his throat. "You will die unshriven!" I lifted the sword and jammed it into his mouth so that he could not curse me. I felt the tip strike his spine and he died.

"Strip his body and hang it, naked, from the tree so that the birds may feast on this evil man." Leaving Edward and my men to do as I had bid I strode over to Tancred's son, Geoffrey. The blood of his father still dripped from the end of my sword. I saw him recoil in fear and even Harold looked terrified. My eyes blazed with anger. I kept my voice low as I jabbed the point between the youth's eyes. The tip broke the flesh and a tiny ribbon of blood dripped down the side of his young head. I saw that he was barely eighteen. "Now boy it would not take much to end your life too."

"I yielded to your squire!"

"But not to me! It will be no sin if I push this sword to end your life now!" I roared out the last word and he recoiled. "Understand me, boy! I will keep you alive only as long as you are useful to me. You are still alive because I do not wish to dishonour my squire. He is more important to me than either you or your worthless father. If you attempt to escape I will hamstring you. If you try a second time I will castrate you. If you try a third I will blind you." I paused so that he understood. "Harold here is the only reason you live. Take off your mail and give it to him. Harold, dress him in the clothes of the dead man at arms. If he tries to run you know what to do."

Harold was terrified, "Aye, my lord." I heard the fear and awe in his voice.

We rode back to the manor of Norton in the dark. None of my men dared approach me. Tancred's lame horse had been destroyed but those of his men at arms carried the armour and weapons we had captured. By the time we had packed the horses, my men had returned from their fruitless pursuit of the fleeing knights. The last of the butchers had fled to Hartness. It confirmed the conspiracy. I would visit there but first I had to bury my father.

Father Peter had cleaned and laid out the bodies of the dead. Of father's oathsworn only Wulfstan was without a wound. Athelstan had been struck in the leg and arm. He would never fight again. Osric had lost an eye to the blow from the mace. They all stepped back when I entered. I stood over the bodies. Although I spoke to all I addressed my words to the dead who would be just a little way above my head.

"I have avenged my father and his brave oathsworn. Tancred de Mamers is no more. Robert De Brus will be punished in due course." I heard sobbing and saw Harold kneeling over Branton's body. I was not the only one to have lost family. I turned to face my people and the survivors. "I am now Baron of Norton as well as Stockton. I hereby appoint Osric to be the castellan of Norton and to guard it in my father's name. What say you?"

He dropped to his knees. "I swear I will protect this castle with my life."

"Athelstan, will you be a steward?"

He looked confused, "I am no cleric, my lord."

"Father Peter will help you I am sure."

"Then I accept. I will serve you unto death."

"Edward, ride to Stockton. I need William to begin to build my father's tomb." He wearily climbed his horse and left. "Father Peter, we will have to dig up your floor. My father wished to be buried beneath it."

"I promised him that he would rest there until judgement day."

I nodded, "So be it." As I looked down at my father I felt the world begin to swim and darkness consumed me.

Chapter 23

I opened my eyes and looked up into the face of Father Peter. He looked relieved. "What happened?"

"Your squire said the Norman hit you with his mace in the battle. You have an angry bruise on the side of your face. I fear you have contused your brain. I was going to release some blood but Wulfstan would not let me. He said you would recover in your own time." He smiled, "He was right."

"How long have I lain here?"

"It is almost dawn." I tried to struggle to my feet but he restrained me. "You can do little. Your men have taken up the floor and dug the grave for your father."

"And his oathsworn."

He looked shocked, "But your father said nothing about those being buried in my church."

"It is not your church, it was my father's and it is now mine and I say that his four oathsworn will be buried around him. They guarded him in life and they can continue to do so in death. If you wish me to rest longer then give the commands."

He nodded, "You are harder than your father."

"I was made by my father. I have his heart but it is true I am not as gentle." I shrugged, "It is the way I am, father. If it is any consolation I will be at Stockton more than I will be here."

"I do not judge, God does that."

As he left I said, "Amen."

I lay in my father's candlelit room staring at the ceiling. I wished now that I had never brought those cattle north. They had been too great a temptation for my enemies. As I lay there I heard my father's voice in my head. I knew it was my father for it was gentle. When I heard my own voice in my head it was always angry.

"It was wyrd, my son. It was meant to be. They would have come anyway. The cattle were an excuse. I had the chance to die with honour amongst my oathsworn. I was useful in the end. I did not linger on in my dotage to be a burden to you and my people. I will sleep beneath the church and I will be happy. Now you must live. You must find a wife. I will watch over you with Aelfraed for we are together once more. I am happy my son. I am happy."

When I opened my eyes it was daylight. Had I heard my father or dreamed the words I wanted him to say? Only time would tell.

The next three days passed in a blur. We laid my father and his oathsworn in the ground. The Latin Father Peter spoke would not have been my father's choice but it seemed fitting for the occasion. The last three of his oathsworn and I stood at the four corners of the grave and threw in the soil. We each had something of my father's. Osric laid his helmet within, Athelstan his Gonfanon and Wulfstan his shield. At the last, I laid his sword along his body. It was the sword he had carried since before Stamford Bridge. It was ancient now and would fight no more but he would have it in the afterlife. Then we covered him with the stone. William had already begun to carve the new stone which would be placed on top of the grave. It would have my father's name and those of his oathsworn. We needed neither Latin nor any message for posterity. None of us would ever forget those four brave warriors who had died defending their lord. The carved stone would tell the following generations of the courage of the Baron of Norton. I made sure that William was paid in advance. He wanted no payment but my father had always told me that a good workman is worth his hire.

After the funeral, we stripped to the waist and repaired Norton and made it even stronger. We cut fresh trees and made good the wall. We cleared the dead from the ditch and replaced the traps. We added stones to the base of the gate to make it even stronger. When we finished I looked at the castle with the critical eye of an attacker. We would need more men at arms but my father had left me well endowed and I would use all of it to make his home safer. At the end of the three days, we were ready to go to war. Wulfstan tried to talk me out of it as did Richard. I would not hear any argument. Had we addressed the problem before then my father might be alive today. We would attack Hartness. I left my hostage in the charge of the priest. I think he was grateful to be away from my baleful stare. I knew that I had terrified the boy.

Under our fluttering banners, we rode to Hartness in our war gear. Everyone's eyes were drawn to the rotting corpse that had been Tancred de Mamers as we passed beneath his swaying body. His eyes had gone already and the movement below the skin told us that maggots were feasting. I was pleased that I had left his son in the charge of my priest. It was not a sight for a son to see.

Hartness promised to have many more men than I was bringing with me. We would be outnumbered. None of my men had either objected or complained but I knew that they had worked out the odds. I had, however, a plan. I would challenge Robert De Brus to single combat. He might refuse me but he would lose too much face if he did so. I was quite willing to lay siege to his castle if I had to. Of course, he had a port and could bring supplies in by sea but I had to face him now or else I would forever be in his shadow. With just three knights and less than thirty men at arms, we were not a huge army but I had witnessed what Robert of Gloucester had achieved with less than fifty knights. I would see what happened.

As we approached the castle the first thing I noticed was the lack of ships in the harbour. There had been a number of cogs and knarrs the last time I had visited. The gates were open but, as we approached they slammed shut. I halted just out of bow range. "Harold, come with me. Wulfstan, take charge of the men."

"Would it do any good to tell you that this is foolish?"

I took off my helmet. "No, my friend but I do not think my life will end this day. I am drawn here. Let us see what the weird sisters of my father and Ralph have in mind for us."

I approached the gate. There was no drawbridge and no moat. The wall was, however, too high to climb without ladders. I waited patiently until a face appeared. It was an old man at arms. The grey hairs and the scarred face told me that he had survived longer than most.

"What do you want my lord?"

"I wish to speak to the lord of the manor."

"The Baron is not here. He and all of his men have left."

I had not expected that. "Left? Where have they gone?"

"He has taken the cross and he goes on a holy crusade."

I almost smiled. He was fleeing to his mentor, Count Fulk. It made sense. He would be able to tell him that his plan had failed and it extracted him from any criticism. He was going on crusade; what could be nobler than that?

"I am Baron Alfraed of Norton and Stockton. My father was treacherously slain three days ago by Tancred de Mamers. He stole some cattle. I would like to seek any of de Mamers' men and my cattle inside Hartness." That was almost a lie. Only two cattle were unaccounted for and Wulfstan was certain that they would return of their own accord but it was a legitimate excuse to enter the castle and to search it. I believed the old soldier but I needed confirmation. If De Brus had fled then I would follow. He was a cunning knight and he might be hiding within the walls of Hartness.

The elderly guard disappeared and the steward appeared. I had met him during my first visit to the castle.

"My lord, I cannot allow you to enter the castle without my lord's permission. Sorry."

"I am going to enter your castle. There are two ways I can do this. You can open the gates and I can enter and search. I give you my word that if I do so then I will only take any of the men I seek or the cattle which are missing. If you refuse then I will assault the castle. As Norton has been attacked twice by your lord and his treacherous allies I know how to do this. The choice is yours but be aware that if I assault I will not be kind to those who resist me." I heard the church bell sound. "You have to the count of a thousand to make up your mind. The bell is God's warning to make the right decision!"

It was not a bluff and now that I knew the castle was not garrisoned I could easily take it with my men at arms. The steward knew that too. A short while later he returned to the gate. "I have your word that you seek only de Mamers' men and the cattle?"

"I swear!"

As we rode through the gate I did not know what I would do. I was ensuring that the Normans had gone but having been let in so easily I knew I would not find any of my enemies. I also knew that I would not find any cattle but I was making a point. I decided to ride to the harbour and then leave. The doors were all shut as we rode through. The people of Hartness hid in fear from me. I rode slowly to show I was not afraid of their departed master. I was also humiliating him even though he was not here. I reached the harbour and dismounted. I looked around the empty port. It was likely that he had fled to warmer climes.

Mounting Star I retraced my steps. I did so slowly examining every stone and every building as I rode through the bailey. As we passed the hall I heard a scream and then a young slave hurtled through the doors and threw herself at my leg. Star whinnied. The girl's eyes pleaded with me as she looked up into my face. "My lord I claim sanctuary. I have been abducted and held prisoner against my will!"

The elderly guard, clutching a raked face, and a hatchet-faced woman appeared. The woman pointed a bony finger at the girl and hissed, "She is a slave, a runaway. You are bound by law to return her to us."

I held up my hand, "Archers cover them. One false move from any of them, and you have my permission to release your arrows." No one moved although I heard doors opening behind us as the villagers watched the tableau before them. "Child, come here." The girl was no more than sixteen years of age and looked to have been beaten and starved. "What is your name?"

She raised her head and said proudly, "I am Adela the daughter of the murdered Lord of Norton Guy de Ville and I have been held prisoner this past year and more. My mother was abused and died of a broken heart and I am all that remains of those who lived in Norton. I throw myself on your mercy."

I looked at Wulfstan who shrugged. None of us had ever seen the old lord of the manor but I did know he had had a daughter.

"Where is the rest of your family?"

She turned and spat in the direction of the old woman, "Dead! These are worse than animals. I have been abused and ill-treated my lord! Will you give me sanctuary?"

I dismounted, "Harold, watch the girl. I want no harm to come to her."

I strode over to the steps leading to the hall. The old woman looked defiantly at me but the man at arms looked ill at ease. I could see where she had scratched his face.

"You were a soldier?" He nodded. "Take out your sword and hold it before you." He did so. I saw that his hands were trembling. "Does the girl speak true? You hold the sword and it is in the shape of a cross. Swear."

He looked at the old woman. "Keep your mouth shut you old fool!"

I pointed my sword at the hag. "I have neither struck nor killed a woman before but if you open your mouth again then I shall have two new experiences this day." Her mouth narrowed into a slit. I looked at the soldier and held his gaze. "Swear that she lies or swear that she tells the truth. There can be no other answer."

His head dropped and he said quietly, "She speaks the truth. I swear."

"Louder!"

He jumped at the ferocity of my words. "She speaks the truth she is no slave. I swear it."

"Then find her a horse now!" I turned to her, "I will take you to Norton. You are safe now!"

In answer, she threw her arms around my shoulders and began to sob uncontrollably. I felt her emaciated body as it was wracked with spasms.

I glared angrily at this nest of vipers. I should burn it to the ground but I knew that I would not and now I knew why I had come here; it had been ordained. It was father's weird sisters weaving once more.

I had forgotten about the corpse until we actually passed it. I looked at the young girl we had rescued. Surprisingly she did not seem afraid of it. Rather she looked at it defiantly and then spat. "Abuser of girls!" were the only words she spoke but I saw hatred in her eyes. During the last couple of miles before we reached Norton, I put my mind to her future. I could not just abandon her once we reached her old home. What could I do with her? My father had been acutely aware of the lack of fine ladies in the two villages. The women who were there were farmers' wives and daughters. The fine women who had been with Adela had been killed or sold into slavery. It was yet another problem for me to solve.

When we rode through the gates of Norton all eyes were upon us. I suspect many had thought that they had seen the last of us and we were riding to our deaths. That fate would be some time off. There were those old enough to remember Adela and I saw older women pointing to her as we rode into the bailey. Father Peter came from his church with the hostage. He recognised her immediately. The girl ran sobbing to his arms. He smiled gratefully at me over her shoulder, "This is a miracle my lord and your entry into heaven is guaranteed by this act."

"Care for her, Father Peter, whilst I put my mind to the problem of her future."

His face fell. He had not thought ahead of the warm welcome he was giving the girl. Harold took the horses away. "Wulfstan, Richard, come to the hall I would have conference with you both."

The slave brought beer and wet cloths for us to refresh ourselves. "What do we do with the young lady?"

Richard looked surprised at the question, "Do? Nothing. You have done your duty and rescued her."

Wulfstan looked at me and shook his head. Poor Richard had not been brought up properly as I had. He was a knight but he thought nothing beyond the end of his sword. "She is a young girl who is alone in the world. We now have a responsibility to care for her."

Wulfstan nodded, "You are your father's son. But you are correct we do have a problem."

I often found silence was the best provider of answers. Wulfstan knew me well. Richard went to speak but Wulfstan put his huge hand over the knight's hand and said, "Ssh!"

Richard shrugged and finished his beer.

I began to speak. I did not know where why words would take me as I began but they seemed to take on a life of their own and devise a solution as they were spoken. "Osric and Athelstan can manage Norton for me. I will leave them enough warriors to defend my father's burgh. You, Wulfstan, will return with us to Stockton. Your wife is there now and it is more comfortable for you. Faren is kind and the closest to all of us. She can be a guardian for the girl. Your new child might help the girl forget the horrors of her past." I saw Wulfstan nodding his agreement. "We will hire more men at arms and we will take ship for Normandy as soon as we can. You will watch my ward and the castle while I fulfil my obligations to the king. I will take my prisoner to King Henry and there I can present the case of Adela, daughter of Guy of Norton. I will beg leave to pursue De Brus. Perhaps the king will grant my request."

Wulfstan banged the table and poor Richard actually jumped. "A good plan my lord but I should be with you."

"I know but who else can I leave to watch our lands?" Richard flushed and looked offended. "Richard, you are a fine knight but you seek land and power. You are with me because I bring you both. You would not be content to sit behind Stockton's walls and grow fat."

He laughed, "You are right, my lord."

Wulfstan finished his ale. "I am not sure I like the word fat."

"I meant no offence, my old friend, perhaps I speak bluntly because you are an old friend and I do not need to make a face to deceive the faces that I meet."

Just then we heard a disturbance outside. We left the hall and saw Aiden and his dogs driving the last two cattle into the bailey. He was grinning. "These animals should be used for breeding my lord. They led the Normans a merry dance and took them into the swamps. After I had slain them with my arrows they happily returned with me. They are warriors like Edward."

Alan began to laugh, "With just a little more sense than Edward!"

Chapter 24

Faren was already feeling maternal with a six-month-old child within her body but the sight of the emaciated girl made her burst into tears. She took her under her arm and whisked her away. Before she left she snapped. "The child needs her own room, my lord."

Wulfstan shook his head, "I will deal with it, my lord."

After I had changed from my armour I went into the village. Alf was as close to a headman as we had. I went into his smithy where he looked like Thor himself beating out a plough. "Come, Alf, I need words." He nodded to his apprentice who took over.

"We have rescued the daughter of Guy of Norton who was kidnapped."

He crossed himself, "That is a good thing, my lord. Perhaps it is the hand of God. He took away your father and replaced him with the girl."

I had not thought of that but it made some kind of sense. I nodded. "Perhaps. I have discovered a web of lies and treachery which I need to present to the king. I will be seeking passage on a ship to take me and my men to Normandy. I will leave Wulfstan to rule in my stead."

"Good. He is a fine man and his wife has won the hearts of all. And what of the girl?"

"I will leave her here but I know that she will be safe. She has suffered much already and she needs to heal from within."

"She will, my lord. You have my word on that."

"I hope that I have discouraged all of our enemies but I will be leaving the two manors perilously short of warriors. You and the other men need to practise with your bows each Sunday. If every man in the manors can use a bow then we will be safe."

"I will make sure that happens and I have many arrowheads already prepared. Old Tom has many trees which he can use to make arrows. He has begun life as a Fletcher."

Old Tom might not be an archer any longer but he used his skill to make the finest arrows in the Tees valley. He soon became not Old Tom but Tom the Fletcher.

"Good. Can you ask your brother in law, Olaf, if he can take twenty of us to Normandy in the spring?"

"His ship would not be big enough but I am sure he can hire another captain." He laughed, "He would be as rich as Ethelred! He envies my big brother who is now the richest man in the village."

Leaving Alf I wandered down to the river, the better to look at my castle. It was not the largest tower I had ever seen and it was not the most imposing but it would do. I knew that an enemy who was determined could assault and capture it but it would take many men to do so. It would cost an attacker more than he might gain. I could leave it in the hands of Wulfstan and ten men at arms knowing that, with the aid of the villagers, they could sit out a siege. I hoped that I had discouraged our enemies. The Jedburgh family would have warned other Scots of the perils of Stockton and the Viking ship we had sent packing would have done the same in the east. With De Mamers and De Brus gone, for the moment, there would be peace and, I hoped, prosperity.

As I returned I put my mind to the voyage we would make. Once inside I sent for Harold. "Bring our prisoner. It is time I questioned him some more." As they returned I noticed that the two of them were closer. I would have to warn Harold of over-familiarity. Geoffrey was our prisoner and as valuable to us as gold itself.

I questioned him for an hour and I was not gentle with my words. I saw fear in his eyes. He did not yet know his fate and he told me all that I wished to know. When I mentioned the girl he looked around fearfully, "I never touched her, my lord. You have to believe me. I will swear it on a Bible!"

He was so adamant that I believed him but his words made me wonder just what she had had to endure. I could never ask her. I now owed her a duty greater than I could have believed a month earlier. I hoped that King Henry would have a solution to my problem.

Faren wrought huge changes in the girl. She had the slaves make fine clothes for her. She used all sorts of potions and oils to make her hair and her skin gleam but the most important thing she did for the girl was to make her smile and laugh. We learned, within the first month, to keep Geoffrey from her sight. He was a memory of her past and her enforced captivity. He was a constant reminder of the abuse she had taken from his father. It was ironic that we were treating him far better than she, a young girl, had been treated in Hartness. As Faren neared the birthing time then Adela became a nurse to her mentor. I was happy. She had purpose in her life and had little time to dwell on the past. The problem had been solved, at least for the time being.

When I had returned from Hartness I had sent messages to Durham, York and to London informing them of the death of my father and the ensuing conflict. The reply from Durham was noncommittal but the letter from Henry's Regent in London confirmed my title of Baron of Norton and Stockton. Had I not received it then I would have continued in my role but my position would have been parlous.

Olaf secured me a second, larger ship which would be able to transport our horses. He seemed happy to be the middleman, "I will handle the financial arrangements, my lord. If we agree a fee I will pay Captain Selwyn. I have arranged a cargo for us to take. We will all profit."

He was so happy that I was certain he was cheating the other captain but the price we agreed was reasonable. The month after Christmas was a busy one as I had to prepare for the voyage and leave the affairs of the two manors in a good state. Alf fitted new shoes to all of the horses and sharpened every sword, axe and polearm. We would have neither farrier nor smith with us. We would be reliant upon whatever we found in Caen and Normandy.

Just before Candlemas, it was so cold that the Tees had a thin sheen of ice upon it and it was too cold to venture forth. I sat with Wulfstan in my hall with a fire blazing away and some mulled wine in our hands. "There is, however, one dilemma, Wulfstan."

We had spent every waking hour going over the logistics of the campaign. We knew exactly what we would be taking with us and what we would need to sustain us over a summer's campaign.

He frowned as he answered. "I believe we have covered every eventuality."

"All but one. King Henry is expecting three knights and thirty men at arms. The men at arms are not a problem. We can ride to Durham and hire some but it is the knight. When I promised three knights you would have been the third. I cannot take you now as I need you to watch over my lands. We have not been visited by any travelling knights. I am one short and we have less than three weeks before we set forth."

"You are the lord of the manor now, my lord. You can knight whomsoever you please. They should be over twenty-one but as most men do not know their age that is not a hindrance."

"Harold?"

Wulfstan considered my choice. "He is a fine bowman and his skills on a horse are improving but I do not think he would thank you yet for such an elevation. He has much to learn. King Henry will want experience in his ranks."

"Then who is there? Had disaster not struck us then Osric or Athelstan would have been worthy choices."

"Edward, my lord. He is well experienced in war. He is a fine swordsman and a fine rider. He can learn the skills of the lance. Alan would make a good squire for him."

"Can I do that?"

He laughed, "You are the lord of the manor and as the king has given you the title so you have the power. You will need to equip him as a knight."

I wondered about that. Did I have the resources?

Wulfstan answered, "He can have my destrier or the one belonging to Geoffrey de Mamers. He has a suit of mail already. I can see no objection, save from him."

It was a good solution to a difficult problem. I sent for him, Alan, Harold and Richard. Richard arrived first and I explained what I intended. He shrugged. It would not affect his rewards as King Henry wanted three knights. Richard was a good soldier but he was difficult to like. While I knew that Wulfstan would be happy for Edward Richard cared only for himself. He and Carl, his squire, kept very much to themselves. They did not mix with my other men.

When the others arrived I said, "Edward, I have a mind to knight you and make you a household knight. What say you?"

He was speechless. Alan grinned as did Harold. Edward was a popular sergeant at arms. Their reaction was in direct contrast to the indifference of Richard.

"Come, answer the Baron!" Wulfstan was smiling as he commanded.

"I would be honoured, my lord. But I do not deserve it."

"That is for me to decide. Kneel and you too, Wulfstan."

"Me, my lord?"

"Aye my father always intended to knight you but events conspired against him. This way I have two household knights."

They knelt and I dubbed them. "Alan, will you be Edward's squire?" He nodded and beamed a huge grin. "Good. Sir Wulfstan says you can have his destrier or that of Geoffrey de Mamers. It is your choice." For the first time, I saw a hint of displeasure on the face of Richard. Both animals were better than his. Then his face became a mask again.

As they all left I said, "Harold, a word."

When we were alone he said, "Yes my lord?"

"I had thought to knight you too but Wulfstan said that he thought you were not ready. I do not like to take another man's word for such things. What say you?"

"He is right, my lord. One day I may be ready but I am young and I am learning all the time. I still prefer the bow to the lance and my manners need improvement. When I am ready I shall tell you, my lord." He hesitated, "I hope I have not disappointed you, my lord?"

"Truth and honesty never disappoint me and besides I would have missed you had I made you a knight. We have many adventures ahead of us yet."

He smiled, "I am honoured that you explained this to me. You did not need to do so." I suspect that I had made Harold even more loyal to me but I had not said what I had for that reason. I had spoken from the heart.

I sent Edward and Alan to hire more men at arms. Since De Brus had departed there were many such men seeking a master. Edward was the perfect choice to hire them. He knew how to discriminate between those who had bad luck and those who were bad luck. By the time he returned we had enough men for both castles and for the campaign. The gold from the ransoms came in handy and we were so prosperous that I knew we would have enough taxes when the tax collector returned.

The day before we were due to leave I had one of the cattle butchered to make a feast for my men. We had the prime cut in the hall. I would have invited Geoffrey but Adela seemed different when she saw him and I was keen to be able to speak with her. Geoffrey feasted with the men at arms. They would watch him. Edward, Richard, Wulfstan, Harold and Faren made up the numbers. Faren ran the kitchen and the cooks ensured that the beef was perfectly cooked and everything was as it should be.

It was one of the happiest times we had had in the castle. Faren was close to giving birth and had that comfortable and content look. I knew that it would be good for both Adela and Faren to share in this experience. I also saw the relief on Wulfstan's face that he would not have to leave his wife at this time.

Richard left the table as soon as the beef was finished. He was hard to get close to and kept himself very much to himself. He did not engage in small talk and women seemed to bore him. In the event, that helped us all. Adela seemed to relax more once he had gone.

"Baron Alfraed I have not thanked you properly for coming to my aid. I know that you risked much."

"Had I known of your plight sooner then I would have come earlier."

She hesitated, "De Brus hates you, you know."

"Hates me? But I barely knew him."

She shook her head. "This goes back before you were given the manor. He killed my family to win the manor. He bribed Richard Fitzherbert to put in a good word with the king but then you were awarded the manor and his plans were ruined. He wanted more land across the river."

It all made sense now. The king must have had an idea of the problem when he tried to appoint one of his Norman knights. It must have been a godsend when we arrived. "His plans?"

"Hartness is a poor manor. The harbour is the main source of income. He has lands at Guisborough. With the manor of Norton and the river under his control he would have been able to rule the whole of the Tees Valley and most of the coast."

"How did you know all this?"

"I was used as a slave, a pretty slave and when he was in his cups he would boast to de Mamers and other visitors of his plans."

"I see. Thank you for the warning."

"There is more."

"More?"

"He is also one of Count Fulk's men. He has been promised much by the Count in Normandy."

"Then he is not in the Holy Land?"

"No, my lord. He sailed to Anjou to help the Count. His people were told to tell you that he went to the Holy Land. I think he hoped you would try to follow him there and suffer an accident along the way. You will be expected."

I had no doubt that De Brus' spies would have kept him informed about the date of our departure and even our route. It was too late to change it now. At least we had a warning. I put my hand on hers, "Thank you, Adela, you have repaid my rescue now and more. I am eternally grateful to you."

She withdrew her hand, "You will still go? But it is a trap." I saw the shock on her face. I was walking, nay running, willingly into a trap. To her, it must have seemed foolish. It probably was.

"I gave my word to my king that I would go to Normandy. I cannot be foresworn."

"But surely the king would understand."

I shook my head. "He is king and would not worry about the danger to one knight. Besides a trap is only a trap if it is a surprise. This is not a trap. We know we will be attacked. It may be at sea or it may be in Normandy. We will just have to be ready." I looked at Edward who had taken in every word. "What say you? Do you regret becoming my household knight?"

He laughed, "My lord I will never regret that. It is an honour that I could have only dreamed of. No, you are right, we can prepare. We have the finest archers I have ever seen in our company. Harold here could hit the eye on a Mayfly if he so chose. We divide the archers between the two ships and make sure that they sail closely together. As for the land and an attack there… with the men we lead I fear no-one." He smiled at Adela. "You have never seen Baron Alfraed fight, my dear. I have never seen his equal. We will return from this campaign as rich men. Do you agree, Wulfstan?"

"I do indeed. I am not afraid, Adela. Alfraed is like his father and a more honest and noble knight I have yet to meet. The difference is that Alfraed here has a ruthless streak which terrifies me and if I were de Brus I would hide rather than seek him out."

"Nevertheless, I would that you take care." She reached behind her neck and undid a locket. "My mother gave me this and I kept it hidden during my captivity. I would give it to you to keep you safe." She put it in my hand and closed the fist around it.

"I cannot accept this. It would be base."

"It would be base to refuse a gift from a maiden my lord. Besides, I will sleep easier knowing that you wear it. Please… for my sake."

And so I took the charm. It was a beautifully carved piece of jet in the shape of a deer. Perhaps it was Adela's charm that kept me safe.

With extra arrows and other preparations for ambushes made we sailed from Stockton a week later. Wulfstan still awaited his child but Father Peter, who blessed us we left, said that perhaps God was waiting until the castle was empty. Perhaps he was right. We heard, much later, that Wulfstan's son, Ridley, was born three days after we had sailed.

Chapter 25

Edward, Richard, Aiden and the horses all travelled with half of the men in the larger ship, the '*Mary*'. We sailed with Olaf on his ship, the '*Serpent*'. We carried the armour and the gold on Olaf's ship. We told both captains of the dangers we might face but they seemed philosophical about the whole thing. Olaf was actually looking forward to someone trying it on with his crew. "Half of them are the sons of Vikings. They are hard lads who enjoy nothing better than a good fight and besides," he had said looking at the weapons we brought aboard, "your men look like they can handle themselves."

As we headed south Olaf concluded that we would be more likely to be attacked closer to Normandy as the Channel was narrow there. "That makes it easier. We only have to worry about the sea!"

I found the voyage much easier than when I had first braved it three years earlier. Perhaps I had grown up or more likely I was not the spoiled aristocrat I knew I had been. I found myself becoming embarrassed at some of the things I had said and done. I squirmed inside as I remembered my petulance. Sadly only three of my companions remained and only Wulfstan was whole. I knew that none of them would regret their decision to return to England. It was their home and it was where their hearts lay. Nor would they regret their death. They had died, swords in hand, defending their lord. They had had their warrior's death.

I spent every waking hour with Harold, honing his skills. I was more determined than ever that he would become a knight. I owed it to Branton and to my father. I could do nothing about his skills with a lance until we reached solid ground once more. However, he soon became almost as quick as I was with a sword. It helped that he had an archer's eye and could react to movement quickly. His shield work was coming on too but unlike me, he had not had to hold one from an early age. He had the strength but not the reactions to use it as a weapon of offence as well as defence. That would come. When riding a horse it mattered little as you used your left hand, along with your knees, to control the horse. He was lucky that he did not have to use a destrier yet. That would be an interesting experience for him.

Before we sailed we planned our voyage and our defence carefully. We knew nothing about fighting at sea; but we knew how to defend a position and between us, we came up with a plan which, we hoped, would thwart any attempt by De Brus to attack us whilst at sea.

I was beginning to believe that we would escape the notice of our enemies as the coast of France loomed up and Captain Olaf told us that we had but two days left at sea. The lookout at the masthead shouted down the unwelcome news. "Sails to the south. There are three ships, master."

We had discussed at length what to do. That had been the day before we sailed. The leading ship, '***Mary***', took in sail and we increased speed so that we sailed but forty paces from each other. Both captains reefed their sails and the two captains matched speed and converged their courses. As the three ships approached from the southwest, ropes were thrown and our two ships were pulled closer together. We used spare sails to pack between the ships and we became, effectively, a floating castle. The sails were tightly reefed and we were just making way. We had archers on both sides of our floating castle. Two archers squirmed up the mast to use that elevated position to target key sailors. We had thought out what we would do. We could not manoeuvre very well but we were a solid fighting platform.

The three ships which approached were smaller than we were but they were packed with men. Both of our captains had just two men each on the rudder and two men at the sail. All of the rest were ready for war. All had a weapon of some description. I joined all the other men on the starboard side with my bow and the quiver of arrows.

The three ships which approached had three choices: they could attack over the bow. That would diminish the effect of their numbers. An attack over the sterns would prove equally wasteful. The only solution to our unique defence was to divide their attack over our sides. That, too, was not as easy as it might have appeared. The wind would keep their ships moving north unless they turned and sailed a parallel course. That proved to be the choice they made.

It allowed us the opportunity to thin their numbers with our arrows as they sailed north, ready to turn. The three ships made the mistake of sailing too close to us. They were just fifty paces from us and our archers could not miss. Harold showed his skill when his first arrow plunged into the head of the steersman. He tumbled over the side and the ship veered away to the west. As others in the crew tried to remedy the problem they were struck by archers like Dick and John who did not miss either. We were not killing the men at arms but the ship's crew were even more valuable. They struggled to regain control of their ship. I assumed that Edward and his men were having equal success.

Olaf ordered a little more sail and our two Titans of the sea sailed a little faster. It made the task of the three ships chasing us even more difficult. They had taken to protecting the crew with their men at arms who used their shields. The sailors shouted down, "The coast of Normandy on the port bow."

We were tantalisingly close to safety but the River Orne was some way off. The first ship began to close with us on our steer board side. Now we concentrated our arrows on the knights. Two of them were hurled to a watery death and the others retreated behind a wall of shields. Once again Harold, Dick and John picked their targets. I was just aiming my arrows at the ship and hoping for success but they were targeting key figures on the other ship. Two men fell from the top of the mast and the enemy sail remained unfurled. They needed to reef it slow themselves down. The ship began to overtake us. Our bowmen then aimed at the huddle of men by the rudder. All of them died and the ship began to veer across the bows of the third ship which had reefed its sail and was heading for our stern.

I began to think we might have won when I heard a shout from '*Mary*', "They have boarded us, my lord!"

I had expected something like this. "Harold, keep them at bay with the archers. Wulfric, Edgar, bring your swords and shields."

This was my kind of fighting. After donning my helmet I grabbed my shield and pulled myself onto the side of the ship. There was a gap between them but I was confident. I leapt across the narrow gap and landed on my feet. Edward and my men were being forced back by the men of Anjou. We had managed to appear at the end of their line. I looked behind me and saw that my two men were safe. "Wedge!" Three men did not make a strong wedge but we would have weight and we would fight as one.

The two of them tucked in behind me and I launched myself at the end of the enemy line. They did not expect the attack. The three of us hit the end man who tumbled to the floor. A moving ship needed good balance. Edgar stabbed him in the face with his sword and I brought my sword under the arm of the next man. Wulfric swung his sword over his head and split open the skull of the next man at arms.

Suddenly they were in disarray. They outnumbered us but we had a solid line facing them while three of us were working our way down the line attacking the shield side of the men of Anjou. It is hard to fight two men at once. Edward roared a battle cry and he used his own wedge to break into their line. The two knights they had with them fell to Edward and Alan and the others broke. They had thought to have an easy victory and instead they were being slaughtered. They threw themselves back to the safety of their own ship. Barely a third of them made it. The rest either fell to their deaths between the ships or the archers and spearmen killed them as they jumped.

"Over to '*Serpent*.' Let us end this!"

The ship which had attacked '*Mary*' was drifting towards the rocks, out of control. There were still two ships on the other side of the '*Serpent*'. I found it easier leaping back but some of Edward's men struggled. It did not matter. The extra archers who joined Harold and the others showered the attacking ship with so many arrows it was as though a cloud had burst above them. They began to pull away as the sails filled and the steersman edged the charnel house to safety.

We waited until they had moved far enough away to show that they were defeated. Then Edward and his men returned to their ship and we severed our ties. We now had parity of numbers but, more importantly, enough leaders and key sailors had been killed to render another attack impossible.

We had won. As we rounded the headland towards the Orne I knelt and said a silent prayer of thanks. Ominously the ships did flee but waited to the north of us. When the lookout shouted down we knew why.

"The river is blocked! There is a chain across the entrance."

We had used just such a chain at Constantinople. Count Fulk must have brought the idea back with him when he returned from the Holy Land. It was simple but effective. With both ends guarded he prevented any ship from entering or leaving the port of Caen.

"That is it, captain, we cannot reach Caen!" It was annoying and frustrating to come so close and have victory snatched away.

Olaf laughed, "We can land you on the beach just south of the river."

"Will we be able to disembark?"

"Your horses can swim. So long as you do not try to land in your armour you should be safe. Once the horses are ashore then the '*Mary*' will ride higher in the water anyway and we have a shallow draught. You might get your arse wet but that is all!"

We drew close to the other ship and the two captains conferred. It was decided that we would land first and be ready to receive the horses. I took off my armour and we put it in the chest. I wanted it neither doused nor damaged. I put my scabbard and sword over my shoulders and I lowered myself from the side. The water came up to my chest and a rogue wave soaked me but I waded ashore and then, with sword drawn, waved the rest to brave the sea. Some suffered the indignity of falling into the surf and all were soaked but they all made it. With my men in a defensive circle, the '**Serpent**' pulled away and '**Mary**' edged in. I was glad that it was Aiden who supervised the loading of the beasts. He wisely chose Scout to be the first one to be sent ashore. They rigged a cradle beneath him and then lowered him into the water. Aiden jumped into the water to release the strap and I shouted encouragement to my horse. The brave horse fearlessly swam towards my voice.

Aiden sent the palfreys and the rouncys next. I saw that the ship rode higher and the captain brought her a little closer inshore. It made the journey shorter and the animals all made it to the beach safely. The most nerve-wracking part was the landing of the destrier. Aiden sat astride Star as he was lowered into the water. My master of the horse spoke to him all the way down and then hung on to his mane as he swam ashore. We only had three destriers and Aiden had to perform the same action with them all. They were all landed successfully. The freedom I had given my slave had repaid me many times over.

With the horses landed we were able to land the armour and the rest of the men. It was almost dark when it was completed but we were ashore and had lost neither a man nor a horse. The two captains waved as they headed away from the darkening shore and we were alone in Normandy. Now, all we had to do was to get to Caen. The question was, where were Count Fulk and his army?

It was too late to scout and we built a camp in the dunes. We ate cold rations but the delay in beginning our march proved a blessing in disguise as it allowed our horses to recover a little from the voyage. The attack by the three ships had resulted in some more armour and treasure from the dead bodies. Edward shared it out between the men at arms. It was a good start. We all shared the sentry duty, much to the annoyance of Richard who wondered why we had men at arms if the knights had to be sentries.

I sent Aiden off to the east before dawn. I needed to know if there was any danger ahead. He disappeared into the east and we prepared for our journey. We donned our war gear. It galled me but we had to use four of my men at arms to guard our chests and supplies. We had too few men as it was and I did not need to waste four men in such a way. I had my hostage with them and they were under clear orders what to do if he attempted to escape. Until we joined King Henry's army we were in danger and I could not risk my hostage warning De Brus and Fulk of our presence.

"Wulfric, I want you and three men to guard the spare horses and the supplies. Take Geoffrey de Mamers with you. If he attempts to flee then you know what to do."

"I gave you my word! I have honour."

"And this will be a test of that honour. I have spoken with Adela and know how she was abused. I have treated you well up to now so do not complain!" He nodded. "Wulfric, you and your men will ride in the middle of the column. Our supplies and our spare weapons need to be guarded."

"Aye my lord."

"Edward, take four men and guard the rear." With those measures in place, I waited for Aiden. "Dick, have half of the archers on the left flank. John, take the other half on the right."

I now had just seven of us at the front of the column. We were the van and it would be up to us to meet any danger, head-on.

Dawn broke and I saw Aiden appear over the dunes. "I saw the men on the chain but no others, but…"

"But what?"

"I saw many fires in the distance. There may be a camp ahead."

I expected a camp but I thought that it would be that of the King. It now seemed unlikely that this was the case. The chain across the river suggested a siege. "You have done well. Take charge of the three destriers. They will need time to recover from the voyage." I could forget the destrier if Aiden was watching them.

We crossed the dunes and headed north to find the river. I knew that Caen lay to the east of the coast along the river. The fact that the port was blockaded was worrying. If we could not join the king in Caen, then what would we do? Once we reached the river we were able to ride close to the trees along its side. It gave us some protection from observation. We soon began to come across bodies. There had been fighting in this area. It looked to have been some time ago. The bodies had been stripped of all valuables and weapons but it made me even more cautious.

Scout saved us again. The land rose a little to a small ridge and Scout whinnied. I waved Dick forward. He was a woodsman and could hide in plain sight. He slipped from his horse and nocking an arrow he disappeared into the small stand of trees some hundred paces from us. He seemed to be away for a long time and I contemplated sending John after him. He returned just as I was about to wave John forward.

"There were two sentries my lord. They are both dead. They wore the same livery as those that attacked us. Ahead is the camp of Anjou. They are laying siege to Caen."

We were trapped on the wrong side of the enemy. Thanks to the deadly accuracy of Dick's bow we were able to watch the enemy's dispositions from the top of the ridge. Our small numbers meant that we could hide whilst observing our enemy.

"We need to get inside Caen."

Richard shook his head, "It is impossible. We are as likely to be attacked by our own side as the men of Anjou."

"We cannot know that. We need more information about the enemy and the defenders. Richard, take charge here and let the men rest. We may need to move tonight." I could see that he thought the situation was hopeless. Now I knew why he had become an impoverished knight. I saw obstacles as something to be overcome. He saw them as a barrier. Sadly I was stuck with him. King Henry expected three knights.

There was still plenty of daylight and I went, with Edward, a little closer to the walls and the defences. I had to see what Fulk was up to. Harold and Alan came with us. Their bows might be the difference between sudden death and survival. I had thought that there would be more men outside than we actually found. Then I realised that the king had asked for the muster to be a few weeks later. De Brus had warned Count Fulk and he had attacked while the king had small numbers inside Caen. That worked in our favour. We might be able to force a passage. The numbers were not huge. It would, however, require cunning. This was where I missed Wulfstan and the others. They had done this sort of thing before. For me, it was my first time. I used the knowledge and skills that they had given me. *'First, gather all the intelligence you can. Second, exploit the enemy's weakness.'* I looked again. The main camp was opposite the main gate. There looked to be over two hundred men camped there. There was a smaller one at the east gate. It looked to have a handful of tents only. That would be our best opportunity to get in.

"The problem is, Edward, that Richard is correct. Unless we can let the king know that we are coming we will be attacked as if we were the enemy."

"I hate to agree with him but unless we can find a way to fly a message in then we are stuck outside."

Harold suddenly laughed, "Then we can get a message inside."

"How? Witchcraft?"

"No, my lord, archery." He pointed to the hill to our right. It was just three hundred paces from the castle wall. "If I released an arrow from there, with a message attached I could drop it into the castle and the king would know we were coming."

Edward clapped him on the back. "He is right, my lord and if we used Dick and John too then we would have three times the chances of one of the messages reaching the king."

I thought about it briefly. It was our only chance. This might be a glorious failure but I believed it would succeed. "Very well, Edward, fetch the men while Harold and I write the messages and prepare the arrows."

Although we had some small pieces of sheepskin we had used to protect our weapons on the voyage we had no ink. Harold proved himself to be ever resourceful. He went to the dead fire of the sentries we had killed and brought a piece of charcoal. He selected one with a fine point but which would not break easily. I wrote the same message on each one. Harold trimmed the sheepskin to make it as small as possible and then he tied each one on a carefully chosen arrow.

"The extra weight will shorten the distance the arrow travels but the hill helps us, my lord. We can loose the arrow high and it should descend over the wall."

While he finished his task I looked at the problem we faced. The drawbridge was raised. We would have to clear a path to the moat and then shout for the bridge to be lowered and the gate opened. That meant we had to eliminate the camp before us and do so silently so that Fulk's men did not come from the main camp to stop us. The problem ruled out a headlong charge. We would need to use silence. My archers could help but then it would be down to the speed and skill of our swords. There was still enough light to see the numbers who faced us. There were eight men close by two pavises forty paces from the bridge. They would be our last obstacle. The main camp was two hundred paces from the moat. There were twenty warriors there and they too had a number of pavises strategically placed for protection. I could see no sign of any knights. This looked to be a small force of men at arms who were there to stop any messenger escaping through the small side gate. Even as I watched, they carefully changed the guard at the moat. They did so under a wall of shields. I saw the sentries on the wall looking for an opportunity of sending arrows their way. They were careful and the defenders wasted no arrows. I took a guess that they would do this every four hours. It would keep the men alert. They had a hard task. Their eyes would have to remain on the gate and the bridge. I began to see the possibility that we might succeed although the odds were still against us. We had to wait until night and then try my risky strategy.

Chapter 26

Edward and Richard brought the men up. While Harold and his two fellow archers adjusted the messages on the arrows to maximise the range I spoke quietly with my two lieutenants. Edward nodded but Richard looked at me in amazement. "You mean you think there are but a handful of men within and you want us to join those who are trapped? That is foolish. We should seek the king's forces that are beyond these walls. Perhaps the king is not even here at all. He may have stayed in London. There would be no dishonour in finding our ships and returning to England. To attempt to join a small garrison inside a castle is madness."

I could not believe this talk. "Our ships are long gone and I gave my word. So long as you follow my banner then you will obey my decisions and my commands." He nodded. "I have no doubt that this castle can hold out. It is the best castle I have seen outside of Constantinople. Fear, not Richard, we shall prevail."

I hoped that I had convinced him but I would not waste any more words upon him. He served me. Harold nodded, "We are ready my lord."

"Then God be with you."

The three of them walked forward a little to gain the maximum advantage of their position. I knew that Harold would have chosen his best shafts. The three arrows would be the best that we possessed. It was now in God's hands. They knew their business and they aimed across the gate between the two towers. I knew that behind would be the bailey and hopefully, the arrows would not strike an unwary defender. They loosed together. Two of them sailed over but perhaps the fletch on one came loose. Whatever the reason one arrow veered a little and it clattered on the roof of the tower to the left and then slid down to fall on the walkway. The guards at the moat looked up at the tower. They had only recently come on duty. The noise would have alarmed and worried them. I was glad then that we would be waiting until dark before we risked an attack. I wanted them weary and waiting for relief. The guards on the ramparts ran to the sound of the arrow. I prayed that they would heed my message.

We ate dry rations as we waited. "Well the errant arrow did us one favour, my lord, they would have found it."

They say that hindsight is a wonderful thing and always perfect. I should have asked the defenders to give me a signal to show that they had read the message. I had been too keen to send the message over as quickly as possible. I did not know if they had understood the message or, more importantly, believed it.

We waited until dark. I wanted the guards at the moat getting towards the end of their shift so that they would be tired and I wanted those at the main camp eating and resting. I took my two knights and their squires as well as my ten archers. The rest of my men would be needed to get the horses and equipment to the bridge as soon as possible. We had counted the men in the camp and knew their numbers. There were six within the tents when we approached and the others were gathered around their fires. They kept no watch around the camp. They felt secure. We had to wait until there were just ten men around the fire. That way my archers could do their job. Harold, Dick and John were masters with the knife but we had to make sure that we were silent.

Two men left the camp to make water. I nodded to Edward and Alan who slipped after them. When another went into the tents I began to feel hope rising. A third man rose and, rubbing his guts came directly towards us. I whispered to Harold, "Ready your men."

The man at arms had his head down and he was still rubbing his gut when I plunged my sword into his painful middle and ripped it up to kill him instantly. I caught him before he could fall and make a noise. Edward and Alan appeared next to me with bloodied blades. The arrows soared and I led my men into the camp as the arrows descended. Nine of the men died silently. One arrow had struck a shoulder and the man turned as Richard sliced down and ended his life. There was no sound and no alarm. I let my archers enter the tents to use their knives. I watched with Edward and Richard. There seemed to be too much noise coming from within the tents but I knew that the noise would not carry. The next camp was at least half a mile away. My men emerged without casualty. We ran back to our horses.

The last part of my plan was the hardest. Each man at arms led two horses while my archers filtered down the track to the moat. There was no fire there and their victims would not be highlighted by the fire. They would need to close as closely as they could and be incredibly accurate. We waited out of sight while my archers loosed death.

Harold suddenly appeared. "It is done, my lord."

"Lead the men down. Richard, watch the rear." The bodies lay behind their shields. All had died silently. As I stood there I knew that I had to break the silence but, as soon as I did the noise would carry to the other camp.

I took off my helmet so that my voice would not be masked. I prayed there was someone inside who recognised both me and my voice. "This is Baron Alfraed of Stockton. I am here at the orders of King Henry. Open the sally gate and grant us entry."

There was an ominous silence. Suddenly a flaming arrow soared high in the sky. As it came down we all looked up and I glimpsed faces on the walls. I heard a voice shout, "Open the gate and get inside. Be quick about it." I recognised the voice. It was Robert of Gloucester.

Unfortunately, the arrow would have alerted the other camp. I knew that Robert of Gloucester had had to make sure we were who we said we were but we now had to get our horses across a narrow drawbridge and through a tiny gate. I turned and went to Richard at the rear. There was no sign of him. "Edward, Harold, come here. Wulfric, get the men inside." I watched as he used the flat of his sword to push our hostage into Caen. There would be no flight for him.

I heard the bridge slam down and the gate creak open. Light from the castle illuminated the bridge behind me.

Of Richard, there was no sign. "Dammit, where is the man?"

"Perhaps he needed a pee, my lord."

I almost laughed at Harold's words. "Then he picked the wrong time to go."

I heard Robert of Gloucester shout, "Hurry! We cannot leave the gate open for too long."

"Inside, I will follow!" I peered in the dark. What could have happened to him? I suddenly worried that we had not killed all of the guards. Perhaps he had been taken. I owed it to him to help. I began to turn and caught sight of the broadsword which sliced down at me. It was Richard!

I managed to deflect the blade. "What are you doing Richard? It is me."

"I know, my lord, and I am sorry for this." He swung the sword at my unguarded head and I barely blocked it in time. I saw sparks in the dark as the swords met. "I think you have picked the wrong side in this war. Count Fulk will pay me for your head and the land here looks better than that in England. I will take my chances here. King Henry is finished." He swung his sword again and stepped forward. "There is too much treachery at home. He cannot hold on to his kingdom." I was being pushed back. I did not have my shield with me and my only defence was the helmet I held.

I heard the sound of hooves as reinforcements galloped towards the camp.

"Hurry Baron Alfraed or you will be left outside!"

I heard the urgency in Edward's voice. As my feet felt the wooden bridge, Carl, Richard's squire thrust his spear at me. I blocked it with my sword and Richard swung his sword at my head. I whirled my helmet at the sword and managed to block it. If I wanted to escape I had to buy some space. I whipped my blade around and slashed at the spear. I heard it crack and split in two. I put down my shoulder and ran at Richard. He was not expecting that attack. I hit him under his arm and he fell to the floor. An arrow thudded into the ground next to me as Count Fulk's men arrived. I swung my sword at Richard lying on the ground. He blocked it but my sword managed to slice across his face. He rolled away as his bare cheek began to bleed. I now had a chance and I took it. I turned and ran towards the bridge. I saw my men in the doorway with shields ready to protect me. It felt as though I had been thumped in the back and I pitched forward onto the bridge. Helping hands dragged me inside as the gate and then the draw bridge were showered by arrows. We were safe. When the gate slammed shut I dropped to my knees.

Robert of Gloucester was grinning at me, "You are not content to fight my father's enemies alone. You bring your own enemies with you." His face became serious and he pointed beyond the door, "What happened?"

"He decided that your father was on the losing side and he switched allegiance."

Edward's face clouded, "Treacherous bastard. I never liked him, my lord."

I shrugged, "He was a good knight. He was never pleasant but he did his job." I looked at Robert, "Where is the king? Our ships could not get beyond the chains."

"He went to visit the Holy Roman Emperor, his father in law. He seeks his support against Count Fulk. He will be back ere long."

"Then he had better hurry. De Brus has joined Count Fulk and he has a powerful army. It will only get larger."

Suddenly Harold said, "Hold still my lord." He pulled at my back and held two arrows for me to see. "You were lucky again, my lord! You can thank your armourer."

I had been lucky. I turned to Richard, "How many men do we have to defend the castle, my lord?"

He led me into the castle, "Your men have made a big difference. We now have fifty men!" I laughed at the absurdity of it. We had just a handful of knights and a few men at arms to hold off a whole army. "I am pleased you have not lost your sense of humour. We may need it before too long."

He had food sent for and we ate, in his hall, a hot meal. It made all the difference. We told him about our journey. He seemed impressed. "Then with the men, you killed on the ships and in the camp, you have whittled his numbers down at no loss to yourselves."

"Most were just men at arms."

"They are the ones who will assault us. Get some rest for I fear that your traitorous knight will have given him your numbers. We had Count Fulk believing that the King was within. It will be hard to maintain that illusion now. Count Fulk may decide to risk all before reinforcements arrive."

"I have a hostage who may be able to supply information about the Count's intentions. Harold, bring Geoffrey." My squire hurried off.

"I think we knew the Count's intentions, Alfraed, capture Caen and defeat my father."

"I think it is more complicated than that, my lord. The plots at home involved a whole host of people. When your father took De Brus with him and chastised the Seneschal of Durham he thought he had ended the problem. I do not think he has."

Geoffrey arrived looking quite worried. Robert of Gloucester stood and took out his dagger. "You are the prisoner of Baron Stockton. He is one of my knights. If I chose I could end your life here and now. I could blind you. I could emasculate you." He smiled. "I tell you this so that you are under no illusions. Tell me all that you know of the plot of Count Fulk."

His voice rose in fear, "I only know a little."

"Then tell me a little and I will decide your fate."

"My father and the Baron of Hartness were to capture Stockton and then close the road to Durham. King David of Scotland would then advance south to join them. With Durham captured and the road south opened they were to invade England. My father said that either King Henry would have to abandon England to the Scots or return home and abandon Normandy to Count Fulk." He shook his head, "Either way we would be on the winning side."

Richard looked at me, "You were right. This is more serious than we thought. When my father arrives he will have much to ponder." He sheathed his dagger. "You have bought yourself some more time young de Mamers." He turned to me. "I will take over as his gaoler now. But you shall share in any reward."

I saw the disappointment on Harold's face. He would learn that we were at the bottom of this food chain. We took the scraps the great and the good left for us.

The castle smith repaired my helmet and my armour which had been damaged in the fight. As we manned the walls, the next day, my men were incensed at the treachery more than anything else. Carl, it appeared, had been as unpopular as his master. My men wanted to get their hands on the two of them rather than Count Fulk whom they did not know.

The enemy host appeared at noon. Their numbers were greater than we had seen the day before. I noticed the banners of De Brus amongst the host and I saw Richard's banner with them too. At least we knew where he was. Count Fulk had been reinforced. These events were preceded by negotiation. It was in the Count's interest to try to achieve the surrender of the castle without loss of men. He sent a knight forward to begin the discussion.

"Count Fulk does not wish an unnecessary loss of life. He demands the surrender of the castle. He will allow all within the castle to leave with their arms as a gesture of goodwill. We know that the king is not within and the castle is in the hands of Robert the Bastard."

I glanced at Robert. He did not seem at all put out by the insult. He saw my look of surprise and shrugged, "What can I say? I am a bastard and grandson of one too. It is not a mark of dishonour. These petty insults show that they are not confident of taking us. Well, I suppose I had better give an answer to this blowhard."

He leaned forward and cupped his hands around his mouth. "I defend my father's castle against all. Tell your master he may try his best but he will leave even more of his knights and men at arms dead if he does. We will not surrender to a usurper and his band of traitors."

"That is your final answer?"

"It is!" They turned and rode away. "I am pleased I have your archers with me. I wish you had brought all of Sherwood's men with you. We could have defeated this Count Fulk before he could reach the moat. If he has any sense he will attack at a number of different places. He must know he has superior numbers."

"Where do you want me and my men?"

"Leave half of your archers here with me and take the rest to the gate you used last night. They may attempt a ram there." He peered at their camp. "They do not appear to have any serious siege engines. I dare say they will be building them as we speak. Hopefully, our reinforcements will arrive." He laughed, "I wish they were all as early as you!"

I made sure that I had Harold, Dick and John with me. My other archers were good but those three were the best. This would be a test of my leadership for I would be responsible for the defence of half of the castle. I had not experienced such a siege before. This was my first. I noticed that Aiden had joined us. I gave him a questioning look. "The horses are quiet my lord. I might as well defend the castle too." He held up his bow.

I was proud of all of my men but particularly Aiden. He might have begun life as a slave but he had proved as loyal and valuable a warrior as any.

We watched as the enemy moved the huge pavises forward. Harold laughed. "They hope to use them for defence."

"They will work though, will they not?"

Dick shook his head, "No, my lord. They can nock their arrow behind it but they must pull and step back to release. We can have them then. We have the advantage of height." He patted the battlements. "We can shelter behind these mighty stones."

My archers were as good as their word. They waited patiently until the Count's archers had stepped back to loose at us and then my men released. By the time he had lost ten irreplaceable archers, the sergeant who commanded them stopped that attempt.

Edward shook his head, "He has learned his lesson, my lord. He is bringing up crossbows."

Even I knew that they were a different matter. They did not need as much skill to use and they could be used behind a pavise. The crossbowman did not need to step back. He could cock his weapon in the shelter of the pavise and then lift it over the top. "Harold, fell them before they reach the pavise."

Before they could reach the safety of the wooden shields they had to run the gauntlet of my men's arrows. The men at arms tried to shield them but they paid a heavy price. Half of the arrows found flesh. However, once they were in the shelter of the shields then my archers had to take cover as the deadly bolts were released. Unlike an arrow, they did not arc and many pinged off the battlements. My men could release their arrows high and the plunging trajectory could strike behind the pavise but a hit was a matter of luck. They caused few casualties but they kept our heads down. We heard the relentless beat of the ram at the gate.

Four men at arms appeared next to us with a pot of boiling water which Robert of Gloucester had sent. "The oil is not yet ready, my lord but the constable thinks that this will slow them down a little."

There were channels built into the walls and they poured the boiling liquid to cascade down onto the men below. The outlet made a waterfall of boiling liquid that insinuated its way through armour and jerkins. We did not venture our heads beyond the battlements but we heard their screams as they dropped their ram and they ran. There was a brief hiatus as they prepared their ladders. Count Fulk was getting desperate but I knew that this was his best chance. If he mounted three or four ladders his crossbowmen could keep us from hurling them back and once he had gained a foothold on the walls then we were doomed. He had enough knights and men at arms to swamp our defence.

Harold saw my dilemma. "Do not worry, sir. Once the ladders are up we can concentrate on the crossbows. They will be aiming at you and not us. Come on boys." He led the archers away from where we stood so that they could release obliquely at the sides of the pavise. The crossbows would have a choice then; target the archers or us. They could not do both. I risked a peek over the top and saw the ladder resting against the wall. The bolt pinged off my helmet and then I heard a cry as the crossbowman was felled by an arrow. It became a game of dare as I watched the progress of the climbers and the crossbows tried to hit me. Our archers were few in number but they kept both the crossbows and the climbers at bay. Inevitably, however, through the sheer weight of numbers, the climbers made progress.

"Edward, you take that ladder. Wulfric, behind me."

"Aye my lord."

I saw that Wulfric had a poleaxe with a wicked-looking hook on it. He grinned at me. "This'll give the buggers a surprise, my lord."

I saw a crossbowman as he took aim at me. I watched in horror as the bolt sped towards me. I jerked my head back and it clanged off my helmet. It spun off and stuck in Edgar's cheek. He was a tough man and he jerked it out and spat the two broken teeth to the ground. He hurled the bolt over the walls.

"That was lucky, my lord. Had it not struck your helmet I might be a dead man. I am not meant to die today!" He hefted his shield and stood next to me on the battlements.

Wulfric waited until the sergeant at arms who was leading the attack was standing at the top of the leader. The sergeant raised his shield and then tried to swing his sword at me. It had little force behind it as he was trying to keep his precarious balance at the same time. As I swung my sword at him he held his shield up to block the blow. I swung again from the side and as I did so the tip of my sword connected with his eye sending him tumbling to his death. Another soldier began to climb from a position a few feet below where the sergeant had been. Wulfric hooked the hook around one of the rungs and the side of the ladder. I had not realised how strong he was but he began to march down the ramparts, backwards, pulling on the poleaxe. The climbing soldier slowed down Wulfric's progress somewhat as the increased weight made it difficult for my warrior. I saw what he was doing and I began to batter the sergeant at arms who was climbing towards me with his sword held out. Harold and the others were hitting those lower down who were ascending the ladder and suddenly the whole ladder began to slip down the wall. The sergeant and the others screamed as they saw the moat below them. They crashed to either die immediately or lie with shattered limbs in the bottom of Caen's moat.

Edward had had less success and I could see that one knight had gained the ramparts and was beating Edward and his men back. I ran towards the knight. As I did so I heard the sound of a trumpet. I had no idea what it foretold. I had to get to my men or the castle would be lost. There were now three knights who had clambered up their ladder and they were racing to face me. Others were forcing Edward back. They had managed to split my tiny force. I had to contend with the battlements on my right-hand side. It restricted my swing and it forced me to swing down from a height. They could swing at my shield. The first knight had an axe and I knew already what damage they could do to my shield. My anger at Richard's treachery gave my arm added power. It struck the side of the first knight's head for he was too slow to raise his shield and he overbalanced to plummet to his death in the bailey below. I did not give the second man a chance to strike at me as I reversed my thrust and brought up my sword, sideways, under his raised arm. He had no armour beneath his arm. I took the arm off at the shoulder and I used my shield to punch his body into the man behind. The last knight could not raise his own sword as his companion lay against him and I stabbed and twisted my blade into his throat. It was not an elegant blow but it was effective and he died. He fell gurgling at my feet. Wulfric had hooked the second ladder and, as it fell to earth, Edward killed the last intruder.

I looked over the wall and saw the men of Anjou and their allies fleeing. I could not believe that we had defeated them so easily and then Aiden shouted, "My lord, it is King Henry. He is here. We are safe! The siege is over."

I dropped to my knees and thanked God. I had expected to die but we had triumphed. God was truly on our side.

Epilogue

We had lost men and others were wounded. Once I had recovered, we saw to our casualties. Many of my men had suffered wounds. Two lay dead. It was less than I expected and was a warning to me of the dangers of attacking a castle that had not been weakened by siege weapons. Then we descended to the bailey.

"You are wanted in the hall, my lord." The man who spoke to me was one of the King's household. I gave my shield and helmet to Harold. I was not presentable but one did not keep a king waiting. He was talking with Robert of Gloucester when I entered.

"Here, my liege is the reason we survived this day. If Baron Alfraed had not arrived early for the muster then I fear we would have fallen."

The king nodded and smiled, "Once again it seems we are indebted to you."

"I also came, my liege, to warn you of treachery."

"Treachery?" He frowned and beckoned me closer. "Tell me more."

"Count Fulk bought Tancred de Mamers and Robert De Brus. They were hired to ferment rebellion in the north and draw off your forces. King David was also involved."

The king shook his head. "And he is related to me!" However, it is those knights who swore allegiance to me whom I must deal with first. It is time both De Mamers and De Brus were punished. But have you any proof of this? De Brus has powerful allies."

"I killed Tancred and captured his son. He is within the castle walls. Robert of Gloucester heard his confession." The king's son nodded. "De Brus fled here. He tried to ambush us at sea but we fought him off."

"I like you more and more, son of a Varangian. Then when I have interrogated his son I will make a judgement on this traitor. I shall elevate you further for you have richly deserved it. Your father will be proud of you."

"My father and most of his oathsworn were treacherously slain by Tancred and the men of Hartness."

"Then I am sorry for your loss."

"I also rescued Adela de Ville and she is at my castle. I would know what to do with her, my liege?"

"A noble deed, indeed. Then I shall make a judgement. She shall be your ward until she attains the age of twenty-one. Perhaps I can find a place for her as one of the ladies in waiting for my daughter. That is for the future. I have much to do in England once we have dealt with the problems here. I would have been here sooner, Baron Alfraed but I was escorting my daughter. She and her husband are, er, well they are having difficulties. She should be joining us soon. I would have you and your men protect her while she is with us."

"I would be honoured my liege."

The doors opened and a vision walked in. On that first day when she strode into the hall at Caen, I saw a young and beautiful twenty-one-year-old woman. She looked every inch a princess. She looked helpless and vulnerable at the same time. I was dumbstruck. I had no words which I could summon up. And, thus, I met Matilda, Empress of the Holy Emperor and daughter of King Henry for the first time. I fell in love with her the moment I laid eyes upon her. She would be the woman I worshipped and never attained. She would be the cause to which I would dedicate my life and I would fight a king for her. My life changed irrevocably that day and I never regretted the meeting for one instant. My life and that of Matilda had been woven into the web by the weird sisters and no one could break that thread. Not even the man who would become Stephen the King of England.

The End

Glossary

Battle- a formation in war (modern battalion)
Conroi- A group of knights fighting together
Destrier- war horse
Gonfanon- A standard used in Medieval times (Also known as a Gonfalon in Italy)
Maredudd ap Bleddyn- King of Powys
Moneyer- a man who makes official coins
Musselmen- Muslims
Palfrey- a riding horse
Pyx- a box containing a holy relic (Shakespeare's Pax from Henry V)
Sumpter- packhorse
Tagmata- Byzantine cavalry
Ventail – a piece of mail that covered the neck and the lower face.
Wulfestun- Wolviston (Durham)

Historical note

The book is set during one of the most turbulent and complicated times in British history. Henry I of England and Normandy's eldest son William died. The king named his daughter, the Empress Matilda as his heir. However, her husband, the Emperor of the Holy Roman Empire died and she remarried. Her new husband was Geoffrey of Anjou and she had children by him. (The future Henry II of England and Normandy- The Lion in Winter!)

When the king died the Empress was in Normandy and the nephew of Henry sailed for England where he was crowned king. A number of events happened then which showed how the politics of the period worked. King David of Scotland who was related to both Stephen and Matilda declared his support for Matilda. In reality, this was an attempt to grab power and he used the Norman knights of Cumbria and Northumbria to take over that part of England and invade Yorkshire. Stephen came north to defeat him- King David, having lost the Battle of the Standard fled north of the Tees.

The Scots were taking advantage of a power vacuum on their borders. They did, according to chroniclers of the time behave particularly badly.

"an execrable army, more atrocious than the pagans, neither fearing God nor regarding man, spread desolation over the whole province and slaughtered everywhere people of either sex, of every age and rank, destroying, pillaging and burning towns, churches and houses"

"Then (horrible to relate) they carried off, like so much booty, the noble matrons and chaste virgins, together with other women. These naked, fettered, herded together; by whips and thongs they drove before them, goading them with their spears and other weapons. This took place in other wars, but in this to a far greater extent."

"For the sick on their couches, women pregnant and in childbed, infants in the womb, innocents at the breast, or on the mother's knee, with the mothers themselves, decrepit old men and worn-out old women, and persons debilitated from whatever cause, wherever they met with them, they put to the edge of the sword, and transfixed with their spears; and by how much more horrible a death they could dispatch them, so much the more did they rejoice."

Robert of Hexham

Meanwhile, Matilda's half-brother, Robert of Gloucester (one of William's bastards) declared for Matilda and a civil war ensued. The war went on until Stephen died and was called '***The Anarchy***' because everyone was looking out for themselves. There were no sides as such. Allies could become enemies overnight. Murder, ambush and assassination became the order of the day. The only warriors who could be relied upon were the household knights of a lord- his oathsworn. The feudal system, which had been an ordered pyramid, was thrown into confusion by the civil war. Lords created their own conroi or groups of knights and men at arms. Successful lords would ensure that they had a mixture of knights, archers and foot soldiers. The idea of knights at this time always fighting on horseback is not necessarily true. There were many examples of knights dismounting to fight on foot and, frequently, this proved to be successful.

Squires were not always the sons of nobles. Often they were lowly born and would never aspire to knighthood. It was not only the king who could make knights. Lords had that power too. Normally a man would become a knight at the age of 21. Young landless knights would often leave home to find a master to serve in the hope of treasure or loot. The idea of chivalry was some way away. The Norman knight wanted land, riches and power. Knights would have a palfrey or ordinary riding horse and a destrier or warhorse. Squires would ride either a palfrey if they had a thoughtful knight or a rouncy (packhorse). The squires carried all of the knight's war gear on the pack horses. Sometimes a knight would have a number of squires serving him. One of the squire's tasks was to have a spare horse in case the knight's destrier fell in battle. Another way for a knight to make money was to capture an enemy and ransom him. This even happened to Richard 1st of England who was captured in Austria and held to ransom.

At this time a penny was a valuable coin and often payment would be taken by 'nicking' pieces off it. Totally round copper and silver coins were not the norm in 12th Century Europe. The whole country was run like a pyramid with the king at the top. He took from those below him in the form of taxes and service and it cascaded down. There was a great deal of corruption as well as anarchy. The idea of a central army did not exist. King Henry had his household knights and would call upon his nobles to supply knights and men at arms when he needed to go to war. The expense for that army would be borne by the noble.

The border between England and Scotland has always been a prickly one from the time of the Romans onward. Before that time the border was along the line of Glasgow to Edinburgh. The creation of an artificial frontier, Hadrian's Wall, created an area of dispute for the people living on either side of it. William the Conqueror had the novel idea of slaughtering everyone who lived between the Tees and the Tyne/Tweed in an attempt to resolve the problem. It did not work and lords on both sides of the borders, as well as the monarchs, used the dispute to switch sides as it suited them.

I can find no evidence for a castle in Norton although it was second in importance only to Durham and I assume that there must have been a defensive structure of some kind there. The church in Norton is Norman but it is not my church. Stockton Castle was pulled down in the Civil War of the 17th Century. It was put up in the early fourteenth century. My castle is obviously earlier. There may have been an earlier castle on the site of Stockton Castle but until they pull down the hotel and shopping centre built on the site it is difficult to know for sure. The simple tower with a curtain wall was typical of late Norman castles. The river crossing was so important that I have to believe that there would have been some defensive structure there before the 1300s. The manor of Stockton was created in 1138. To avoid confusion in the later civil war I have moved it forward by a few years.

Vikings continued to raid the rivers and isolated villages of England for centuries. There are recorded raids as late as the sixteenth century along the coast south of the Fylde. These were not the huge raids of the ninth and tenth centuries but were pirates keen for slaves and treasure. The Barbary Pirates also raided the southern coast. Alfraed's navy had been a temporary measure to deal with the Danish threat. A Royal Navy would have to wait until Henry VIII.

The Welsh did take advantage of the death of the master of Chester and rampaged through Cheshire. King Henry and his knights defeated them although King Henry was wounded by an arrow. The king's punishment was the surrender of 10,000 cattle. The Welsh did not attack England again until King Henry was dead!

Books used in the research:

- The Varangian Guard- 988-1453 Raffael D'Amato
- Saxon Viking and Norman- Terence Wise
- The Walls of Constantinople AD 324-1453-Stephen Turnbull

- Byzantine Armies- 886-1118- Ian Heath
- The Age of Charlemagne-David Nicolle
- The Normans- David Nicolle
- Norman Knight AD 950-1204
- The Norman Conquest of the North- William A Kappelle

Griff Hosker November 2016

Other books by Griff Hosker

If you enjoyed reading this book, then why not read another one by the author?

Ancient History

The Sword of Cartimandua Series
(Germania and Britannia 50 A.D. – 128 A.D.)
Ulpius Felix- Roman Warrior (prequel)
The Sword of Cartimandua
The Horse Warriors
Invasion Caledonia
Roman Retreat
Revolt of the Red Witch
Druid's Gold
Trajan's Hunters
The Last Frontier
Hero of Rome
Roman Hawk
Roman Treachery
Roman Wall
Roman Courage

The Wolf Warrior series
(Britain in the late 6th Century)
Saxon Dawn
Saxon Revenge
Saxon England
Saxon Blood
Saxon Slayer
Saxon Slaughter
Saxon Bane
Saxon Fall: Rise of the Warlord
Saxon Throne

Saxon Sword

Medieval History

The Dragon Heart Series
Viking Slave *
Viking Warrior *
Viking Jarl *
Viking Kingdom *
Viking Wolf *
Viking War
Viking Sword
Viking Wrath
Viking Raid
Viking Legend
Viking Vengeance
Viking Dragon
Viking Treasure
Viking Enemy
Viking Witch
Viking Blood
Viking Weregeld
Viking Storm
Viking Warband
Viking Shadow
Viking Legacy
Viking Clan
Viking Bravery

The Norman Genesis Series
Hrolf the Viking *
Horseman *
The Battle for a Home *
Revenge of the Franks *
The Land of the Northmen
Ragnvald Hrolfsson

Brothers in Blood
Lord of Rouen
Drekar in the Seine
Duke of Normandy
The Duke and the King

Danelaw
(England and Denmark in the 11th Century)
Dragon Sword *
Oathsword *
Bloodsword *
Danish Sword
The Sword of Cnut

New World Series
Blood on the Blade *
Across the Seas *
The Savage Wilderness *
The Bear and the Wolf *
Erik The Navigator *
Erik's Clan *
The Last Viking

The Vengeance Trail *

The Conquest Series
(Normandy and England 1050-1100)
Hastings
Conquest

The Aelfraed Series
(Britain and Byzantium 1050 A.D. - 1085 A.D.)
Housecarl *
Outlaw *
Varangian *

The Reconquista Chronicles
Castilian Knight *
El Campeador *
The Lord of Valencia *

The Anarchy Series England 1120-1180
English Knight *
Knight of the Empress *
Northern Knight *
Baron of the North *
Earl *
King Henry's Champion *
The King is Dead *
Warlord of the North
Enemy at the Gate
The Fallen Crown
Warlord's War
Kingmaker
Henry II
Crusader
The Welsh Marches
Irish War
Poisonous Plots
The Princes' Revolt
Earl Marshal
The Perfect Knight

Border Knight 1182-1300
Sword for Hire *
Return of the Knight *
Baron's War *
Magna Carta *
Welsh Wars *
Henry III *

The Bloody Border *
Baron's Crusade
Sentinel of the North
War in the West
Debt of Honour
The Blood of the Warlord
The Fettered King
de Montfort's Crown

Sir John Hawkwood Series
France and Italy 1339- 1387
Crécy: The Age of the Archer *
Man At Arms *
The White Company *
Leader of Men *
Tuscan Warlord *
Condottiere

Lord Edward's Archer
Lord Edward's Archer *
King in Waiting *
An Archer's Crusade *
Targets of Treachery *
The Great Cause *
Wallace's War *
The Hunt

Struggle for a Crown
1360- 1485
Blood on the Crown *
To Murder a King *
The Throne *
King Henry IV *
The Road to Agincourt *
St Crispin's Day *
The Battle for France *

The Last Knight *
Queen's Knight *
The Knight's Tale

Tales from the Sword I
(Short stories from the Medieval period)

Tudor Warrior series
England and Scotland in the late 15th and early 16th century
Tudor Warrior *
Tudor Spy *
Flodden*

Conquistador
England and America in the 16th Century
Conquistador *
The English Adventurer *

English Mercenary
The 30 Years War and the English Civil War
Horse and Pistol

Modern History

The Napoleonic Horseman Series
Chasseur à Cheval
Napoleon's Guard
British Light Dragoon
Soldier Spy
1808: The Road to Coruña
Talavera
The Lines of Torres Vedras
Bloody Badajoz
The Road to France
Waterloo

The Lucky Jack American Civil War series
Rebel Raiders
Confederate Rangers
The Road to Gettysburg

Soldier of the Queen series
Soldier of the Queen*
Redcoat's Rifle*
Omdurman

The British Ace Series
1914
1915 Fokker Scourge
1916 Angels over the Somme
1917 Eagles Fall
1918 We will remember them
From Arctic Snow to Desert Sand
Wings over Persia

Combined Operations series
1940-1945
Commando *
Raider *
Behind Enemy Lines
Dieppe
Toehold in Europe
Sword Beach
Breakout
The Battle for Antwerp
King Tiger
Beyond the Rhine
Korea
Korean Winter

Tales from the Sword II

English Knight

(Short stories from the Modern period)

Books marked thus *, are also available in the audio format. For more information on all of the books then please visit the author's website at www.griffhosker.com where there is a link to contact him or visit his Facebook page: GriffHosker at Sword Books or follow him on Twitter: @HoskerGriff or Sword (@swordbooksltd)
If you wish to be on the mailing list then contact the author through his website.

Printed in Great Britain
by Amazon